A SIMPLE TWIST OF FATE

TJ Medeiros

Copyright © 2024 TJ Medeiros

All rights reserved.

ISBN: 9798330364022

He hears the ticking of the clocks
And walks along with a parrot that talks
Hunts her down by the waterfront docks
Where the sailors all come in
Maybe she'll pick him out again
How long must he wait?
One more time, for a simple twist of fate
-Bob Dylan

PROLOGUE

David Stone, the CEO and founder of Stone Technologies, strode down his company's wide mahogany halls towards the boardroom. The sound of his Italian loafers on the imported marble floors echoed throughout the mostly empty corporate headquarters. The board of directors had been waiting for him for over thirty minutes. With the IPO scheduled in 48 hours, questions had to be answered, and concerns needed to be addressed. This was the first time since he started StoneTech that he was less than thrilled to meet with the board.

Stone approached the massive African Blackwood double doors, the tension rising in the back of his neck. The shiny red-black of the ten-foot-high doors starkly contrasted the white marble floors and the deep red of the mahogany walls. As he stopped and gathered himself in front of the boardroom doors, he couldn't help but be reminded of the scene in The Wizard of Oz when the rag-tag group first met the Wizard. In this case, HE was the Wizard; and he was beginning to wonder if his board members had the brains to comprehend what he was trying to accomplish. He opened the manila folder he was carrying and looked at his notes. This had to work. Hearing the low murmuring of the board, he could only imagine what they were discussing. He began working on this project while still a student at Stanford, long before he started StoneTech. Before any of the board was involved. Most of whom didn't understand a damn thing about what he was doing.

Taking a deep breath, he pushed open both doors and strode confidently into the room and to the head of the long, wide table. Immediately, the conversations stopped, and their eyes all followed his path. He sat down and looked across the table at the chairman, Alex Benton. Alex and David had met at Stanford, Stone getting his degree in biochemistry and Benton in accounting. They conceived the idea for StoneTech soon after. They had been close. Until now.

Stone scanned the faces of the other board members and then looked directly into the eyes of his friend, trying to sort out what he and the board might be up to. He had an idea, but he was ready to fight. For his job, his company, and his project. Benton spoke first.

"I'm sure you know why we called this meeting, David."

"Money?"

Stone knew it was always about the money with Benton. He couldn't think long-term. He had a problem seeing the end game here.

"Yes, money. Your R&D budget is out of control. We should have reigned you in long ago, and now we must explain this to potential investors. They will want to know what we have to show for it. Actually, the entire board wants to see what we have to show for it."

"We're close. You know it. You've seen the status reports. The results of our first tests. They've all been very promising."

"Promising isn't what we are financing, David. You know it. The board wants to see a live demonstration. With results. Can you arrange that?"

Benton knew this pushed the CEO into a corner. He would have to produce or face the consequences.

"Yes. In the lab. Tomorrow. 11 am."

Stone responded with no emotion. Slowly scanning the faces of the others in the room, people he had handpicked to be on the board of HIS company. Executives from other companies that he was going to make rich. Fools. They don't have a clue.

Stone gathered his composure, picked up his folder, and slowly rose from his chair. He made his way to the large double doors of the boardroom, pushed them open, and before heading out, turned around and said quietly, "See you all tomorrow."

Benton excused himself and followed Stone out the large doors before they closed.

"What do you want now?" Stone growled without turning around and continued walking towards his office.

"I want to make sure you're clear on what just happened."

They had both reached the outer door of Stone's office. Stone opened the door, walked around his desk, and sat down. Benton followed him and was waiting for an answer. Something. Stone slowly swung back and forth in his chair, looking at Benton, measuring him, scrutinizing him. After what seemed like an eternity, Stone stopped moving and, without taking his eyes off of Benton, slowly leaned forward.

"I want to make sure YOU'RE clear of what will happen. I'm only going to say this once, so listen up. If you think I'll let you and the board stop me, you're crazy. This project is too big. I expected this from those idiots, but not you. What happened to you? We are on the verge of something huge. You know it. You've known it since I first brought this idea to you."

Stone slowly put both hands down on the top of his desk, raising himself and leaning even further forward, his eyes now at the same level as Benton's. Without blinking, he continued.

"So, here's what's going to happen. Tomorrow, you and the rest of the board will be in the lab at eleven. I'll give you all the demonstrations you want. Then you are going to convince them to continue funding this project. Do you hear me?"

"Yes, but, ..." Benton replied.

"No, but. Because if you don't make that happen, you're as good as dead to me. Now get the fuck out of here. I have somewhere to be."

CHAPTER ONE

Javier Lopez didn't know it, but this would be the last day he would come to work. As the morning fog slowly burned off, he sped along in his department-issued golf cart; the tool-laden wagon bouncing along behind as he traversed the compacted dirt paths of Golden Gate Park. As the head gardener, Javier handled a small crew of gardeners that maintained the expansive thousand-acre park on the western edge of San Francisco. Unlike most city workers who rose to the supervisor level, Javier worked alongside the rest of his crew. It was a work ethic learned from his father, who had held the same position as Javier over forty years ago. His father learned from his father, who had worked in the Park when it was built over a hundred years ago.

Javier spent most days ensuring his crew of young men were working, not hiding out, smoking pot, drinking, or doing anything to avoid work. However, a few of the guys on his staff had been there for years, were hard workers, and enjoyed learning about the Park's extensive plant collection. The rest of his workers resulted from city government nepotism, local rich kids needing work experience hours before heading to Berkeley or Stanford, and the occasional kid looking for an isolated part of the Park to grow pot and get paid while doing it.

Today wasn't a typical day. There were two no-shows, and the rest of the crew was busy doing maintenance, prepping the Park for the usual annual review from city hall. It wasn't as if the suits from downtown cared about the Park. Over the last decade, the City had reduced funding to where Javier had to maintain the vast area with ever-dwindling resources. It was challenging to keep the good workers, who found they could make more money mowing the small patches of grass that adorned the front yards of homes in the Sunset and Richmond Districts that bordered the north and south boundaries of the Park. It also meant that park security was out-sourced with a rent-a-cop contractor that Javier had never seen, and neither did the ever-increasing number of homeless people taking up residency in the many hidden pockets of the Park.

No, today wasn't a typical day. Today Javier was on his way to replace a dying rhododendron at the far eastern edge of the Park where the city would hold their review. It was just another photo op, Javier thought. They always used the same three locations in the Park. The Beach Chalet at the western edge of the Park, the museums in the middle of the Park, and the McLaren Lodge at the eastern end near Kezar stadium. This was where the dead, or nearly dead flower bush needed to be replaced. It was always the same. Add several new, healthy-looking plants, clean up all the trash tourists left behind, and roust any homeless so the city council members were happy.

As he pulled up to the lodge, the Gothic stone structure loomed amid the last swirls of fog as the sun poked through the still leafless branches of the trees. Even though Javier had been at work for over an hour, the surrounding city was still sleeping, the sun just now rising over the hills to the east. He caught the unmistakable smell of sourdough French bread baking from the Haight Street Bakery several blocks away. In this same spot during lunch, nearby pizza parlors would replace that smell.

Javier loved this part of the Park and especially the lodge. McLaren Lodge was constructed in 1896 as the home for the first caretaker of the Park, John McLaren. It had been vacant since he died in 1943. Anytime Javier did any work at this end of the Park, he usually tried to plan it around his lunchtime, so he could sit on the nearby bench and dream of being that first caretaker. His grandfather had worked with Mr. McLaren, something he would proudly speak of many times to his grandson. Those stories had as much to do with Javier eventually working at the Park as the fact his father had worked there. Javier could only imagine what it might have been like to work with John McLaren, let alone be the Park's original superintendent. Those were dreams he had whenever he was in this part of the Park. He wouldn't have time for those dreams today.

Javier jumped off the golf cart, took a long draw from his water jug, and grabbed the round-point shovel to remove the dead bush. The ground under the bush was still damp from the night dew, but it also meant it would be easy for Javier to replace. He didn't have the new shrub yet, but he'd come back later and put it in, closer to the time of the photo op, so it looked as fresh as possible. Javier just wanted to remove the old one and bring it to one of the many compost piles around the Park. He made a note to check the irrigation in this area since the rhododendron had always been one of the healthier bushes. Who knows? Maybe one of the idiot rich kids cut a line when planting pansies earlier this month.

Javier jammed the point of the shovel into the ground under the bush. He cut a circle around the plant, slicing the dead roots as he went, prying up on the plant to break it free from the earth. The bush was close to the building but not so tight that the gardener couldn't work around it with the shovel. He remembered when this was planted years ago by one of the college kids he trusted to work on his own. It had looked healthy until a few weeks ago. The north side of the building shielded it from the scorching sun in the summer, and the ordinarily moderate climate in San Francisco, along with the always present morning fog, was perfect for these kinds of plants.

The root system was more extensive than Javier thought as he widened the hole he was digging. He continued to work around the bush in a circle, gradually gaining some leverage and eventually popping the dead plant out of its hole. He dragged the dead plant over to the wagon attached to the golf cart and tossed it in. As he walked back to the now vacant hole, he saw the remnants of roots that would need to be removed before planting the new bush. Javier took the point of the shovel and used it as a cutting tool, stabbing at the exposed roots repeatedly, and cutting them away from the edges of the hole. Time after time, the shovel landed in the hole's bottom, cleaving away a bit more of the dirt as it went. Javier scraped out the roots and left them in a pile next to the hole, figuring he would haul them away when he came back to plant the new bush.

As he pushed the shovel along the bottom of the hole to scrape out the last of the dirt and roots, Javier heard the distinct sound of metal on metal. "Shit, damn water pipe," he thought. As he more gently used the tip of the shovel to expose what he thought was an old water pipe used to deliver water to the Park from the nearby street service, he realized it was something else. Shaped like a box, he continued to clear more and more dirt from it until he had the top exposed. Measuring about a foot and a half square, made mostly of what looked like some sort of metal, Javier stepped back and thought, "What have we here?"

Javier dropped to his knees and pulled out a small spade to clear more of the dirt from the sides of the box. The more he removed, the more he could see that the box was a mix of wood and metal. The corners of the top of the box had large metal corners protecting the wooden top. He tried to bush off the wet dirt, but that just smeared it more. He'd have to get the box out and give it a good cleaning, but it looked like something he might make a few bucks off. Who knows what might be inside?

As he continued to remove dirt from the sides, Javier eventually exposed enough to see that the lid had a latch with a small lock holding it closed. The backside had hinges made from the same material as the top corners. Javier worked faster now. The excitement of what he might find inside spurring him on, Javier finally uncovered the entire old box. Prying it up and out of the hole with the blade of his shovel, he could finally see that it resembled something of an old cigar case, just deeper and wider. He flipped the box around in his hand, checking all sides, inspecting it curiously, wondering how it came to be buried there, under the dead rhododendron.

At first, the gardener thought of trying to remove the lock without damaging the box, just in case it was worth something. He picked at it with a small pocket knife, trying to leverage the hasp open. When that failed, and eager to see what was inside, he placed the box on the ground and aimed the blade of his shovel at the lock. First gently tapping it, then pulling the shovel back a foot or so, Javier let go with a quick and accurate strike to the lock. It came off easier than he thought. The years of being buried in the moist soil must have weakened the metal.

He removed the remnants of the lock and slowly opened the box. Not what he had hoped...no gold coins or rare stones. No jewelry, nothing that appeared to be worth anything. Just a nondescript notebook and nothing like the crafted box it was in. The notebook reminded Javier of something a schoolchild would put together. A stack of papers with rudely placed holes on the edges and a cheap twine laced through the holes to keep the pages together. At least it looked like the box had kept the notebook intact and dry. Javier reached in and carefully removed it. As he carefully pulled the notebook out, he realized the construction wasn't as simple as he first imagined. Instead of cheap materials, the cover and backing were of soft leather and what he thought was twine holding it together was thin strips of leather. The pages inside were thicker than the paper he was familiar with. Still appeared to be paper-like, yet rougher. Maybe made of something else.

Slowly flipping through the notebook, Javier didn't seem to understand exactly what it was he was looking at. The text wasn't English or Spanish, he obviously could read both. No, this was in a language he had never seen, if it was some language. The letters or symbols all looked the same. Well, similar. They were like C's, but some with lines on top of the C and some with what Javier thought looked like tails. Others looked like fish hooks and weird shaped E's. No, he had never seen writing like this before. As he flipped through the pages, he saw that there were hand drawn diagrams, some on pages by themselves, and others drawn between the weird writing. The symbols made no sense to him. No treasure here.

He tossed the notebook back into the box and started gathering his tools. His thoughts returned to the task at hand as he walked his tools back to the gardener's cart. The new plant was back at the main shed near the center of the Park. Javier decided he would get the plant now instead of waiting for later in the day. He pulled the cart around to head back to the maintenance shed. He had too much prep work for the quarterly review and the sooner he completed it, the sooner he could get back to normal maintenance. As he spun the cart around, he realized he had left the box lying beside the hole. Who knows, maybe it is worth something. He threw it into the back of the cart along with his tools, got back in the golf cart, and sped back to the maintenance shed. Taking the several winding paths back towards the center of the Park, Javier enjoyed seeing the many trees and flower beds that had become like his own private backyard.

He pulled the cart into the double-wide opening of the large wooden shed. He hopped out and walked towards the row of recently potted plants, grabbing the new rhododendron and carrying it back to the cart. As he lifted it into the back, the box again grabbed his attention and he had another look at the notebook. He quickly flipped through the pages. Javier thought he might know who to ask about the notebook and if it was worth anything. Someone that might know what it all meant. Someone that was the smartest person Javier knew. It had been years, but he was sure he could help. Maybe this was worth something.

He grabbed his phone and took a picture of one of the weirder pages, and scrolled through the contacts on his phone. He knew someone who might know what this was or at least point him in the right direction of someone who would. When he found the contact he was looking for, he pressed the phone icon to dial their number. He heard the phone ring several times before someone picked up and said hello.

"Stookie! long time, no see. This is Javi."

"Javi! How have you been? Still working the Park?"

"Yeah, hey look. I found something and I'm not sure what it is. I'm hoping you'll be able to help me. I'm going to text you a picture. Can you have a look?"

"Sure boss, anything for you."

Javier clicked on the text icon on his phone, added Stookie to the contact field, and attached the pic he had just taken. He clicked send.

"Just sent it. Let me know when you get it and what you think."

"Got it."

Stookie's tone had changed, but Javier didn't notice.

"Where did you get this?"

"I found it buried in the Park today just now. There are a lot of other pages. It's a whole notebook. Looks old. Is it important? Worth anything?"

It took a while before Javier got a response and at first; he thought maybe the call had dropped.

"Can I see the rest? In person?"

This time Javier heard the change in Stookie's voice. The friendly banter had dropped, and now it felt cold and flat.

"Sure, come by my place after work. It will be good to see you, have a few beers, catch up on old times, and you can have a look."

Before Javier could say anything else, he heard the click of the connection drop.

CHAPTER TWO

Kevin Dillon held the chair for Mary Quinn as she slid into the seat by the window at the Buena Vista. On the weekends, this could be a very busy restaurant and bar, with tourists coming for their famous Irish coffees. But tonight, it was relatively quiet, and it looked like they wouldn't have to share their table, a requirement when it was standing room only. Mary thought that was a good thing, because after dating Kevin for nearly a year, she was ready to take down the walls she hid behind and let Kevin in, and she had plenty to tell him.

The couple had been to BV several times, usually for a nightcap after walking around Fisherman's Wharf, or having dinner at one of the many Italian restaurants in the area. Tonight it was Capurro's on Jefferson, where they shared a large bowl of Cioppino and then the oven roasted Dungeness crab, paired with a nice Napa Chardonnay. Mary liked the fact that Kevin knew his wines and was born and raised in the Bay Area. Coming from Sacramento, she had a rather sheltered life, so moving to San Francisco and meeting a man like Kevin was what she needed at just the right time.

The right time. Tonight was that time. Mary liked how their relationship was developing and she knew that before it went much further, she needed to let Kevin know more about her. And why she had moved from Sacramento. She stared out the window at the bay, and then back at Kevin as he took his seat across from her. Just as she was about to reach across the table for his hand, a waiter quickly approached and asked if they wanted something to drink.

"Couple of Irish Coffees, please," Kevin replied.

Mary liked that about Kevin, too. He took charge, not in a domineering way, but in a confident way. This offended some women. A man being so forward as to order for them. Mary thought it was romantic, being taken care of. She was raised this way, and it made her feel warm inside having a man in her life who treated her well. She extended her arm across the table and took Kevin's hand. He took hers and they looked into each other's eyes. She didn't realize it, but she was squeezing his hand tighter.

"Is everything ok?"

"Wonderful."

Mary let up on his hand slightly. Nerves, just nerves. But why was she nervous? This man loved her, and she loved him. She had nothing to be nervous about. She had just never let her defenses down with anyone. At least, any man. Before she came to San Francisco, her life was good. Mary had a good job at a bank in Sacramento and lived with her parents. She had lived her entire life there and, until a little over a year ago, never thought she would live anywhere else.

Though the place was only half full, there was still a buzz in the air as tourists watched the experienced bartender make a dozen Irish Coffees at once. As he went through what looked like a complicated process of filling the heavy glass flutes with hot water, then sloshing it out, everyone at the bar whooped. Kevin and Mary looked over just in time to see him drop sugar cubes in each glass and then expertly fill them with coffee by pouring it from one glass to the other, filling the dozen glasses in one motion. They turned back and smiled at each other. They had watched this many times. It intrigued Mary the first time she saw this performance. Now it was something that intensified those feelings that this was so right. Her life now. With Kevin. And being in the city. She felt like the smile on her face would never go away.

Mary thought back to the day she first met Kevin. She had come to San Francisco to interview for a position at the bank on Geary. When she walked through the door and headed to the manager's desk, she glimpsed him out of the corner of her eye. As the manager walked her back to one of the small conference rooms for the interview, she could feel his eyes following her. It was a bit unsettling, but that had more to do with the past she was leaving.

Three weeks later, on her first day as a teller for the bank, Kevin proved to be the friend she needed. She found him to be sweet and endearing and within a few weeks; they were having lunch together every day. He slowly gained her trust and after a month on the job, they were officially dating. Now, nearly a year later, their relationship had blossomed to where Mary was ready to tell him everything.

The waiter returned with their coffees and asked if they were ready to order. Kevin let him know they were just there for the coffees and the waiter left. They sipped their drinks, making small talk, Mary's mind only partly there. She kept waiting for the right moment, a break in the conversation, so she could open up to Kevin and explain why she had moved to San Francisco. That it wasn't just for the job, or to move away from her parents.

"You know I love you, right?"

"Of course. I love you, too."

Mary's gaze dropped to the tabletop as she thought about the next words she was going to speak.

"Kevin, you had asked me a while ago why I moved to San Francisco. What I told you was true, but not the entire story."

"What do you mean? You didn't come for the job? You didn't live with your parents?"

"No, no, that was all true. But there was another reason, the main reason I moved. I've never really told anyone, not even my parents. But now, I feel I can trust you."

"You're kinda scaring me. Where is this going?"

"Don't be. I love you and just want to be completely honest. Make sure you know everything about me. I'm the one who is nervous as hell to tell you. I've been afraid that if you found this out about me, that you'd leave. Not want to see me any longer. But I think our relationship is strong enough now. And I see this going somewhere. I hope you do, as well."

"I thought so, and, yes, I think this is going somewhere too. But you're making me nervous now."

"OK, let me just get this out, and then you can ask me questions. I lived with my parents. I never really had any reason to move out. They are great that way. Gave me my space, understanding. You know, the cool parents. They always encouraged me to follow my dreams, to find what my passion was. They grew up in the 60s if you know what I mean."

"Anyway, after several jobs, I worked for a bank in Sacramento as a teller. I really liked it. Good co-workers and good customers. Close to the state capital building and Old Town Sac. You know, after you've been with a bank long enough, you have your regular customers. It was no different for me. Mostly retired couples depositing their social security checks, the occasional capital employee, and local business owners making their nightly deposits."

"Then there was this one guy. Middle-aged, good-looking, normal-looking, you know? He would come in like clockwork, every Tuesday and Friday. Tuesday withdrawals, Friday deposits. He would make small talk, any plans for the weekend, stuff like that. Pleasant enough, not creepy or anything. At least not at first."

"It didn't take long for me to realize that the deposits were in the same amount as the withdrawals. Of course, you're supposed to alert your supervisor if you suspect anything out of the ordinary. The amounts weren't that great, so I really thought nothing weird was going on. And, again, he was just this quiet, nicer, middle-aged man. Not threatening in the least."

Mary had been looking out the window at the lights reflecting on the bay as she relayed her story. Her head slowly turned and for the first time saw the look of bewilderment on Kevin's face. She continued.

"So, I didn't report it. Probably should have. Looking back, I definitely should have, just to have a record of it. Anyway, this went on for a few months. Nothing really changed. Until about a couple of months before I quit. He shows up on a Monday and just stands by the deposit slip table, staring at me, not getting in line or anything. No one else noticed anything except me, because I was so used to his routine. I kept looking up at him after I finished with each client, would smile, make eye contact, and get nothing back. Just this blank stare. He finally gets in line and makes his way to the front, again, waiting for me ever though there were other tellers open. Never taking his eyes off me."

"When he finally walks up to my window, I noticed he had nothing in his hands. No deposit slip, no withdrawal slip. Nothing. I ask him how he was and what could I do for him today. He leaned forward so only I could hear him and says, 'I want you'. At first, I wasn't sure if I heard right or not and said, excuse me. He leans in again and says the same thing. 'I want you.' I kind of laughed it off and said how sweet that was but that I was seeing someone. Obviously, I wasn't, but he was like thirty years older than me. His face turned red, and I thought I had embarrassed him. He just turned and left. I thought that was the end. He didn't show up for his usual Wednesday withdrawal and Friday deposit that week, so I figured he didn't want to show his face since I turned him down."

"Until two weeks later. He started coming to the bank every day. Same routine, walk-in staring at me, go to the deposit slip table, fill out something, stare at me some more, and then just leave. Didn't get in line or anything. That went on for another week and then nothing. Didn't come in again. I had told no one, not even my parents. I thought it was over until one night when I was leaving work. I swear I thought I saw him standing across the street just watching me, but when I looked back, there was no one there."

"Anyway, I went to the police to report it. Even considered getting a restraining order, but the police said they really had no reason to issue one. That's when I started looking for another job, in another city. I gave my two weeks' notice and applied to several banks in San Francisco, thinking it was big enough to get lost in. I don't know, maybe I was just scared. Until that last week. I actually saw him watching me. Nearly every night when I left work. I made sure that he wasn't following me, but I was never sure."

Mary stopped and just stared at Kevin, looking for his reaction. And even though she had been nervous to tell him, Kevin turned out to be the man Mary thought he was. Compassionate, understanding, caring.

"I'm sorry you had to experience that. I can't imagine what that must have felt like. To have someone stalk you. But I don't understand why you would be afraid to tell me this. From the sounds of it, you did nothing wrong."

"I don't know. Embarrassment? Maybe feeling like it was my fault? That I somehow led him on? I don't know. I guess I feel better after talking about it."

"That's good. I don't think you have any reason to feel you did anything wrong. Probably just a creep and embarrassed that you shot him down. And now you're here."

"I know. Now I'm here with you. I guess it all happened for a reason. Forced me to move and meet you. I have to tell you, though. I had a lot of anxiety for the longest time. Constantly having this feeling that someone is watching you, following you. It's a terrible feeling, very unsettling. And you hallucinate things, see things that aren't there. Just last week, I thought I saw him come into our branch."

CHAPTER THREE

Javier sat at the old gray Formica table in the kitchen of the small apartment he rented in the Sunset just blocks from Golden Gate Park. Sunlight filtered into the room and danced off the specks of dust floating in the air. The smell of a microwaved burrito clung to the eighty-year-old kitchen cabinets. The only things adorning the faded paint on the walls were a couple of dime store paintings, a Team Mexico poster from the 1976 World Cup, and a black-light, felt painting of Christ. There were a couple of outdated Giants schedules, and a forgotten shopping list being held by old magnets on the fridge. Javier's furniture, a worn brown velvet couch, a black pleather armchair, and a mid-century modern coffee table he had purchased from garage sales in the neighborhood. The sorry acquisitions of an aging bachelor. Not that Javier minded. To him, the apartment was his castle, some place that he could relax after a long day at work. He was proud that he could live so close to the park. The area had gotten so expensive since he first started living there thirty years ago. Even though his house had sold a couple times, luckily it was to investors that had appreciated the long-term tenant. Basically, built in income. He had the rent raised several times, but it was modest because of the rent control laws of San Francisco.

The homes in the Sunset were originally two-story single-family homes built before the war for middle-class families. They were "shotgun" style homes with no side yards separating them from the neighbors. Constructed individually, but stacked against each other with barely an inch of space between them. They didn't share a wall, which made them relatively quiet, even on rare warm summer nights when windows were open. The faint sound of music or TV wafting down to the street. There were no front yards to speak of, save a potted plant or two. They were all stucco, most with gated entries and single-car garages. When first constructed, not everyone owned a car, public transportation was extensive, and there were corner stores nearly every couple of blocks, which encouraged walking. Times were slower back then.

Javier's apartment was on the second floor on 22nd Street, two blocks from the park. Downstairs, what used to be a garage, was now a small one-bedroom apartment. Smaller than Javier's but perfect for a single young person commuting to downtown or Silicon Valley. The current tenant was a young woman that Javier rarely saw. Mostly because he left for work before the sun came up, but also because Javier rarely socialized. Although they had passed each other a time or two, it embarrassed Javier he couldn't remember her name. Something he was sure she had told him when they first met.

He liked the idea that he was so close to the park he could walk to work, something Javier used to do when he was younger, and probably still should. But the hard work of being a gardener had taken its toll on Javier's body. Constant back aches from bending over and lifting. Instead of walking, he drove a late 70s Chevy step-side pickup, the same one he had purchased new when he first started working for his dad at the park. That and the couple of Tecate beers he had every night after work helped ease those pains.

As he sat at the small table and sipped from the beer, Javier flipped through the old notebook he found today. Most of what was in the notebook was foreign to him, but there were a few symbols and words that looked familiar. He couldn't place exactly where he had seen them or what they meant, but they looked familiar. His attention turned to the box. This might be worth something. I mean, it's old, he thought. And why would someone bury it unless they wanted to hide it because it was worth something? It had to be special. He pulled his phone out and snapped a few pics of the box, one on each side. Might get a few bucks for it at a secondhand store. He pushed the box aside and returned to the strange notebook. Absently, he took more pictures of the pages as he downed the last of his first beer.

Javier stood and walked across the kitchen to grab another Tecate from the fridge. He twisted the cap off and took a long draw of the cold liquid. He walked back to the table and sat, waiting for his friend to come. Javier always liked Stookie. He had worked for Javier for several years before he went off to Stanford and continued during the summers the first couple of years. Stookie was one of the few kids Javier had hired that actually took a liking to plants, asking questions, interested in how plants grew, what fertilizers worked best. He was also a hard worker. Rare these days.

As he waited, he realized that before today; he hadn't spoken to Stookie in years. He wasn't even sure what he did now, where he worked. Javier missed the conversations he used to have with Stookie during his school breaks, working in the park like he did before he went to college. Those times were different. Before he went to college, it was Stookie that would ask the questions and Javier providing the answers. Mostly about plants, sometimes about life. He was certainly interested in the park and all of its history. But after that first year in college, the roles reversed. It was Javier that now asked the questions and Stookie providing the answers. What classes are you taking, what subjects do you enjoy the most, how was he liking college life? Stookie was like the son that Javier never had.

He took another long sip of the cold beer. Yeah, Stookie will know what this is and if it's important. He was a smart kid. He looked over at the kitchen clock. Nearly seven-thirty. As he raised the bottle to his lips, ready to take another sip, the sound of the gate buzzer jerked him out of his thoughts. Finally. He put the beer down, stood, and walked over to the intercom. He pressed the "talk" button and asked, "Stookie?"

"Yeah," he heard and pressed the button that unlocked the gate. "Come on up, I have a cold one for you!"

Javier went to the front door and opened it so Stookie wouldn't have to knock when he got to the top of the stairs.

As he pulled the door back, his friend was already on the stoop. Javier excitedly grabbed his friend and embraced him in a long hug.

"My friend! Can I get you a beer?"

"Sure Javi, thanks."

Stookie walked past him into the small living room, looking around. He followed Javi into the kitchen and immediately went to the small table. Without a word, he sat down and went through the notebook, slowly, page by page.

"Yeah, that's it, look it over. Strange, huh?" Javi handed his friend the beer.

Javier sat down across the table from his friend and watched as he intently looked at each page. Slowly flipping from page to page, staring at it for a while, then turning back to a previous page, then forward again. Repeatedly. Getting to the last page and closing the notebook, he finally looked up at the old gardener, "This is all? This is all you found? Nothing else in the hole?"

"Yes," Javier responded. "That was all that was in that box." he motioned with his bottle to the box on the table. "Is it worth anything? Do you think it's one of those treasure boxes that was supposed to be buried in the park? Every once in a while, I have to chase people out for digging in the middle of a flower bed. You know they are supposed to apply for a permit, but most don't."

"I've heard about that, but, no, I don't think this is one of those."

"So, what is it, then?"

The young man was silent for the longest time. He reached for his beer and took a long slow drink from it, nearly finishing the bottle. He continued to look at the notebook and finally looked up at his old friend. "Honestly, I don't have a clue."

"OK, but do you know what any of those words mean, those symbols?"

"Not really, and it's probably nothing, but it wouldn't hurt to have someone else have a look. Mind if I take it with me?"

"Not at all, my friend, but if it's worth something, I want it back!"

"Of course. Listen, I wish I could stay and catch up more, but I need to get going. Thanks for the beer" Stookie stood and picked up the old notebook and box. "Call you as soon as I know anything" And without waiting for Javier to respond, he turned and headed towards the door. Javier followed him, opened the door, and thanked him again as he watched him descend the stairs, open the gate, and exit without another word.

"It was good to see you. It's been too long." Javier called after his friend.

Javier closed the door, walked back to the kitchen, grabbed another beer from the fridge, and sat down. Looking at the clock, he realized it was later than he thought. He downed the beer, got up, turned the lights out, and walked down the narrow hall to the rear bedroom. He peeled off his work clothes, turned down the covers, and crawled in. As he lay there in the dark, he thought about the book and those strange words and symbols. He knew he had seen something like them before, but he couldn't place it. He mulled them over and over as his eyes got heavy, and he slowly slipped into a deep sleep.

Outside his apartment, as Javier was slipping into bed, a car pulled up with its lights out and slid into the open parking spot across the street. The spot that fell between two of the ancient sodium lamps that lit the street. No one got out. The car sat there. The driver waited, observing. He was there for one purpose, his only purpose, to get rid of loose ends.

Evening turned to night and night closed into dawn, that brief time before any light was in the sky. The quietest point of the night. This was the time he waited for. He quietly opened the car door and slipped out, walking slowly but purposely across the street to the apartment he had been watching. His skills were many and the security gates so popular in this part of town posed no challenge. With quick, deft movements, he skillfully unlocked the gate and slipped inside, closing the gate behind him. He stood in the lower foyer of the stucco building, not moving, listening. Again waiting. Patiently.

As Javier slept, unaware of what would happen soon, a shadowy figure slowly made his way up the concrete steps to the front door. Again, with quick movements, he had the door open, its key lock breached with ease. He closed the door behind him as he stepped into the small apartment. Familiarizing himself with his surroundings, years of training had taught him. Where his target was, his points of entry and exit. And the kitchen. This one would be quick and easy. He made his way to the kitchen and looked around. The stove.

The gas stove. With purpose, he walked to the stove and turned on all the burners. Not fully, because when you turned them on all the way, the sound of gas can wake light sleepers. I can't have that, he thought. No, he just turned them all to "simmer", just enough gas to do its job without waking the mark.

His task complete, he headed for the door. As he opened the front door and walked down the same concrete steps, headlights illuminated the foyer. A car was pulling into the driveway. The man silently slipped through the gate as the car had just finished parking. He hurried across the street to his car and slid in, closing the door behind him, and waited. And watched. The car was parked; the engine was off, but no one was getting out. He waited. And waited. Still, no one was getting out. Ten minutes, twenty minutes. What is the driver doing? Just as he was about to start his car and leave, the passenger door opened and a young woman exited the car. He couldn't hear anything since his car's windows were closed. But he knew why it took so long now. The passenger was out on a date, her friend was dropping her off, and they were saying goodbye. A nice long goodbye. The sort of goodbye that can leave the windows steamed, he thought to himself. This wasn't something he had planned on, but it might be better.

The young lady waved to her companion and opened the gate. She closed it behind her and walked into the apartment. Her friend started the car, pulled out of the driveway, and drove down 22nd Ave. When it made a turn on Judah and was out of sight, he started his car and waited. Won't be long now. As much as he wanted to stay and watch, he knew he couldn't. He put his car in gear and pulled out into the street, heading for the corner. At the end of the block, he slowly turned the corner. He counted to himself... one... two... three... how long before she turned on the light? Or maybe she won't. She knows her apartment. He was now a block away... four... five... six. Maybe she just heads to her bedroom without turning on the light. No late-night snacks, no nightcap. Two blocks away now... seven... eight... nine. Nope, I guess she just heads off to bed... ten... eleven...

As he drove his car along the northern border of Golden Gate Park, heading for the great highway that ran parallel to the Pacific Ocean, he heard the faint sound of a muffled explosion and saw the bright flash of light in his rear-view mirror. I guess she wanted a snack.

CHAPTER FOUR

The cell phone vibrated on the nightstand, making an irritating yet distinct sound. Its rhythmic vibrations made the phone gradually move across the table until it bumped into the empty beer bottle. Now the vibrations against the wooden nightstand, combined with the phone vibrating against the glass bottle, finally woke Terry Eckhart from his sleep. He reached for the phone, still half asleep, and searched for the button to silence the call. It was from the Taraval station watch commander's desk, and he reluctantly picked up.

"Yeah?"

Eckhart wiped the sleep from his eyes and tried to shake the alcohol-fueled fog from his head. It was Harry Dawson, the on-duty watch commander.

"Good morning to you too, sunshine. Sorry to wake you from your beauty sleep, but we have a couple of deep-fried stiffs in the Sunset, 1415 22nd Avenue. Fire and a couple of officers are already on the scene."

"You could use it more than me. Ok, I'll be there in 20."

He hung the phone up and rolled onto his back. As he did, his arm hit the unmistakable feel of warm skin. He turned his head slightly to see the blond tussles of hair on the pillow beside him. 'Crap'. He slid out from under the covers and stood there, trying to reconstruct the events of the night before. It had been a rough stretch and the first night off in over a month. The kid killer trial had started, and he needed to blow off some steam.

Eckhart lived just outside the San Francisco city limits in the 'Gateway to the Peninsula' town of Daly City. His home, in the Westlake neighborhood, was walking distance to his favorite restaurant and bar, Westlake Joes. There were many a night he closed that neighborhood bar down, complimenting his Manhattans with the chicken parmigiana or ravioli. Two golf courses and Lake Merced also bordered it. Eckhart wasn't a golfer. He had no time to waste hitting a little ball around the lawn for six hours, but he liked the idea of the courses nearby.

He remembers being at Joe's and having a Manhattan or two, and then things got fuzzy. Someone helping him into a car. His car? No, he walked over to be safe. Whose car was it? Maybe blondies? Why does she look familiar?

He dialed the number of his partner, Nick Fowler, and let it ring a few times before hanging up. I'll try him after my shower, Eckhart thought. He didn't enjoy having a partner, and his history with them wasn't good. He enjoyed working alone, did his best work that way. Eckhart had been through several unqualified rookies and didn't have time to train them. At least Fowler was different. He had a sense for detective work and Eckhart didn't feel he needed to babysit him. Captain Jordan warned him if another partner requested reassignment, it would be Eckhart who would be transferred from Taraval to the Tenderloin.

He padded down the hall to the bathroom, relieving himself while scratching his unwashed hair. He had time to jump in the shower. It would help wash some of the brain fog from too many cocktails the night before. He brushed his teeth and ran a razor over his stubble-covered face. Ten minutes later, showered and dressed, he walked by his bedroom to leave, when he heard a voice from the room.

"Terry, you ok? You were having a rough night."

He stopped and peered into the room. Eckhart's fog had lifted enough to remember Liz, the waitress at Joe's, and her helping him home after Joe's closed.

"Still a little foggy. Thanks for getting me home. I hope. I mean. That whatever happened…"

"Terry, relax. Nothing happened. I got you to bed and stayed to make sure you were all right. As much as I would have liked…"

Eckhart smiled uncomfortably. The only thing worse than having a partner was being in a relationship. His history with both wasn't the greatest.

"Listen, I have to head out. Take your time and make some coffee if you like."

"Thanks, I will. And Terry? Take care of yourself, OK?"

Eckhart smiled at Liz and left the house, dialing his partner again as he was getting in his car. This time, he picked up.

"Just got a call, two stiffs on 22nd. Patrol is already on the scene. Want me to pick you up or just meet me there?"

"I already heard. I'm at the station house. I'll just meet you."

Eckhart started his car and pulled out of his driveway. The radio was still on KNBR from listening to the Giant's game the night before. This morning, the two sports jocks were lamenting the poor hitting of the team and wondering if they still had a chance at catching the Dodgers in the standings. Eckhart changed the station to KGO and immediately caught the tail end of the news report of the explosion and fire at 22nd Avenue. The reporter stated the SFFD had no idea if this was an accident or something else. Eckhart thought the last thing he needed was a reporter mucking up his investigation. And like the SFFD, he had no idea if there was really anything to investigate yet.

The Sunset was just a few minutes north on 19th Avenue and it wasn't long before Eckhart pulled up to the scene. The sun was just breaking over Twin Peaks, and the fire crew was mopping up. Two uniforms were interviewing the few neighbors and keeping them away from the scene. Eckhart walked over to Fowler, who was holding two cups of coffee, offering one to Terry.

"What do we got?"

Eckhart took a sip of the coffee. He was a twenty-year veteran of the SFPD, the last 10 as lead detective out of the Taraval station in the Sunset. Fowler was his third partner since he made detective, and his second since moving to the Taraval station. The first two didn't last long because they lacked the attention to detail that Eckhart was obsessed with.

Fowler learned quickly and seemed to have that same eye for detail as Eckhart. He also had Terry's work ethic for police work.

"Two dead, female downstairs, male upstairs. The female was found in what looked to be the living room. The male was found in bed. Body retrieval is here waiting for us to release them to the M.E. I had them wait to give you a chance to have a look."

Eckhart stared at the burned building in front of him, his hand slowly rubbing his goatee-covered chin. He took out a small notebook and pen and started jotting down details. Looking up occasionally at the scene, then back down to his notebook. The smoldering wood and stucco building on 22nd Avenue was still being tended to by the SF Fire Department. The flashing lights of the patrol car and two fire engines threw a strange kaleidoscope of light over the scene. The blues and reds reflecting off of the two homes on either side of the charred building in the middle.

"At first, the fire investigators thought it might have been an accident. The neighbors we canvassed all said they heard an explosion around four this morning. SFFD thinks it was a possible gas leak. The arson investigator thinks the stove was the probable cause. All the burners were on and nothing was on the stove. Suicide?"

"Maybe. Have the victims been ID'd yet?"

Eckhart had seen it all, or at least that's what he kept telling himself. Yet every year some fuck head came along and proved him wrong. It never surprised him how cunning or completely twisted some people could be. At least what he was looking at now was something normal. If you consider two dead in a burned house, normal. But looks can be deceiving. If he's learned one thing in those twenty years, it was never to assume anything. Investigate, dig, find the truth. Most of the time, it was the simplest answer. The obvious was usually the conclusion he came to. What did they call that? Akum's Razor?

"Not positive, but the owner of the building gave us the names of his two renters. Young woman was Mary Quinn, twenty-six, single. She was a teller for Community Bank on Geary. Lived downstairs. We're trying to contact next of kin, but we'll need to confirm her identity using dental records."

"And the male?"

"Javier Lopez, lived upstairs, sixty-four, city employee, head gardener for the park." Fowler nodded towards Golden Gate Park.

"Have the forensic guys been able to recover anything yet?"

"Not much. Miss Quinn's computer and cell phone, and Mr. Lopez's cell. Doesn't look like he had a computer. Other than that, we won't know much until they finish digging through the site. Looks like Mr. Lopez's apartment was pretty sparse. Bachelor pad? Not really much more in Miss Quinn's, either. Looks like they both lived alone. I sent the phones and computer to the tech guys back at the station."

"OK, I think we have enough for now. I don't need to see the bodies. In their condition, only the M.E. and a tox screen are going to tell us anything." Eckhart turned and started walking back to his car. "Oh, Fowler, one last thing... the stove, which one?"

"Which one? Oh, upstairs. Only stove in the place. Just a microwave downstairs."

"OK, see you back at the station."

Eckhart opened his car door and slid behind the wheel. Accident? Can't be an accident. No one accidentally turns on all the burner knobs. But suicide? Why would a gardener commit suicide? And people don't commit suicide that way anymore, for several reasons.

Suicide by gas didn't go out of style - it just became a lot less convenient. The gas piped into homes today is not your grandfather's gas. Modern gas companies deliver "natural gas", a naturally occurring fuel that is a mixture of methane and ethane. It only smells terrible; it's really not that lethal. Turn on your gas jets and yes, you will die, but only after the gas displaces most of the oxygen or, more likely, reaches the pilot light and explodes. Who has that kind of patience? And who can stand that smell that long?

The gas it replaced, "coal gas" was another matter entirely. Manufactured locally at "gasworks" from coal heated in airtight chambers, the gas produced a mixture of methane, hydrogen, and carbon monoxide. This not only burned beautifully but was perfect for the suicidally inclined. The active ingredient was, of course, the carbon monoxide. With blood having over 200 times the affinity for carbon monoxide than oxygen, it doesn't take much to saturate the blood and starve your brain and nervous system of oxygen.

A few breaths of 1% carbon monoxide is enough to knock you out; a few minutes of breathing it will kill you.

Of course, this type of information isn't something you pick up as a beat cop or even a detective. At least Eckhart didn't pick it up that way. About five years into his career as a cop, they paired him with a kid fresh out of the academy. Someone Eckhart would call a real smartass, the type of kid that raises his hand every time the teacher asks a question, the type of kid that over answers. The type of kid that gets "trashcanned" in high school for being a nerd. After only a week of riding around with the kid, Eckhart had gone to his captain and asked for a new partner. The damn kid just wouldn't shut up. He wasn't a poor cop, but Eckhart could tell he wasn't cut out for that type of work.

When his request was turned down, Eckhart started calling the kid 'Professor'. After a few months, the professor grew on him. At the end of that first year, he came to really care for him. Eckhart schooled him on street smarts, something the Professor had obviously never acquired. And all those hours riding around with him, he picked up stuff from the Professor that he never thought he wanted to know. Every case they caught, every crime scene they investigated, the Professor would drop these 'little known facts' on Eckhart. They became quite the team.

Until they caught that last case. It was a rare hot day in San Francisco. Most summers were spent in fog and moist air. But towards the end of summer, when kids were back from vacation and heading back to school, the City warmed up. By September, you could have days hit the high eighties. This was one of them. They were making their rounds in the cruiser when they got a call from dispatch about an armed robbery at a small corner store at Taraval and 19th. They were close and when they arrived, they saw someone matching the description heading down 19th in a sprint. They chased after him until he cut across Larsen Playground. Trying to cut him off, Terry sped up, took a hard right on Vicente, and pulled right in front of him on 20th.

They both jumped out of the cruiser, pulled their weapons, and ordered him to the ground. That's when it all went to shit. The call was an armed robbery, so they both assumed he had a gun. The last assumption Eckhart would ever make. What happened next was a blur... and a mess. He doesn't remember asking for ID, but Eckhart can't be sure if he didn't either. The 'perp' reaches for something and Terry hears a shot.... the runner hits his knees and a red, wet pool forms on his chest from the perfect center shot. A second later, he's dead, and he face-plants on the turf. Eckhart turns around and sees the professor still pointing his weapon, the barrel smoking, his hands shaking. The first and last time the kid would pull his service revolver. Everyone that watches crime dramas on TV thinks it's easy for a cop to pull their weapon and just as easy to shoot someone. It's not. Most cops, and I mean most, want anything but pulling their weapon.

No weapon was found near the perp, but during the investigation, one was found close to the store that was robbed. The perp's prints were on it. He was the guy that pulled the robbery, but he had dumped the gun before he took off running the 100-meter dash down 19th. They were both cleared by IA, but that didn't clear Eckhart's conscience that the call could have gone better. That he could've trained his partner better. That maybe, just maybe, they both could have handled the situation better. But the professor never recovered. He resigned the next day. Killing someone can do that to you.

The professor left the force and went back to school. With Terry's urging, he got his teaching degree and went to work at one of the local high schools. The Professor, Miles Ward, quickly moved from high school to the community college and after five years there, got a job teaching biochemistry at Stanford. Eckhart stayed in touch regularly the first few years Miles had left the force. The calls between the two were less and less frequent as the years moved on and Eckhart realized he hadn't heard from the professor since he got the job at Stanford.

Eckhart's thoughts returned to the case. His initial gut feelings were usually right, and right now he didn't think this was a suicide or an accident. So why would anyone want to kill a gardener? Since the gardener's stove was the only piece of evidence at the moment, he had to be the target, if, in fact, it was foul play. Unless the forensics guys found something else, that's all Eckhart could conclude. Motivation for murder was usually one of three things. Vengeance, jealousy, or greed. Sure, there were the random whack jobs that just got off on killing people, but those were usually done in public, with no concern for getting caught. And then there were gang-related crimes, but this didn't feel like either of those. No, if this were a murder, it was for one of the big three.

He started his car and slowly pulled away from the scene and down 22nd towards the Taraval station, about ten blocks away. Terry had been at the station for the last 10 years, and he loved it. He transferred there to get away from downtown. Less homeless, more families, quieter, and since he lived in Westlake, it was closer to home. That's when he got paired up with Fowler. The station itself was small. The building used to be a library, but he liked the proximity to the park and beach. He was one of a handful of detectives at the Taraval station, most with less time on the force than Terry, but they were all great guys to work with.

Best of all, working at the Taraval station meant less violent crimes. Until today.

CHAPTER FIVE

With the sounds of sirens and the glow of the fire in his rear-view mirror, he headed west on Lincoln toward the beach. The sun was just coming up, and breaking through the morning fog. The avenues were waking up, people leaving for work, shops opening up, the city coming to life. He loved this time of day. Peaceful, not a lot of ambient noise to cloud his mind. The only time of day he didn't have those visions.

He needed to clear his head. The years had taken a toll on him. That and the constant nagging of the thoughts in his head. The visions. Some days, the thoughts were like pieces of dreams when you first wake up. When you first wipe the sleep from your eyes and then little pieces of a movie appear. Disjointed and obscure. But then a second and a third image appears and the memories of that dream take shape. If you could call it that. It was like watching a movie where the film has been cut and spliced so many times there is no continuity, but it's something you've seen before, so your mind could fill in the blanks. It switches from black and white to color, no sound, but you know what everyone is saying.

Other days, the bad days, the thoughts were thick. So thick he couldn't avoid them. Thick enough that it clouded his actual vision to the point he needed to sit and just take them in. But they were as clear as they were thick. So clear, like that same movie is in digital and all one piece, unedited. Images of a future he won't be able to avoid, no matter how hard he tries. Not that he tries as hard as he did as a youth. No, now he accepts them as part of himself. But those are the days he also feels the most alive, energized. And then the planning starts.

He didn't look at the visions as a problem. At least not during the early years of his life. He assumed everyone had them. Why wouldn't he think that? He was like other kids in every other way. Why not this one, too? But he also didn't discuss them with others. He kept the visions to himself because no one else talked about theirs. And, of course, they must have them too, right? Maybe because he was embarrassed by his visions, he never considered a therapist. When he heard other kids talking about having to see a therapist and what they talked about, he knew it wouldn't help. Mom didn't breastfeed him. He wasn't nurtured as a child. Dad beat him or wasn't around enough to provide a father figure. He was picked on at school. None of it was true, of course, so why bother talking about that stuff with a stranger?

He actually had what he thought was a pretty ordinary life. His parents were successful, and from all appearances, loved each other. He had a brother and sister that he got along with. As well as any siblings got along. He did well in school, although he got easily bored. Looking back, he knew the boredom came from not being challenged, since most of the work came so easily to him.

He dated, although not as much as he would have liked, as most of his dates found him odd. Maybe it was when he made the mistake of telling one of his high school dates about his visions and it got around school. It was a girl he trusted. They had been going out for longer than any other girl he had dated. He had actually thought he might be in love. After a movie date, he was walking her home, and he brought up the visions. In a matter-of-fact way, like you would mention what foods you liked or disliked. They were holding hands and his head was down. His comfort and feelings of being safe with her led him to just blurt it out. A vision he had the night before, and he asked what kind she might have had. He really doesn't remember the detail in which he described his vision, but he does remember that he thought it was completely normal. Until he felt her hand pull away and becoming mostly silent the rest of the walk home.

He brushed it aside until the next day in school. As he walked to his locker, nearly everyone in the hall turned and looked at him. He retrieved his books from the locker and headed to his girlfriend's locker. She was there, but she was talking to two of her friends. All three turned as he approached and the smiles on their faces and the look in his girl's eyes told him all he needed to know. He didn't get angry. More sad than anything. From that day forward, he never shared his gift with anyone. Because of that experience, most of his dating ended until college, and he kept those thoughts locked away. But a pretty average childhood. He thought.

No, he didn't need to see a shrink to know what was wrong with him.

As far as he was concerned, there was nothing wrong with him. He enjoyed what the visions prompted him to do. And with his education, he was never lacking a job. For the next forty years, it never impeded him from holding down a normal job, but these last ten years, that had become more difficult, the visions were coming more often and with greater intensity. It was harder and harder for him to push them aside during work. The distractions were getting more intense and disruptive.

But as the visions became more intense, so did his ability to focus on the planning. The attention to detail became unsurpassed. He marveled at himself as he planned each of his outings. But the planning also interested him more than his job. And the planning was perfect.

Except this time. He hadn't thought this out as carefully as he normally did. He usually avoided the possibility of there being witnesses. It was all about the planning. Making sure that no one else was around when he worked. This time, the planning wasn't up to his normal standards. Whoever else was in that car could have seen him. Might be able to identify him.

As he pulled into the parking lot by the beach, the sun had risen high enough in the sky for the fog to burn off completely. It was one thing he loved about San Francisco and especially the beach. You could count on the fog to be there in the morning. Those quiet, chilly mornings. Its silvery tendrils snaking off the coast and through the streets, low to the ground, reaching inland as far as it could before the sun rose and forced it back to the ocean. Then it would advance again in the early evenings, making its way through the Golden Gate, rolling over the cliffs and covering the city in a soft white pillowy blanket. It was probably the chilly air that he liked best. You could think clearer when it was cooler. He did his best work in the evening's cool air. Or at least before the sun rose, and the day warmed up.

He slipped into a parking spot and shut the engine off. He stared out the windshield and over the concrete abutment that held back the sand. The cold Pacific waters foamed and rolled onto the beach as he watched. Just like clockwork, the waves continued their never-ending advancement onto the sand. Pushing and pulling at the tiny granules, causing them to sparkle in the morning sun. He watched as you would a campfire. Each wave differed from the last, yet somehow the same and comforting. Relaxing, tranquil... exactly what he needed after his job.

It was nearly eight, and he could hear the sirens from the cops and fire engines heading to the scene. In the past, that was something he would have stuck around for, not for any thrill, more so to see the cops fumble around trying to figure out what happened. Here, he thought they might actually tell this was no suicide, but there was never any fear of getting caught. There was never any connection between him and his victims. Sure, when he was first starting out, he made a mistake or two. But he learned from them. Fixed them. Made notes and studied more to make sure he didn't make the same mistakes again. It was all in the planning.

He sat and watched the waves. It always relaxed him. The smell of the salt air, the sound of the waves gently crashing on the immense sandy beach. From where he was parked, he could see the Cliff House on the rise to the right and the curve of the beach towards Daly City to his left. He loved this place. He had spent most of his life coming here, first as a kid with his dad, when there was an amusement park here. Then later, as an adult, as his means of shutting things down, returning to those times when things were simpler and his mind was quieter. He let his head slowly slip back against the headrest and closed his eyes. Just a few minutes of shut-eye was all he needed. He didn't need a shrink to do any analyzing. Besides, from what he heard, they always want to talk about your mother.

As he slipped into a light sleep, he quieted the noise in his head and slowly replayed the past forty-eight hours. Like his dreams, the images came in fits and spurts, disjointed pieces of memories, sewn together like a quilt, no two pieces alike. The patchwork was comforting to him, wrapping him up in recollections of pleasure. Echoes of the past reverberating with the assurance of a heartbeat.

Unlike his dreams, these were images he had already lived, so he knew the before and after parts, no need for them to be laid out in order. His subconscious did that for him. He watched as they flew past him, with just enough time to mark them and file them away. Depictions of moments in time, laid bare for him to enjoy, to elicit feelings of both pain and pleasure. He could almost see that they were all attached with a thin thread, running off into a never-ending horizon of near blackness.

The images came slowly at first, slipping out of the darkness and then growing in size and focus as they neared, then pushing past in one beat, quickly disappearing behind him. The next image replacing the last and so on and so on. He felt his body floating, falling into a vortex of darkness, the images following his path or him following theirs. As he slipped deeper into sleep, he felt his body fall back into a prone position, the images now flying above him. He could watch them come towards him and as they passed over his head.

It was usually at this point that he either woke up in a start, or fell completely into a deep sleep, images fading away. If sleep, then all that was left were varying degrees of darkness, with a faded, distant light on a horizon he would never reach. If he woke, he'd be covered in a cold sweat, shivering as if he had just stepped in from subzero weather.

Today, it was the latter. His head snapped up, his body quivering, his shirt drenched. He looked at his watch and saw that he had been asleep, if that's what you call it, for less than an hour. He opened the window of his car and although it was windy outside; it felt warmer to him.

He didn't know if this was normal or not. And he really didn't care. But he knew that this was one of those things he would keep to himself. He always had. He didn't need any head shrinker to go poking around in there and pulling this out of him. As much as it bothered him sometimes, it was comforting and part of who he was. And he wanted to keep it that way. Besides, he knew they would just want to talk about his mother.

And what would the shrink say if he told him he killed her?

CHAPTER SIX

Eckhart arrived back at the Taraval station house. He pulled his department-issued sedan into the parking lot on 24th Ave across the street from the station. Facing McCoppin Square playground, he sat in his car for a few minutes thinking about the scene he just left. He was still trying to wrap his mind around why anyone would want to kill the gardener or the young woman downstairs. The gardener had to be the target. It was his stove that was used to vent the gas and cause the explosion. At least that's what the crime scene techs thought at first glance. He made a mental note to go back to the scene later and poke around in case there was something they missed. They were good. Good and thorough, but you never know. Second set of eyes and all that.

Eckhart watched a group of kids play catch with a man who appeared to be their dad. He wondered if the gardener had kids. Maybe living with an ex? He hoped not. Eckhart had those kinds of conversations way too often in his career, and he didn't need another one right now. Especially after the case he just closed. Anytime kids were involved, either as children of a victim or the victim themselves. The only thing worse than notifying the next of kin after a murder or accidental death was doing it when there were kids involved. No, Eckhart hoped that the poor guy was single, or divorced with no kids.

He didn't think the teller had any kids, but he would check on that too. She was in her early twenties and the techs mentioned nothing about any evidence of kids. He would also have to check on significant others, next of kin, and anyone else in her life. Some of this he knew he could get from her employer, but there were always those people in someone's life that no one knows about.

The gardener, Javier, was his focus now. The evidence pointed to him being the target. Eckhart would look for the motive first, and that usually led to a suspect. If divorced, that opened a couple of possibilities. Insurance or alimony. If the death proved accidental, an ex would stand to get the insurance money. If there were any. And if he was paying alimony, she could get the rest out of any assets he had after his death. If this was accidental, and Eckhart didn't think it was.

Mental note... check the gardener's financials. Drug problems, bad loans, gambling. The autopsy would tell him if there were traces of drugs in his system. They were all possibilities. Fowler pulled up beside him and he snapped out of his thoughts. They both got out of their cars and walked across the street and up the short flight of stairs to the entrance to the police station.

Taraval station was in what used to be a neighborhood library, and it still had all the architectural elements of one on the outside. The city had reconfigured the inside, but only to the extent of housing the police department. The large open area was left virtually intact, with the beat cops having their desks in the bullpen. A small crime lab and the detective's office were in the back of the building where rooms had been sectioned off with eight-foot-high walls and no ceiling. This sometimes made for a noisy environment, especially since the Taraval station handled the largest jurisdiction of the entire SFPD. Its boundaries set by Golden Gate Park to the north, the ocean to the west, the San Mateo county line to the south, and the foothills of SF to the east.

Eckhart thought he could still smell the familiar scent of old books when he first walked into the station every morning. It was a smell he liked, but he also felt it was mostly psychological since the aroma of burnt coffee replaced it by the time he reached his desk. This morning, he still had the smell of the fire scene in his nose and couldn't smell books or coffee.

Fowler headed to the detective's room and Eckhart checked in with Captain Jordan. It wasn't something he enjoyed doing, but Frank Jordan liked to second guess all the detectives. He expected them to give a rundown when they caught a case.

"So, I heard you got a couple of burn victims on 22nd. What have you found out so far?"

"Two vics, one male, one female. Both look like cause of death was the fire. Won't be sure until we get the MEs report back. Could be an accident, maybe not. Fire says the cause is gas. Looks like the stove was on, not lit. They'll have more when they complete their investigation."

"What do the witnesses say?"

"Neighbors heard an explosion, didn't really see anything. Fowler and I have a couple of leads we'll chase. Couple phones and a computer are in the lab. See what we get off them."

"OK, well, keep me in the loop. Do it by the book."

"Don't I always?" Eckhart turned and left without waiting for Jordan to respond, not that he was expecting a response and certainly wouldn't wait for one. He had been on the job long enough, he didn't need to be hovered over. It was hard enough for Terry to have a partner. He hated being micromanaged.

He went down the hall to the detective's room and sat at his desk across from Fowler. Like any big city strapped for cash, police and fire were pretty far down the list with budget priorities. Because of that, Terry sat in the same chair since he moved to Taraval. The desk was even older. Although private businesses had ergonomic experts, adjustable chairs, and computer-height desks, most of the Taraval station office furniture was from a time before computers.

"What did Cap want?"

"Bust my balls. He lives for it. Can you check on next of kin?"

Eckhart absentmindedly flipped through a pack of phone messages. Nothing urgent, a couple of calls from the neighbors reporting the explosion, and a message from the assistant DA, Ally Wilder, most likely a follow-up from the last case. Most likely prep for the trial that he had been called as a witness to. He liked Ally and wouldn't mind spending time with her going over his testimony.

Eckhart put the messages aside, got up, and headed to the lab. He was interested in finding out what the forensics team might have gotten from the gardener's phone. He walked down the hall to the lab at the back of the station. It wasn't as large and well-appointed as the forensics lab at headquarters downtown, but it was plenty good for most of the cases they handled in the Sunset. Even though they covered the largest portion of San Francisco, the Taraval station didn't get the number of violent crimes that the Tenderloin and Central stations got. And since the Giants built their new stadium, and the Warriors moved back to San Francisco, the Southern station activity shifted, especially during the World Series runs in the early 2010s.

"Hey Tim, were you able to get anything off the phones and computer recovered on 22nd?"

"They were pretty bad, Terry, but I pulled the drives and I'm scanning them to see what I can recover from them. We can always send the hard drives up to Novato and see if Drive

Savers can recover any more. Should have something for you by the end of the day."

"Let's see what you get first, then we can decide if we need to do a full recovery."

Terry went back to the detective's office and sat down across from Fowler. Gathering as much information as quickly as possible in any investigation was critical. The longer time passed, the more difficult it became to get accurate information, especially when it involved witnesses. In this case, the only witnesses they had were neighbors, and at that hour of the morning, all they really had were people who heard the explosion.

"Fowler, any leads on next of kin of either vic?"

"I just got a hold of Mary Quinn's parents. They live in Sac and driving down to make the ID. They were pretty shaken up. Hadn't seen her in a few months. She called them once a week. Nothing on Mr. Lopez yet."

"OK, let's start with Miss Quinn then."

"Terry, I also got a call from the patrol at the scene. Guy just showed up claiming to be Quinn's boyfriend. Said he had just dropped her off the night before. They took his info and said we'd be in contact. He works at the same bank as her. Kevin Dillon."

"Ok, run a background on him and her. I'll work the gardener."

Eckhart used the department's software to check the background of the gardener. The City employed him in the Parks department. Not married. No record. Nothing. Didn't look like he was ever married. Thank god. No need for 'that call' and the uncomfortable meeting with a wife and kids. He also pulled the names and numbers of his supervisors and made calls to them. First notifying them of the accident and then asking about Javier's co-workers or anyone else he came in contact with.

The supervisor said they had no issues with Javier. He had been working for the Parks department for nearly forty years, the last twenty in the same position his father held before him. There was nothing in his jacket regarding complaints from employees, no disciplinary actions noted. Javier appeared to be a model employee.

"Terry, you think this is something more than an accident or suicide? I mean, everything points to Lopez offing himself, and Quinn is just collateral damage. You know, just a twist of fate. What do you see that I'm missing?"

"You're not missing anything. That is what it looks like. I just have a hunch that appearances aside, this was no accident. And where is the reason for suicide? Plus, I don't believe in fate."

"Who knows? People off themselves for a hundred different reasons. Depression, drugs, money. Why do people jump off the bridge?"

"I know you like to have these cases all tidy and shit. You can just button them up and file them away and move on to the next one. We all do. And maybe this is one of them. But we need to do the job first. Due diligence man. If not for the vics, then for her parents or the gardener's friends. Or for yourself. Follow?"

"I'm just saying I don't see it."

"Well, we work the case until you do. When do the parents arrive? I'd like to have something for them when they get here."

"They said they would be at the morgue tomorrow by noon. I called over and told them to give us a heads up when they get there."

"OK, that gives us a day to see what we can dig up. Let's check the boyfriend and any of Miss Quinn's co-workers. When you have enough material, we can head over to Community Bank and ask some questions. Let's make sure the boyfriend works today, too."

Fowler wasn't one to short-shift a case. Terry wouldn't stand for that in a partner. But age and experience had more to do with Eckhart's push to investigate every case to its fullest. He had been Fowler's age once. He understood human nature to take what you had for face value, and mostly, that led to closing a case successfully. But he got to where he was by making sure he turned over every stone. Following every lead. Let the evidence take you where it may.

"Are you OK, Terry?"

"Yeah, I'm fine, why?"

"Well, getting a call at two am from you isn't the norm. I mean, if it's just me, I don't mind, even on my night off. But Nicki wasn't too happy."

"Crap, I called you? Sorry partner, I just hit a wall last night. The thought of having to testify and see that fuck's face again — well, I just want that case to be over. Apologize to Nicki for me, ok?"

"She's fine. The wife of a cop, she gets it. It's just this past month was hard on her too, me being gone so much and all. Just worried about you. Maybe come over for dinner this week?"

Eckhart didn't want to think about how this past case just went so terribly wrong. Finding the body of a butchered five-year-old will do that to you. Cops hate kid killers more than any other perp. He and Fowler worked overtime to catch this one. And by overtime, he meant nearly ALL the time. Neither one of them got much of a break for the past five weeks, and that took a toll on their bodies, their minds, and their relationships. Well, Fowler's relationship, Eckhart didn't have one to speak of.

It was one of the most intense manhunts he had been involved with. Trying to catch a killer like that and getting closure for a family that was nearly torn apart by what had happened was all they both could think about the past month. It felt like they worked twenty-four-seven for five weeks straight. He was single because of cases like this, so he understood where Fowler's wife was coming from. Unfortunately, the work took priority over your life. And your relationships.

When they found out that the killer had snatched another kid, they upped their intensity, if that were possible. Finding him before he killed another kid, and destroyed another family, was their only priority. So, when they got a lead from a CI that he was in an abandoned house in the Bayview, they didn't wait for a warrant or backup. It was a decision he had to make in a split second and based on the situation and his experience. It could have turned out horribly wrong. But it didn't.

They were focused on saving the kid, and his actions probably saved his life. But not following strict protocol, resulting in a firefight that put both his partner and the child in jeopardy, obviously brought the department and Internal Affairs down on him. And now being called by the defense as a key witness was just wasting his time and the courts.

Eckhart didn't think they compromised the case at all and he was hoping Ally Wilder, the Assistant District Attorney, would see it that way as well. Having to testify regarding his decision to move forward without a warrant or backup weighed on him and the last thing he needed was this guy walking because of his decision.

"Thanks, partner. I'll be OK. And I'll be better once the trial is over and that guy is sitting in San Quentin. Today, let's just focus on this one."

"You got it. Let me make a few calls and then we can head over to Commercial Bank and talk to Mary Quinn's boyfriend."

CHAPTER SEVEN

After leaving Javier's, David spent the next several hours looking through the ancient notebook his old boss had found. He tried to calm any anxiety when he received the texts earlier that morning. How had his boss found the book? He should have destroyed it when he first found it.

As a kid, David's aunt had taken him to the Rosicrucian Society museum in San Jose and it sparked a lifelong obsession with mysticism, psychic consciousness, Ancient Egypt, and specifically, alchemy. Unlike his parents, his mom's sister was an academic, a college graduate, and someone David looked up to. Neither of his parents graduated from college, not that they embarrassed him. He loved them both. But he always aspired for more. When his aunt introduced him to this world, he was hooked. He would devour books on the subjects, returning to the museum as often as he could convince his aunt to take him, and even saving his money so he could visit the King Tut exhibit in San Francisco.

David studied famous people that were also interested in Rosicrucianism and actual members of the ancient order.

Throughout history there were many historical figures that were members, from George Washington and Abraham Lincoln to Isaac Newton and Leonardo da Vinci. Francis Bacon, Michael Faraday, and even Walt Disney. There were rumors that the famous "Big Four" of San Francisco were also in the society, even holding secret underground meetings. None of these meetings were documented, but the rumors alone intrigued David. If Leland Stanford, Collis Huntington, Mark Hopkins, and Charles Crocker were Rosicrucians, then David wanted to learn as much as he could about the society and what they believed in.

When he took the job working in Golden Gate Park, it was partly because he needed the money for college, and partly because he loved plants and wanted to learn more. The real draw was being in the park and the historical connection to his obsession with the Society. David had discovered that the park's original designer and first superintendent of parks, John McLaren, had connections to San Francisco's Big Four and possibly the Rosicrucian Society.

Through that first summer working with Javier, David spent as much time in the park on his off hours as he did working. He explored every corner of the park, even those areas less traveled by tourists and locals. On one of these exploratory days, David discovered an old statue covered in vines and hidden by a thicket of hedges. After clearing enough to read the base, he could read the name of Thomas Starr King, a Unitarian minister and Freemason.

David mentioned his find the next day at work. Javier explained there were statues all over the park.

"Wealthy San Franciscans paid to have them installed in the 1920s. Mclaren hated it. McLaren believed the park was for nature, not for statues. He fought hard to keep the trollies out of the park, also roads. He wanted people to walk among the plants and trees, enjoy life."

"Why are they hidden from view by overgrown shrubs?"

"McLaren wanted it that way. Every time the city installed a statue, McLaren would plant bushes and vines all around them so it would hide them from sight."

"So, you know where they all are?"

"Yes, but don't go uncovering them. My father worked for Mr. McLaren and truly respected him. The City had all the statues uncovered when he passed, but because my father respected him so much, over time he slowly planted to cover them up again."

"Gotcha. But you don't mind me hunting around for them? On my days off, of course."

"Do what you want. I don't know why you'd want to waste your time. You know, McLaren had a nickname for the statues. Stookies. I'm not sure what it means. My father didn't either."

David spent the rest of that summer and the next, discovering all the hidden statues and other oddities of Golden Gate Park. This just furthered his desire to research the Society, its connection to historical figures in San Francisco and the park itself. Through his research, he saw multiple references to alchemy, the ancient forerunner of chemistry. Alchemy is based on the transformation of matter and the ancients tried to use it to transform base metals into rare metals such as gold.

That research and working in Golden Gate Park led to his accidental discovery of something that would change his life. Late in the summer of his last year working in the park, Stone had finished his shift and was spending the rest of the afternoon tooling around the park in one of the old golf carts. David had located most of the statues because of his research. He had more to discover. There just wasn't much information on their exact locations. Since it had been a hundred years, they could have been moved or destroyed.

As he was making his way west towards the de Young Museum and passing the rhododendron dell, he glimpsed the statue dedicated to McLaren himself. In an odd twist of irony, the city commissioned and installed a statue of the original caretaker of the park on his 65th birthday. The person who absolutely hated statues being erected in "his" park thanked the city and put it back in the box, where it sat until his death in 1943. Stone pulled his golf cart over and hopped off. He had seen this statue many times during his workday. It was the only one placed with no plantings covering it up. It's also the only statue in the park that is positioned on the ground, with no concrete base, because of McLaren's love of nature.

Stone wandered through the dell and around the statue. He looked at it again with a fresh set of eyes. Each time he visited any of the statues, he looked for something new and different. Because the life-size statue was built to McLaren's height and was directly on the ground, David could compare his height to his. McLaren was a somewhat shorter, stocky little man. David stood a good foot taller than the statue. He smiled as he walked around the back, to the bronze stump that was part of it. Even though the statue was placed at ground level, David thought there must be some sort of solid base, so the statue wouldn't list with erosion.

He kicked at the dirt around the base. Nothing. He dug his heel in a bit and drug the earth back away from the stump and the feet of the statue. Still nothing. It was getting near dusk and the park was nearly empty, especially in this area where hardly anyone walked. David walked back to the golf cart and pulled out a small spade. As he walked back to the statue, he looked around, making sure he was alone. Not that it mattered. He was still wearing his work clothes, including the gardening-issued shirt with his name on it, but he felt better if no one observed him digging around the base.

He started scraping away at the dirt, pulling it from the bronze feet of the statue towards himself. The ground was loose and damp, probably from the loamy soil being watered so frequently for the nearby rhododendron bushes. It was easy to move aside and within a few inches of soil being revealed; the spade hit the hard surface of the concrete. Just as he suspected, they had placed the statue on a base, just not visible and above ground like the rest of the statues. David quickly worked the spade around the base, exposing more and more of the concrete. Within several minutes, he had removed enough dirt to see that the base was a good four feet square.

As he exposed the edges of the base, David wasn't even sure why he was doing this. Curiosity? Sure. But something else was driving him. The only statue not hidden all these years, out in plain sight, honoring a man who despised statues in his precious park. A man with friends in the elite circles of the San Francisco society of the late 1800s and early 20th century. Friends like Leland Stanford, a man that David was obsessed with. So much so that he planned his life in order to get into Stanford University. Was that why this statue fed his curiosity?

He kept digging as he contemplated why he was doing so. He was working around the edges of the base, exposing several inches down around the perimeter. David was starting to work up quite a sweat and was just about to stop when his spade hit metal instead of concrete. The sound of metal on metal was distinct. He got down on his knees and started moving the dirt away with his hands. In a matter of minutes, he had uncovered a large metal pull ring, a little over five inches in diameter. At first, he thought this might have been used to lower the large concrete block into place, but then he noticed something that made him rock back on his knees and rest on his heels.

Just above the metal ring and a couple of inches below the top surface of the base, David noticed a seam that ran nearly the entire length along the backside of the base. He moved more of the dirt away and saw a seam along either side as well. It appeared to be a cover or an insert of some sort. He needed to clear more dirt to make sure. As darkness swept across the sky, David worked feverishly to expose as much of the side as possible. It didn't take him long to discover that the statue's base was only about a foot thick, and the seam he discovered ran along the entire edge of one side, forming a concrete cover of some sort.

Once he had enough of the side exposed, he tugged at the metal ring to see if it would give. It felt solid and David imagined they had mortared it or that it was just a decorative feature. That the seam was created when the concrete base was poured. He used the tip of the spade and run it along the groove of the seam, seeing if he could loosen anything that might keep it from opening. David gave the ring another tug, and it didn't budge, but David thought he felt it give a bit, if only in his mind. He pulled out his pocketknife and worked it into the gap, pulling dirt and crumbling mortar out as he moved along the seam. When he had scraped the gap clean all the way around, he put his knife back in his pocket and pulled at the ring again. This time, he felt it give. He moved his body in such a way that he could rest a foot on each side of the base and reach between his legs for the large rusty ring.

David steadied both his feet and prepared to give the ring all the strength he had, so he was surprised that when he pulled it and the side fell open, his whole body spilled over backward. When he gathered himself and could move the large, heavy concrete door to the side, he discovered two smaller wooden boxes.

David pulled both boxes out of their hidden perch and quickly put the cover back in place. Before even looking in the boxes, he covered up the hole and the entire base, removing any evidence that the ground beneath the statue had been disturbed. He wouldn't even tell Javier. It felt like stealing, but David convinced himself that it wasn't because no one alive even knew these were there or that they existed.

When he finished, he carried the boxes back to the golf cart and finally opened them to see what was inside. Just a couple of notebooks, but they were filled with such exquisite writings and symbols that somehow felt familiar to him. They intrigued him. Better than money or some hidden treasure. Just old notebooks, but they felt so special and important to him. He would spend the next four years studying the notebooks. The next four years trying to understand them. He would copy snippets of the information from the books and show them to his professors at Stanford, asking for their help in deciphering them. He wasn't sure why, but he knew he shouldn't reveal anything about the notebooks that might raise suspicion.

And now, today, a decade later, those same notebooks had reemerged. The notebooks he had built his business on. As he sat at his table, he wished he had put them back where he found them. He had tried. Several times. But each attempt was met with nearly being discovered. First by Javier, who just so happened to be working later than usual. The second time by a pair of drunk homeless men. His final attempt to hide the notebooks in their original resting place nearly got him arrested.

He had parked out on Fulton and 8th, the closest he dared get to the McLaren statue. The sun had set, and he figured there would be no one around. He had taken the notebooks out of the trunk of his car, along with a shovel, and began walking along 8th to JFK Drive. Just as he was rounding the corner, he saw an SFPD cruiser, the cop inside drinking a cup of coffee. Most likely washing down a donut. He had turned around and given up on trying.

Instead, he decided to bury them where Javier had just discovered them. Near McLaren's lodge at the east end of the park. It was several years later, and police department cuts meant patrolling was a lower priority.

Maybe he should have destroyed them, even against his better judgment. That would have been the safest thing to do. Yet, he knew of their potential historical importance and needed to be preserved. And now, with his company making the contents of them a reality soon, he knew he could never destroy them. No, they had to go back to their original hiding place.

CHAPTER EIGHT

Eckhart and Fowler pulled up outside Community Bank on Geary and found an empty parking spot. Geary was the busiest street in the Richmond district, so finding an open slot was rare. Having an unmarked sedan, with a police department placard, made finding a space irrelevant, but Eckhart didn't like to take advantage of his position when it came to things like that. Most beat cops didn't abuse their position and power to benefit from shopkeepers and store owners to get free cups of coffee and donuts, stereotypes be damned. To Eckhart, it had the same feeling as the mafia or gangs demanding protection money, something to "wet their beak". Not that cops actually demanded or even asked for it. Mostly, they gave it in gratitude for the dangerous job they performed.

Eckhart slid out of the car and looked up and down Geary. Very little had changed in the last twenty years. Some shops were still owned by the same families that opened them. The biggest change he noticed was the shift from mostly Italian delis and restaurants to a majority of Asian fare, something that matched the shift in demographics for this part of town.

Eckhart and Fowler entered the bank and went to the manager's desk, asking for Kevin Dillon. He directed them to a slick-haired twenty-something sitting four desks down. When they approached him, he hopped up, extended his hand, and introduced himself as the branch loan officer. Eckhart got the impression that Dillon thought he had a hot lead on a home loan. He actually seemed a bit too happy, considering what had just happened this morning.

"Mr. Dillon, this is Detective Fowler. I'm Detective Eckhart. We'd like to talk to you about Miss Quinn?"

Dillon's demeanor changed immediately, and a look of genuine sadness came across his face. "Mary was a really special lady. She worked here too, you know. Do you know what happened? I mean, what caused the fire?"

Several other employees began looking over at the three of them, obviously interested in the conversation regarding their deceased co-worker.

"We don't have any answers yet. Is there somewhere more private where we can speak?"

"Sure, we have a conference room we can use." He led them to the back of the branch, where several small offices lined the hall on one side, and a wall of windows exposed a large conference room on the other. He opened the door and led the detectives in. As they sat down, Kevin Dillon released all his pent-up emotions. His head fell into his hands and he started sobbing.

"Are you OK with answering a few questions?" Eckhart asked.

"Sure, sure… sorry."

"So how long have you known Miss Quinn?"

"Since she started here, probably about a year."

"And how long have the two of you been going out?"

"Almost a year. Pretty serious the past few months."

"And last night?"

"We went to dinner at Capurro's and then had a nightcap at the BV. Then I took her home. And that was it."

"And you returned to the scene in the morning. Why?"

"I was picking her up for work. She left her car on Geary when we went out last night and she didn't want to drive, so I told her I'd pick her up and…"

"Do you mind me asking why you're at work today, considering?"

"I've got nothing else. Nowhere else to go."

Eckhart nodded. Understanding more than Kevin Dillon could know.

"And how was Miss Quinn, mentally? Was there any reason to think she was depressed?"

"No, not at all. Do you think this was a suicide? She wouldn't have done that. She was always happy. And I think she... her and I... I think things were going well."

"Well, the fire department hasn't completed their investigation on the cause yet. We're checking every angle." Eckhart said.

"Did she have anyone in her life that might want to hurt her? An ex?" Fowler asked.

"No. I don't think so. She said she hadn't dated in over a year. Everyone here loved her. Like I said, she was a cheerful person."

"How about any customers that might have been upset with the bank or with her?"

"Not really. I mean, we all get the customer that complains about their statement being wrong or that their fees are too high, that sort of thing. And most of them are older. They're the only ones that come in the bank anymore. Deposit their social security checks. They don't trust technology, you know? Most of our younger customers never set foot in the bank. Paychecks are auto-deposited. They use the ATM for cash. Sorry, I'm rambling."

"That's OK, so no one specifically asking for Ms. Quinn. A repeat customer or someone you noticed or remember having an argument with her?"

"Sorry, no. Well, that's not entirely true. Last night, she mentioned a customer she had at her last job in Sacramento. She thought the guy was stalking her. But that was over a year ago."

"Really? Did she mention his name or whether she filed a report?"

"No. No name. I don't think she filed a report either. Thought about it, but decided not to. You don't think he would have done that, do you?"

"Never know. Too early to tell, but we'll check it out. If you think of anything else, please call us," Eckhart finished, handing him his card.

"OK. Do you mind me asking, what happens now? I mean, with her body? What about her parents?"

"Her parents are coming to make an ID. You haven't met them?"

"No. We never got that far. Can you — can you tell them how sorry I am? I'd like to know about any services or…"

"Sure. Sure, Mr. Dillon. We'll let them know. Thanks for your time." Eckhart shook his hand and they let him get back to work.

They spent the next hour speaking with each employee in the conference room. Some didn't really know Miss Quinn, so their time in the room was short. Others that had some sort of friendship with her all agreed that she was a cheerful person who everyone liked. No one could recall any incidents with co-workers or customers that raised any suspicion and certainly nothing that would have justified a homicide.

Eckhart didn't have any evidence to support it being a homicide, but he was going to pursue that line until he exhausted every possibility. He just couldn't see this as a suicide. For whatever reason, someone wanted the girl, or the gardener, dead. He didn't have a clue as to a motive yet, but that's why he needed to follow any likely lead.

The bank manager was the last person they interviewed. They covered the usual areas, like when was Miss Quinn hired? Was she happy at her job? Had there been any disciplinary issues, reasons for her to be upset? The bank manager confirmed what all the other employees and her boyfriend had told them. He had interviewed her for the job and she was an obvious choice based on her experience and personality. Apparently, she had worked at a bank in the Sacramento area and had made the move to the Bay Area. He had checked her references with the bank up there and said everything checked out.

Eckhart figured since the parents were coming from Sacramento, it made sense that Miss Quinn might be from that area. He made a note to check with her previous employer about the same topics. See if there were any things not mentioned in her personnel files, any issues with a customer. He knew he was going to have that difficult conversation with the parents as well. Any exes that might want to hurt her? If they knew anything about this potential stalker? Sometimes the parents know. Most times, they don't. He still had to ask the questions.

When they finished up the questioning, they thanked the manager and left the branch. As soon as they got outside, Fowler asked Eckhart, "Terry, what do you think? Doesn't seem like a suspect to me."

"I agree. Seems genuinely upset with her death. Nothing really there, but I'm keeping him on my list until we get more evidence. I don't think anyone at the bank had any reason to hurt her, and sounds like she didn't have any reason to hurt herself. But let's chase this lead on the stalker. See if anything is there. I could be wrong, but I still think this has something to do with the gardener. Let's head over to the Parks Department and see if they can tell us anything."

They made the short drive from Geary to the McLaren lodge, where the Parks department had their offices in the back portion of the lodge. The front part was maintained as a historic landmark for the park's original superintendent, John McLaren. Fowler parked the car, and they both entered the offices. Although the parks department handled over 200 parks, playgrounds, and open spaces, a relatively small group of directors and office staff managed it. The office space behind McLaren Lodge was a small and cramped two-story space. Eckhart approached the front desk, introduced himself as a detective, and asked for the Director of Parks.

"Let me call Eric and see if he's available." She dialed a four-digit extension and made the typical small talk. When she finished, she notified Eckhart and Fowler that Eric would be right down. Eckhart went through his notes of the Dillon interview as they waited.

"Gentleman, Eric Parks, director of Parks and Recreation. Yes, I get the irony."

"Mr. Parks. I'm not sure if you heard, but —"

"Yes, Javier Lopez passed this morning. Terrible accident. So sad."

"Can I ask how you heard?"

"One of his workers went to his place when he didn't show up this morning. Don't think he's missed a day in years. Doesn't even take a vacation."

"You said accident. How do you know it was an accident?"

"I just assumed. It wasn't an accident? Who would want to hurt Javier?"

"Not saying it was an accident and not saying it wasn't. We're investigating it. So, you have no reason to think someone would want to harm Mr. Lopez?"

"No, not at all. The staff here and his workers loved and respected Javier. He's been here longer than me. Hell, longer than any of us. His father had the same position as him for thirty years. Javier grew up here, working for his dad, and then taking over the position."

"Did Mr. Lopez list anyone as his next of kin? Anyone we would need to notify?"

"I don't think so. As far as I know, Javier was never married, no kids. But I'd have to check his employment records to see if there was anyone else."

"Could you do that? And we'll need a list of all employees that reported to him, past and present."

"Of course. That list might be long. A lot of park workers are part-timers."

"We'll wait. Thanks."

Eric Parks left Fowler and Eckhart waiting in the lobby as he returned to the second floor to retrieve the requested files. He returned sooner than they thought with a thick manila folder.

"Here you go, detectives. This is a file of all the employees that reported to Mr. Lopez over the past thirty years. They're listed in chronological order, with the latest employees first. And I confirmed Javier had no next of kin. No living relatives."

"Thanks, Mr. Parks. We'll call you if we have any further questions."

Fowler and Eckhart left the Parks Department offices and got in the car. While Fowler started the engine, Eckhart flipped through the long list of employees. It had to be over three hundred names in the files. The oldest employees appeared to work for the parks for several years, while the newer employees sometimes didn't last a year. In fact, most didn't stay longer than a few months. It was just a part-time gig now. Eckhart thought that this made sense, considering the salary compared to other jobs today wouldn't be close to a living wage. Looking at the ages of the most recent employees, they were mostly late teens, early twenties. He imagined they might have second jobs as well.

Just as he was about to close the file, something caught Eckhart's eye. He flipped between a couple of pages, going back and forth, finally closing the file and turning to Fowler.

"Interesting. For the last ten years, most of these employees have worked for less than a year. Looks like most might be summer jobs or part-time second jobs."

"Yeah? So, what's so interesting about that? I'm sure it doesn't pay that well."

"I agree. But there's one employee who worked for Mr. Lopez for over three years. A David Stone."

CHAPTER NINE

"What did you learn from the boyfriend?"

Captain Jordan was waiting for Eckhart and Fowler in the detective's room when they returned from the interviews. He had the usual annoyed look on his face. Something Eckhart had no problem ignoring. Fowler hadn't been here long enough to be indoctrinated into his personality quirks. He would eventually.

"I'll put it all in my report as soon as I speak with the lab."

"I'd like a briefing now if you don't mind."

Eckhart did mind, but he also wanted to keep Jordan off his back as much as possible, and giving him a thirty-second update would do that. Eckhart told him about the interviews with the bank employees, including Mary Quinn's boyfriend Kevin Dillon. He also filled him in on what they learned at the Parks Department regarding Javier Lopez. When he finished, and Captain Jordan was satisfied that Fowler and Eckhart were making progress, Eckhart left the room and headed to the lab.

"Tim, what do you have for us?"

"Well, I'm still trying to do a full recovery, but I figured you'd want to see what I have so far. The computer is toast. To be clear, we could pull the hard drive and send it out to a clean room and have them do a sector-by-sector recovery. I believe that is the only way we will get anything out of it. The female's phone was on her and I still haven't been able to recover anything. It was pretty bad as well. Again, we might do a recovery with a third party, but we'd have just as much luck contacting her service provider and seeing what kind of cloud backups they perform. Most of the big cell service providers do automatic cloud backups of call logs, contacts, pictures, texts, and sometimes emails. It's quicker getting a court order to access than to send the phone out."

"We recovered a small portion of information from the gardener's phone. A few texts and a call to the same number. Not sure it's the last, but the time-stamp puts it at yesterday morning. The texts look like they are multimedia, which means they were pics or GIFs of some sort. I'll know more when I finish the recovery process."

"OK, great. Can I get a printout of the call log, or whatever you've recovered so far?"

Tim sent the file to the printer on his desk. The call log from the gardener's cell phone was printed out on a single page. Eckhart grabbed it off the printer and went back to his desk.

He sank down into the worn leather desk chair and leaned back, holding the printouts in his hand. He looked through the call log for any pattern. The thing that really jumped out was the gardener hardly used his phone. It looked like days, if not weeks, between calls and texts were even more infrequent. Obviously, he didn't have the full list yet, but the latest calls and texts from yesterday were all to the same number. Whatever reason he made the call and sent the texts must have been important.

He logged onto his computer and entered the number into Merlin, the reverse lookup for phone numbers. It returned the cell number for a David Stone. He would need to confirm it, but Eckhart was certain this was the same David Stone that had worked for Lopez. This was getting interesting. Why would the gardener be texting and calling an employee that hadn't worked for him for over ten years? And why today?

His address was in Palo Alto. Eckhart pulled up his driver's license and entered David's info into the database software for arrests, employment and any other pertinent info. The results confirmed the address in Palo Alto and also listed his employer as Stone Technologies in the same city. It also lists the City of San Francisco as a past employer, the Department of Parks. It was the same David Stone.

"Fowler, that David Stone is the last call that Lopez made yesterday. Looks like he works or rather started his own company in Palo Alto. Why would his only call be to someone who hasn't worked for him in almost ten years?"

Just then, Eckhart's desk phone rang with a call from the lab.

"Tim. What do you have?"

"I recovered the last few texts and pictures taken yesterday morning from the gardener's cell. You should see this."

"Be right there," Eckhart said, and hung the phone up.

Eckhart entered the lab and spoke with Tim, the lab tech. "What did you find?"

"I'm not sure, but it was the last thing the gardener texted. Have a look."

Eckhart looked over his shoulder at the computer screen. Tim had brought up the pic, and they both stared at it.

"Do you know what that is?"

"No idea," Tim said.

"OK, can you make a printout of that for me?"

"Sure thing. There are a couple of other pictures I recovered, taken around the same time. He didn't text them, but they look related."

"OK, print those out, too."

When the printouts were complete, Tim handed them to Eckhart. He took them, left the lab, and returned to his desk. As he sat in his chair, Eckhart spread the pics out on his desktop.

He picked up the picture and looked it over again. It was of a single page of the notebook, with handwritten symbols that Eckhart was unfamiliar with. It also contained what looked to be mathematical equations. The paper appeared to be old and yellowed. The other pictures were of an old box, one of it in a hole in the ground, partially covered in dirt. In the other he had placed it next to the hole, the dirt swept off. There was a picture of the box opened, with what appeared to be a notebook inside, and lastly, a picture of the notebook. Definitely old. He slid the photos and phone log across the desk to Fowler.

"Have a look at these. The lab finished pulling out the last few texts and calls Lopez made. What do you make of those pics?"

Detective Fowler picked them up and quickly flipped through the stack, then went back and slowly looked at each printout.

"Writing looks Arabic, but the drawings look like chemical symbols and formulas."

"Chemical?"

"Yeah, see the shapes that look like open-ended hexagons with letters at their corners? They remind me of basic chemical formulas. And some of the writing looks like symbols. You know, uppercase, and lowercase for each element, but grouped together? That looks like a specific chemical compound."

Fowler hadn't noticed while he was looking at the pics, but Eckhart was now staring at him with a smirk.

"You got all that from Sesame Street?"

"High school chemistry. I paid attention. All kidding aside, that's about all I remember. I have no idea what any of it means, and we'd have to translate the Arabic, too."

"I might know someone."

Eckhart picked up his phone and dialed the lab.

"Tim, did they find anything at the site that looked like that notebook or the box in those other pics on the phone?"

"Not that I know of, but from what I heard, it was a total loss. Paper and wood wouldn't have had a chance. We're lucky the phone survived enough to recover what I did."

"Yeah, you're right. One more thing. Can you tell when these pictures were taken? Like day and time?"

"Sure thing. The timestamps say they were taken yesterday morning. First pic at 7:35, last one 7:47."

Eckhart flipped through the printouts until he found what he was looking for.

"And the call to David Stone was at 7:50. So whatever this is, the gardener was in a hurry to get a hold of this 'Stookie'. OK, thanks. Let me know if you find anything else," and he hung up.

Eckhart rocked back in his chair and closed his eyes. The gardener has a few pictures of this box and a notebook on his phone. He calls David "Stookie" Stone, who at one time worked for the same department in the City as the gardener and now works for a high-tech firm in Silicon Valley. Seconds later, he texts a couple of pics to the same number. Is any of this even related? Maybe the gardener thought Stone would know what the pics meant?

"Fowler. Why do you think the gardener texted this to Stone?"

"You said he worked for a high-tech company, right? Maybe Lopez just called the only person he thought was smart enough to figure out what it was. Not sure, but we should have a chat with him since it looks like he might be the last person to talk to him."

He picked up the pictures again and scanned through them. Fowler was right. If they were chemical formulas or symbols, they would need someone to explain what they are and why someone might kill for them. He thought he knew the perfect person to help them out. His old partner, the professor. Since they're going that way to question Stone, they may as well make a stop to his old friend first.

"I told you about my old partner, right? He teaches biochemistry down at Stanford. I think he can tell us what these are, maybe what they mean, and if they are important enough to kill over. Maybe we should talk to him before we go see this Stone guy. It's been a while since I saw him, so it would be a good excuse to catch up."

They left the station house, Fowler driving. Should probably call the professor to make sure he's actually available, Terry thought. He pulled out his phone and realized he didn't have the Professor's cell number, or his home number.

He dialed information and asked the operator for the number for Stanford University. The call connected and after a couple of rings, a bubbly-voiced young girl came on the line. "Stanford University, how may I direct your call?"

Eckhart froze for a moment, not knowing how to respond to her question, then said, "Give me Professor Miles Ward, please."

There was a click on the line, then soft Muzak started playing. Just as Terry was getting into the sounds of "Let it Be" played by what he could only imagine was the Lawrence Welk band, the music stopped and a voice stated, "This is Professor Ward, how may I help you?"

"Hey Professor, this is Terry Eckhart. Long time, no see!"

"Terry! How the heck are you? Retire yet?"

"Can't afford to. Besides, you know how much I love what I do."

"Right. So, what's new with you?"

"Hey Miles, I'm sorry I haven't stayed in touch as much as I should have, but I need your help. I have something I'd like you to look at, and my partner and I are on our way to Palo Alto. Can we stop by and show you? Get your input?"

"Sure, Terry. Hey, I could have tried too. Life happens, right? If you're heading down now, I'm free until my next class this afternoon at two. Does that work?"

"Perfect. How do we find you?"

Miles gave him directions to the Beckman Center for Molecular and Genetic Medicine on the Stanford campus, and they agreed to meet within the hour. Terry hung up as Fowler started the car and they left the Taraval station parking lot and headed south to Palo Alto and Stanford University.

"Before we head down to Stanford, I want to take another look at the scene on 22nd. Can you stop there first?"

"Sure, what are we looking for?"

"Not sure, just want to confirm a couple of things, make sure the techs missed nothing."

They were in front of the burned remains on 22nd Street in less than ten minutes. There was still crime scene tape blocking off most of the street in front of the house. Fowler parked across the street and they both got out. Eckhart walked under the tape and approached the granite steps in front. The neighbor was outside watering her singed geraniums. Eckhart sensed her stare and pulled his badge to flash her as he walked up the steps. He didn't plan on actually stepping into the house, as he was unsure how stable it actually was. He was hoping to get enough of a view inside to quell his curiosity.

When he reached the top of the steps, the front door was gone and replaced by a sheet of plywood. Eckhart suspected the door was removed by the FD to fight the fire. The entrance was also blocked by more crime tape. Eckhart tore it aside, pried the plywood off and took a step inside, testing the floor to make sure it would hold him. Although FD had mopped up hours ago, the smell of burnt, wet wood hung in the air. The fire department had soaked the furniture to make sure nothing could reignite. The room was small and Eckhart could see all the way into the kitchen. He didn't see what he was looking for, but he did see the ignition point of the fire, the old gas stove in the kitchen. He took a chance and walked down the charred hall to the back of the home. Although the floors seemed solid, they creaked and gave a bit with each step. The last thing he wanted was to fall through into whatever was left in the apartment below.

Fowler called out to him, making sure he was still OK. Eckhart yelled back just as he got to Javier Lopez's bedroom. He definitely wasn't stepping all the way in there, and from what he could tell, what he was looking for wasn't there either. He backed out and started back down the hall, stopping at the only bathroom to have a peek in. Nothing. He made his way to the front door and down the stairs to the apartment below.

Eckhart called out to Fowler that he was entering the lower apartment and cautiously stepped inside. Because there were fewer windows, just one in front and one in the back, it was darker than the upper apartment. He looked up and saw that most of the ceiling sheet-rock had been burned or pulled down by the FD. Water was still dripping from the beams, and the smell of charred wood was heavier here. He made his way through the studio much quicker since there was only one large, open room. The remains of the bed, a small couch, and a table were the only actual furniture in the room. Eckhart didn't expect to find what he was looking for, but he had to check. He took one last glance around and then turned to head back outside.

When he was finally out, Eckhart realized he had been holding his breath. He let the air out and then took a deep breath of fresh air.

"Wasn't there."

"What wasn't there?"

"The box or the notebook. Let's head to Stanford."

CHAPTER TEN

As they drove south towards Stanford, Eckhart's thoughts turned to motive. If this was a murder, and his gut told him it was, what and who was behind it? It could have been coincidental, but one of the last things the gardener did with his phone was to take photos of this old notebook and the box it came in. What was the significance of that and why text them to this David Stone? There had to be a connection and the reason for their deaths. But why? The pics of the notebook just looked like anything you'd find in a college science book. He was hoping his old partner had some answers for him.

The last time he had heard from Miles was when he left a message with the watch commander asking him to call him back. Eckhart was in the middle of a case and put it off until he forgot. He was always in the middle of a case. There was always something else that took priority. One thing that ended his marriage. Other things having priority. As much as he tried to change that behavior. He couldn't. And as he got older, Eckhart became more inclined to accept it as the way he was. It would bother him from time to time that he didn't put as much value on friends as others did, but it was also what made him who he was. Solving a case, bringing someone to justice, being an advocate for the victims and their families... these are the things that took priority in Eckhart's life. And as much as he didn't want to admit it, he found relationships, both friends and those of the opposite sex, distracting. It was hard enough to keep a partner, let alone a friend.

His marriage had lasted longer than it should have, and the long hours and dedication to his cases eventually wore thin on Lauren. He had come home after another long day of chasing evidence to an empty house. Well, empty as far as her clothes and other belongings. It stung a bit, but it didn't surprise him. And that's probably what hurt more. As he looked back at that period of his life, he realized he was trying to be something he wasn't, all to make someone else happy, when he wasn't happy himself. He didn't want to make that mistake again. The relationships he had after that were nothing more than casual, sporadic encounters that lasted a few months or less.

As they drove south on 280, the roar of planes flying overhead after taking off from SFO snapped Eckhart back to the Lopez/Quinn case and what would have motivated someone to kill a gardener or bank teller? If the teller was the target, why use the stove in the apartment above hers? Makes little sense. And if the target was the gardener, was this missing notebook the reason or just a red herring? And if it was the notebook, where did it and the box it came in go? His brief search of the residence wasn't conclusive, but there was nothing in the obvious places. Whoever opened those burners, if it was intentional, must have taken it. Eckhart was going to take one last look through the home once he got the OK from FD that it was safe to be in there. He knew going in before was a risky chance, but his curiosity got the best of him.

They were up along the skyline hills above the tony but aging enclave of Hillsborough, once the respite for the rich, looking to leave San Francisco for a more peaceful life on the Peninsula. Communities to the south replaced Hillsborough as the elite locale. The wealth of Silicon Valley grew exponentially as startups became multi-billion dollar corporations. Los Altos Hills, Menlo Park, Woodside, and Atherton, places where the nouveau riche could live and play next to millionaire athletes. Players like Bonds, Montana, or

Curry living with the likes of Ellison, Page, and Benioff. Where six-figure incomes were so common, they were low-income. Eckhart's thoughts turned to greed as one of the biggest motivating factors in a lot of the crimes he saw. And it was the same at every economic level. Someone has more than someone else, and the perp always found some sort of justification to equalize things with the vic.

They made the turn onto Sand Hill Road and entered the Stanford campus. Stanford covered over eight thousand acres, and the drive to the Beckman Center would take another fifteen minutes through the tree-lined and meticulously landscaped campus. When they finally reached their destination, Fowler pulled into the parking lot closest to the building where Eckhart's old partner now taught and found an empty stall. Although Stanford has over fifteen thousand students, they are spread over hundreds of buildings, so the parking lots are rarely full. Many of the students choose bicycles and walking, as well as the many provided shuttle services.

Eckhart grabbed the manila envelope containing the prints of the pictures and call log, and they got out and walked towards the entrance of the Beckman Center. It's a fairly new building and doesn't have the same classic California Spanish-style architecture of the original Stanford. Funded by the university to promote research and development, as well as an employee feeder program, a lot of the campus now looks more like a corporate business center than the university built in the late 1800s.

Once through the main doors, the cavernous hallway leading to several classrooms and labs took off both left and right. There was a smell inside the building that Eckhart couldn't place, but it had a chemical, burning quality to it. It made sense, being this was the chemistry building. In front of Terry was the double-wide staircase leading up to the second and third floors and behind that, the elevators that do the same. Knowing he could use the exercise, they head up the stairs to the second-floor classroom of his ex-partner.

When they finally reach the second-floor landing, the hallway looks the same as the first floor, heading off both right and left. The smells up here intensify a bit, possibly because the chemistry labs are on the second floor. The sign on the wall in front of him lists classrooms 201 through 210 to the left and 211 through 220 to the right. Slightly out of breath, but excited to see his old friend, Eckhart and Fowler, head down the right hall to room 216.

Eckhart peeked through the small window in the door to make sure the professor was alone, and saw him at his desk, and what looked like grading papers. As he swings open the door, Professor Ward looks up from his work and a huge smile quickly spreads across his face. He stands to greet the detective, his large six-and-a-half-foot frame filling out the casual attire of a typical university professor. Faded jeans, brown tweed jacket with leather elbow patches, Sperry Topsider loafers — Terry half expected a pipe to be in his mouth or at least in the upper pocket of his jacket.

"Terry, you old fart! How you doing?"

"Living the dream, squirt!"

As Eckhart extended his hand to shake, Miles Ward took him by both shoulders with his hands and pulled him in for a bear hug.

"How the hell are you, Professor?"

"I'm doing great. I was surprised but happy to hear from you. We really shouldn't have let so much time go by."

"I know, I know. I'm not so good at keeping in touch. Miles, this is my partner, Detective Fowler."

"Detective, nice to meet you, you've got one hell of a partner in this old guy."

"Nice to meet you, Professor Ward. Yeah, I've learned a lot from Terry."

"So, Miles, how do you like teaching at Stanford? Is it everything you thought it would be? When I heard you got the teaching gig here, I couldn't be happier for you. It really seems to be the right path for you."

"It is, Terry. I mean, it's not as exciting as chasing down some thug, but you know how that turned out for me. All kidding aside, I love teaching. I love connecting with students and seeing the look on their faces when they finally get some complex formula or theory."

"That's great. I know you only have a few minutes. I can't really tell you too much about the case. We just caught it and we're early in the investigation. We have a victim with some pics on his phone and we're trying to figure out what they are and if they might have any significance to his death. Let me show you. Maybe you can tell us what they mean."

Eckhart pulled the rolled-up envelope out of his coat pocket and dumped the pics on Miles' desk. Miles picked them up and started flipping through them.

"Hmmm, what do we have here? These are very interesting, Terry. Where did you get these? What case are you working on? Do you have any pics of the whole box? Any of the notebooks? Sorry, lots of questions."

"I can't really get into the details. They were pictures on a phone and texted to another individual. The person who texted them ended up dead. We don't know that they mean anything, but it's the last thing the guy did, so we wanted to check out if they meant anything and if they would be worth killing someone over. That's why I'm down here, to chat with the last person the victim spoke with."

"Did the dead guy have them on him when he died? I guess I mean, do you have the actual papers?"

"No, they weren't there. We're thinking whoever killed him took the notebook and box with him, or they burned in the fire."

"Oh. That's too bad. So what did you want from me?"

"Well, you're a professor in chemistry, and Fowler here thought they looked like chemical equations of some sort. Being we were on our way down here anyway, I thought we could stop by and see if anything jumped out at you."

"OK, sure, I can have a look at them. Detective Fowler is right. They are chemical formulas and symbols, for sure. Not sure what they mean, but if I can spend some time studying them, I'm sure I can figure something out. I have a class shortly. Any chance of getting copies so I can study them later?"

"No problem. Can we make copies before I leave?"

"So, you think they killed this victim because of these papers? Maybe the killer thought they were worth something?"

"We aren't really sure of anything right now. Just a hunch on my part."

Professor Ward scooped up all the pictures and slowly flipped through them one more time. "Actually, is there any way I can get an electronic copy of these? It may help if I can zoom in and not lose any resolution."

"You mean like email them?"

"Yeah. Do you know how to do that?" Miles asked with a big grin on his face.

"Yes, you brought me into the twentieth century."

Eckhart reached into his jacket and pulled out what was to him, the latest in smartphones. Miles saw it and laughed.

"Oh, I remember those."

"Ok, ok, let me call my tech and have him email me the pics and I'll forward them over to you. Maybe after you've looked them over, we can meet for dinner and a beer?"

"Sounds good. I need to get ready for class. It was great seeing you. Nice meeting you too, Detective Fowler."

After getting Professor Ward's email address, Terry said his goodbyes, and they headed back down the stairs and to Fowler's car. A smile crept onto his face as he left the building. It was great seeing his old partner. He shouldn't have let so much time pass. Miles was only Eckhart's partner for a short time, but they learned a lot from each other. Maybe Terry was the one that learned the most.

Before they left the Stanford parking lot, Terry pulled out his not-so-new phone and called the station, asking for the lab. He asked the tech to email him everything he could recover from the phone. As he hung up, his phone chirped, and he saw the email notification that the tech had already sent him the files. He clicked forward, entered Miles's email address, and typed 'Here you go' to the email before hitting send.

In his classroom, Miles heard his phone vibrate and picked it up, seeing the email from his old partner. He opened the email and saw that he had sent a handful of pictures to him. He sorted through them one more time and then closed the email.

CHAPTER ELEVEN

They pulled out of the parking lot and headed to the other side of Palo Alto to David Stone's residence. Based on what Eckhart found out about him, he lived in East Palo Alto, which once was one of the worst parts of town. In the 90s, there were more murders in East Palo Alto than anywhere else in the Bay Area. Twenty-five years and several large tech firms later and now you couldn't touch an 800 square foot bungalow for less than a million.

It didn't take long to make their way from the Stanford campus across town to the narrow streets of East Palo Alto. Eckhart had been here before, in the past few years. Mostly for police business, but once to Shoreline Amphitheater for a concert. There was a time when Stanford was the only thing south of The City. It got its nickname, The Farm, because of that. Eckhart recalled seeing an old photo of Stanford under construction. In the distance, you could make out several Native American teepees. Old and new in contrast to each other. His father always complained that the tech industry ruined perfectly good prune orchards. Progress was a bitch. In this case, progress was positive for the area.

They made their way down University, across the Bayshore Highway, and over to Clark Street. Eckhart heard that in the past, east Palo Alto was a war zone. But as high-tech companies continued to grow, their employees pushed into these neighborhoods and gradually the crime rate dropped. That money was also beneficial to services like police and fire, allowing both departments to grow to meet the increasing needs of the city. It took a significant bite out of the once rampant crime scene on the east side. Now, as they passed several fancy private schools and mid-century bungalows with Beemers and 911s parked out front, he couldn't help see how this area had changed.

They drove down Clark Avenue, heading east until they came to Bell Street. Fowler took a left at Bell and pulled up to the fourth house on the street. As they came to a stop, he took a quick look around and realized that the entire block looked deserted. Of course, middle of the afternoon on a weekday. Everyone's at work. They walked up the flagstone path and Eckhart knocked on the door. He stepped back and looked around as he waited. Everything looked well-kept. Manicured garden, probably had a gardener. Figuring Mr. Stone was at work, Eckhart didn't knock again. He walked around to the side of the house and looked over the locked gate into the backyard. It looked as well maintained as the front. Small manicured lawn, cobblestone patio, expensive looking gazebo and what looked like a thousand-dollar Traeger grill.

Eckhart wasn't sure why he thought Stone would be home on a weekday. Of course, he would be at work in the middle of a weekday. From what he heard, tech workers typically worked far longer than a normal nine to five, anyway. He would have preferred to talk to him alone, somewhere that was comfortable for him. Let him be on his own turf. But he had a feeling about this guy. He obviously knew Lopez from his days with the park department. And he was the last call on Lopez's phone. Either fact on its own wasn't much, but together, they posed questions for Eckhart.

"Fowler, do you think it's odd that a CEO of a tech company lives here? In such a small bungalow, in this part of town, instead of up in the hills where the rest of these techie executives live?"

"I guess. I mean, I have no idea what these guys make. And these homes are damn expensive now."

"Just doesn't feel right. I don't know, maybe it's just my stereotype of what these guys are like and where they should live. It's not like when Jobs and Wozniak first started out, that whole rebel persona. Starting in your mother's garage. Now it's just a bunch of venture capitalist making each other rich. Who knows, I could be totally off. It's just what I've read. Maybe he doesn't make as much, or maybe he just likes to live a more austere lifestyle. Guess we won't know until we meet him."

"You'd know better than me. I wasn't around then."

"Funny, smart ass. I wasn't around then either, but I do read. Anyway, let's try his business. I should have thought of going there first."

"Why didn't we just call ahead and see if he's there, or just have him come into the station?"

"I didn't want to give him any reason to be on the defense if he had anything to do with the murders. I'm still not sure he is a suspect. Let's just approach this as a fact finding for the texts and calls, and notifying him of Lopez's death. I need to see his reaction when we ask these questions. And how he reacts to his old boss's death."

They got back in the car to drive to Stone's place of business. Stone Technologies was back across town at 1701 Page Mill Road, among several other large high-tech firms. Page Mill ran from El Camino Real up the hill, west to 280 and was south of the Stanford campus by a few miles. The drive back was longer than the ride here from Stanford, so it gave Eckhart some time to think about his approach in interviewing the suspect. If he was a suspect. Eckhart wasn't sure what involvement Stone had in the explosion at 22nd Ave, but anyone that was the last to speak to a victim was on the short list of suspects. How you approach them, and how a detective handles that initial interview will go a long way to exposing any involvement the suspect might have in the case.

There are two ways to handle an interview in cases like this. Asking the suspect open-ended questions forces them to answer in something more than just yes or no. It was also effective to not respond immediately when they finished talking. It's interesting how people don't like silence and feel a need to fill it. Some of that comes from nervousness, but it's also human nature. In the past, Eckhart had suspects just erupt in a barrage of verbal diarrhea if he let them sit, staring at them. Sometimes before he even read their Miranda rights to them.

Of course, hardened criminals, those who had been through the interview process a lot, clammed up. This could be a sign of guilt, or just that the perp was an asshole. Eckhart had interviewed enough to know that those first few questions were critical. To feel out how involved the suspect was, and if so, how experienced they were.

Either way, a good detective can get a lot of information from just body language and facial expressions. Eckhart was skilled at reading the face of the suspect as they reacted to a question.

The other approach that was used on suspects that you had a pretty good idea were guilty was to treat them as hostile. Firing questions at them, not waiting for them to answer. This worked well in crimes of passion, where this might be the first offense for the suspect. Husbands, wives, business associates, basically crimes of opportunity.

He still wasn't sure how he was going to handle this one. He usually lets the interview take him where it may and adjust as needed. This early in an investigation, there was no telling where it would take him. All he knew at this point was Stone was probably the last to communicate with Javier Lopez.

They arrived at StoneTech and pulled into the large parking lot. A sign directed him to the visitor parking near the front of the building. In one of the older corporate centers on Page Mill, this building looked out of place. Its three-story glass facade, shimmering in the late morning sun. The building stood in stark contrast to the one just down the hill from it. A massive concrete building with no windows, the tiled image of a sine wave on its side, housed the company that was considered the impetus of 'Silicone Valley'. Old and new, side by side.

This part of Palo Alto was all owned by Stanford University and the land was leased to tech companies, most, if not all, started by graduates of the university. The university owns or controls nearly eight thousand acres of prime California land worth nearly twenty billion dollars. All of it exempt from property taxes. The value of Stanford's holdings is larger than Apple, Google, and Intel combined.

They parked and made the short walk into the lobby where a rent-a-cop security guard greeted them. His face made him look like he was still in high school. But he had the body of someone who spent all his off hours at the gym. Well over six feet tall, with the physique of an NFL lineman.

"Can I help you two?"

"Yes, we're looking for David Stone."

"Can I ask what this is regarding?"

"Police matter", Eckhart said, showing the rent-a-cop his badge as he looked around the three-story lobby. The lobby of StoneTech looked like the entrance to a modern museum. The floors were shiny marble, while the walls were stark white. Behind the guard desk and to the left were a set of double doors that Eckhart assumed led to the offices of the employees. To the far left of the security desk was a water feature that extended the entire three floors, water slowly cascading over rippled metal into a huge sunken basin on the floor. Large koi slowly circled amid the expensive water plants.

To the right was a wall of monitors, which looked larger than the scoreboard at AT&T where the Giants played. A constantly shifting slide show of products, office workers, and people garbed in lab coats, faded in and out in different areas of the massive wall of screens. Eckhart also got glimpses of what looked like 'clean rooms' and employees wearing hazmat suits.

The lobby was larger than Eckhart's entire house, furnished with several expensive-looking leather chairs and tables, randomly sprinkled into individual seating pods. They designed the areas for visitor meetings and to have semi-private conversations. Eckhart glanced up, seeing the second and third floors had open balconies that looked down into the lobby. Although he hadn't had much opportunity to visit many high-tech firms in the valley, he had heard stories about the absurd amounts of money spent on aesthetics. Look like you're successful before you actually are.

"What do you guys make here?" he asked the guard.

The guard leaned over the desk and in a low whisper said, "To be honest, I don't have a clue. Some high-tech shit. That's all anyone does in the valley. Plus, this is my first week here."

Eckhart just nodded, still mesmerized by the scenes on the monitors.

The guard picked up the phone and punched in four numbers and waited for the call to connect.

"Mr. Stone, there are a couple of policemen here to speak with you." Pause "He didn't say, sir." Pause "Yes sir."

The guard turned to Eckhart. "He'll be right out. You can have a seat over there. Can I get you two anything? Water, coffee?"

"No thanks", Eckhart and Fowler took seats in a square of very comfy and very expensive couches in the middle of the lobby.

"This is what I'm talking about. These monitors, this furniture. Hell, the koi fish alone probably cost more than his house. Sometimes I think all of this is just for show. You know the whole, 'look successful to become successful.' Wouldn't surprise me if most of these techies are living on credit just to keep up with the others living on credit. Vicious circle man."

"Maybe you're just thinking too much about this."

"Maybe. Hell, I could be completely wrong, and we're just in the wrong profession."

CHAPTER TWELVE

He was like any man when his mind wasn't clouded with thoughts of his "future". Working, living, going about his day, and not being noticed. Nothing about him stood out. He was the classic nondescript personality bordering on complete invisibility.

This was something he struggled with all his life. Struggled? That really wasn't the right word. It wasn't a struggle to just be yourself. It would have been a struggle to be someone that would fit in. Someone noticed by others. Someone that others would accept.

But that was all right. He didn't need to "fit in". In fact, as he got older, he realized that being invisible to others was a benefit in his line of work. He was the person no one noticed walking down the street. The person the store clerk couldn't remember if they paid with cash or a credit card. He was the man no one could remember walking into the store. Everything from his facial features to the clothes he wore was anything but memorable.

These thoughts that ran through his mind that afternoon as he strolled down Geary after just finishing his late lunch at

Café Enchante. He stopped at a news rack, dropped a couple of quarters in, and grabbed the afternoon paper. He glanced at the headlines before folding the paper and tucking it under his arm. He had a pretty good idea of what the lead article would be about.

This was part of his daily routine. An early morning at the beach, catch a small bite to eat at any of the small cafes close by, grab the paper and catch up on any news that he hadn't created himself, then settle in for the afternoon and whatever it may bring. Most of the time, he knew what that was. The images played in mind and, like it or not, revealed what his day and most likely night would be like.

Of course, in his younger days, this time of day was spent working, not relaxing. He would still head to Ocean Beach before dawn when he needed to clear his head, but back then, it wasn't as often as it had become. And he wouldn't have had time to sit in a café and leisurely enjoy breakfast or lunch. Of course, his job gave him more opportunities to satisfy his needs. They helped to clear the images from his head before they drove him crazy. The kind of job that gave him access to people and their personal lives.

He was retired now, not his idea, but nonetheless he no longer had the job as a means of meeting potential victims. No, if it were up to him, he'd still be working. But his busy body boss didn't like the time he spent at certain clients' homes and when he got that complaint from the lady that thought he was a "little too familiar", well, that was the final nail in the old work coffin.

Being able to enjoy a good cup of coffee and watch people come and go. The differences in how people dress, what they ordered, who they were with depending on the restaurant or diner he was in. He was very observant. He noticed things that most people never would. And some things even the most observant person doesn't notice. So, as he went unobserved, he was able to watch people, their patterns, their tendencies.

The way people dress and what it says about their profession or how they want to be seen. Unemployed, retired, still wearing the clothes from last night's date, trying to make a good first impression. And he could always tell when couples were on first dates, the forced conversations about little to nothing. Or couples that were spending their umpteenth routine morning, both with their faces in the paper or their phones, hardly a word spoken by either the entire time.

But the ones he noticed the most, which caught his eye, were the loners, the single women that had that look of loneliness, and no significant other in their lives at the moment. They had a certain walk about them. A look. Everything from what they ordered, how and what they ate, where they sat. Everything. Of course, he fine-tuned those observation skills with years of study.

They made themselves targets, whether or not they knew it. And he was just the person to take advantage of that. He was never quite sure if it was him consciously making that decision or if it was his subconscious and the visions he had. Or were they one and the same? Did it make a difference? It was just a hunger that consumed him. And it needed to be fed.

After yesterday's brief event, he thought his 'urges' would be satisfied for some time. But that wasn't the case. What used to be sizable gaps in time between his visions and urges had grown shorter. More intense. And more random. The days of the slow build-up, the time between finding and then completing a plan, were gone. Now he felt like things happened in rapid-fire succession. Sometimes within a matter of days.

This scared him. For several reasons. The visions increased in intensity and there were days when they wouldn't stop. Instead of minutes, they lasted for hours. And this was happening more often. Recently, he would experience an entire day of visions so detailed it would incapacitate him with terrible headaches when they were over. When that happened, he had to isolate himself for fear that he would act out in public, and do something without the careful planning he had come to expect.

His latest little escapade was an example of what could happen when the planning wasn't precise. The outcome was fine. It was the details that bothered him. Not realizing there was a roommate. Making more of a spectacle than necessary to accomplish the job. The person dropping her off. All issues when it came to his precision and his planning. It bothered him, but not as much as it should. What was that about? It was as if he didn't care if he was getting sloppy. But that wasn't him. That was out of character.

This was one of the main reasons he stayed away from alcohol. Having impaired senses during one of his episodes could be disastrous. But the main reason was a feeling of not being in control. And that was something that he refused to give up. As much as the visions left him feeling like he was losing control, he had no way of counteracting that. But to purposely put himself in a state where he made poor decisions, or put his mind in a fuzzy state, was contrary to what he believed. It's not like he never tried alcohol. But he was younger, and the visions hadn't taken over his life yet.

He remembers the first time he tried a drink. He was with his dad, spending the weekend with him after the divorce, or maybe it was just when they had split up. He doesn't really remember exactly. His dad came out of the small apartment kitchen with a large water glass filled with ice, and what he thought was water. They were watching a game on TV, snacking on pretzels or chips. His dad had left the room and rather than get up to get his own glass of water, he grabbed his dad's glass and downed a big gulp. He quickly realized it wasn't water, but a tall glass of vodka. He immediately spat it out just as his dad came back into the room.

It was the first and only time he thought his dad was an asshole. The way he laughed at him made him feel small and embarrassed, something his father had never done in the past, or any time in the future.

CHAPTER THIRTEEN

Eckhart was just about to question the security guard again when he spotted a well-dressed young man coming through the doors with a huge grin on his face and heading straight for him. He couldn't afford suits like that, but he could sure tell an expensive one when he saw it. This guy was dressed to the nines. What looked like expensive Italian loafers, so soft they must have felt like slippers. He wore a custom-tailored suit, a silk shirt, and the glint of a watch that Eckhart assumed was a Rolex or some similarly expensive brand. Cleanly shaved, premature salt and pepper hair neatly trimmed. That haircut probably cost more than the 15 bucks I spend, Eckhart thought.

David Stone was a man of large stature. He easily stood 6 foot 6 inches and had an athletic build. Between his size and expensive attire, David Stone presented an imposing figure. Someone that commanded your attention, if not, your respect. To Eckhart, he seemed like the kind of man that usually got his way.

"Officers, I'm David Stone. To what do I owe the pleasure?"

Stone extended his hand to offer a shake and exposed the watch to confirm Eckhart's guess. Rolex. And not one of the low-end ones. Eckhart grabbed his hand and shook it. The very slight smell of expensive aftershave lingered in the air.

"It's actually Detective Eckhart, Mr. Stone. And this is my partner, Detective Fowler. We are with the SFPD. Do you have somewhere private where we can speak?"

"SFPD? What brings you to Palo Alto?"

"Mr. Stone, please, somewhere private?"

"Sure, follow me to my office. I only have a half-hour though, detective. We're preparing for our IPO tomorrow and I need to give the board a demonstration of our new process at 10."

"IPO?"

"Initial Public Offering. On the stock exchange. The NASDAQ. It's our way of generating more funding for our projects and the expansion of our company. So, what's this all about, Detective?"

"Just a few questions regarding a case I'm on. Let's wait until we get to your office. What is it you do here?"

"I'm the CEO."

"No, I mean, what does your company make?"

"Sure, sure. What do we make here? Well, I doubt you'd understand, but we develop the technologies that other companies in Silicon Valley use to make their products."

Eckhart felt like responding to the CEO but thought better of it before interviewing him. It was best if he kept himself on an even setting with Stone, even better if he thought he was smarter than the detective. Interview suspects talked more if they thought they were smarter than the person conducting the interview. If they're guilty, that is. Highly intelligent suspects get frustrated when they have to explain themselves to someone, especially if that someone is in a position of authority.

It was also a matter of where you were questioning a suspect. Eckhart was a master of the interrogation process. Partly from experience and being an excellent judge of human character, and partly because getting them on your turf in your environment kept them off balance. When a suspect is on their own turf, their own environment, they feel powerful, like they have the upper hand. Eckhart was aware of that and made sure the suspects felt they were in control of the situation. He wasn't even sure that Stone was a suspect.

"I'm not sure I understand. What do you mean by the technologies?"

"Well, nearly every electronic product that is made has circuit boards in them. You know, the boards that have all the electrical components like resistors, capacitors, etcetera."

"Ahhh, so you make those components."

"Not exactly. We develop the technology used to make the circuit boards. Here, let me show you."

Stone pointed to a door to the left. Eckhart noticed a keypad with a swipe slot that looked like a credit card machine. Stone took his ID card and slid it through the slot. He then entered a series of numbers and there were two sounds. The first was a brief buzz. The second, an audible "clunk" as the door unlatched. Stone pushed through and gestured Eckhart and Fowler to follow him.

"This is one of our testing labs. We take a random sampling of the products we manufacture and run them through several tests to make sure they meet our minimum requirements for production."

The room they entered looked like something out of a movie to Eckhart. There were several long, heavy workbenches. They were stacked with electrical test equipment, microscopes, soldering guns, and lots of other tools that Eckhart had no idea what they were. Stone walked over to a bin and pulled out a rectangular, thin panel that looked plastic. It was about a foot square. When Stone handed it over to Eckhart, he knew he had seen something similar before. It was very thin, probably less than an eighth inch thick, and covered in tiny rectangular parts that couldn't be any larger than a sixteenth of an inch, plus several larger rectangles.

"So, what you're holding is a standard printed circuit board. That particular one comes from a company that makes microwave test equipment called a Signal Analyzer. What my company does is develop the technology for making that board, or what we call substrate. Most people call them circuit boards. They're used in almost anything electrical you buy today. You'll see there is a front and back to that board. Both sides have circuits on them. Small electrical traces that connect the various parts. What you don't see is, there are several layers of those traces inside the board. That one has sixteen different layers, all with very thin copper traces."

Eckhart turned the board over in his hands, looking at both sides while listening to Stone.

"My company develops the actual process of manufacturing that printed circuit, along with the process for attaching the components. The inner layer connections, or traces, are copper. The outer traces, the ones you can see, are also copper. But they have to be coated with something to keep them from corroding. I'm sure you've seen copper after exposure to air and moisture. It turns green. Corrodes. Beautiful as an architectural feature. Not so much as an electrical conductor. These traces are so thin, so very thin, that any type of corrosion would compromise its conductivity. If that happens, the circuits will short out. Not good, especially if it's in something like a shuttlecraft. It could be fatal."

Eckhart looked at Stone. "So, how do you accomplish that?"

"Do what? Keep them from corroding? Well, without going into too much detail, today we protect a majority of the board with a silk-screening process and then electro-statically plate the places where components go with a tin-nickel alloy. That protects the copper from environmental pollutants and significantly retards the corrosion process. That's where our IPO comes in. We are working on a way to cut costs and improve the long-term reliability of circuit boards. Something that will put us well ahead of our competition."

"This stuff is Greek to me. So, if you don't mind me asking, what is this new process you're working on? How is it so different from what you're currently doing?"

"Actually, detective, I do mind. It is proprietary and I can't discuss it. Certainly not before the IPO announcement tomorrow. Like I said, Detective, I really am on a tight schedule today. Can we proceed to my office?"

"Sure. Thanks for the tour. Perhaps I can come back when you have more time."

They left the lab, Stone unlocking the door the same way he did when they entered. They headed down the hall a short way until it dead-ended at an elevator. Eckhart noted that there were doors on either side of the elevator. One to the left labeled 'No Admittance' with the same electronic keypad and swipe as the lab had. The one to the right simply labeled 'Stairs'. Stone punched the elevator up button as they both waited.

"What's in that room?" Eckhart nodded his head toward the 'No Admittance' door.

"Just our basement storeroom. We keep old project files and other documentation stored there."

The elevator doors opened, and they both walked in. Stone tapped the button for the 3rd floor and Eckhart noticed there was no button for the basement. It appeared the only access was through the locked door on the first floor. They were silent for the short ride up, and Eckhart followed Stone out when the doors opened on the 3rd.

Unlike the first floor, these walls were paneled in a dark wood veneer, the floors were marble, which gave the impression that they were in a completely unique building. The long, wide hall had ceilings that were higher than the first floor, probably 10 feet high. At the end of the hall were two huge, dark double doors. Stone started walking down the hall and stopped at the first door to the right.

"Here we are", Stone stated as he opened the door and let Eckhart and Fowler enter first.

Stone followed him in, taking the chair behind the massive, obviously expensive desk. Instead of immediately taking a seat, Eckhart slowly surveyed the office. One wall was covered in somewhat obscure art. Eckhart thought it was ugly, but assumed it too was expensive and original. Just like everything else with Stone. The opposite wall had what at first appeared to be a large painting, but as Eckhart looked at it, the painting slowly morphed into a different image. It was displaying the same information that the lobby wall of monitors was.

"Same technology as our lobby, just smaller scale." Stone offered.

Eckhart looked at Stone and nodded, then turned back to the changing screens of the monitor. Pictures of employees in white lab coats, as well as some sort of headgear. Eckhart had heard of clean rooms before and thought this was the sort of outfit they would wear in one. The next pic showed some similar-looking printed circuit boards he had just seen in the lab, except these were under a microscope, with a similarly garbed employee looking into the eyepiece. Beneath the monitor was a long ornate bookcase that was filled with various texts. Just as he could feel Stone ready to remind him of his tight time-line, Eckhart turned towards him and asked,

"Do you know a Javier Lopez?"

"Of course, I worked for Javier at Golden Gate Park when I was going to college." Stone's demeanor shifted slightly.

"When was the last time you spoke with Mr. Lopez?" Eckhart was looking directly into Stone's eyes, watching his expression.

Stone stared back at the detective and gathered himself, regaining that initial sense of calm and confidence that the detective first saw when he walked through that door. "Actually, he texted me yesterday."

Eckhart eyes were locked on Stone, trying to read him, to see if there was anything that would show he was lying or holding back information.

"Texted you? What about?"

Eckhart could almost hear the gears turning in Stone's head, trying to figure out what Eckhart knew and how best to respond. Yet that same look of confidence and calm remained on Stone's face. Without flinching or stumbling, he answered Eckhart in a measured and exacting tone.

"He said he had found something. Texted me a couple of pics and asked me to come over and have a look. Why, what did he say?"

"And did you?"

"Did I, what? Have a look, yeah. Went over last night, had a beer, we reminisced, and he showed me some old papers he found."

While David Stone was speaking, Eckhart had started slowly moving around the office, taking his eyes off Stone and perusing the book shelve under the monitor. There were standard books regarding different management processes, twelve steps, many technical books that related to printed circuits and their processes, and a couple of books that looked quite old with leather spines and no markings.

"And that was it? What were the papers he showed you?" Eckhart bent down to pull one of the old leather-bound books off the shelf.

"I'd prefer you not touch those. They are quite old and quite expensive."

"Oh sorry, always curious about what books someone has on their shelves. What are those about?"

"Just old science books. But unique, and like I said, old, and very expensive" Stone was getting annoyed and he was getting nervous, not about the questioning, but the impending demonstration for his board of directors.

"So, what were these papers that Mr. Javier showed you?" Eckhart finally turned around and faced Stone.

"I don't know. Just old papers. What's this about? What did Javier tell you?"

Eckhart walked back across the office to the ugly painting and leaned in to look at the signature. He finally looked up and over at Stone, looking at his face, watching him with the expert eye of an experienced investigator.

"He's dead, Mr. Stone, and it looks like you're the last person to see him alive."

CHAPTER FOURTEEN

Stone's face became ashen when Eckhart told him his old boss had died. Stone slumped back into his chair. Eckhart watched his reaction and felt the emotion Stone exhibited looked genuine.

"Dead? How? What happened?"

"That's what we're trying to figure out," Eckhart continued to stare at Stone. "There was an explosion at his home. Gas. Looks intentional. What time did you leave Mr. Lopez's?"

"Not Late. I was only there a short time. Maybe seven. I had to be back here for a meeting. My board of directors called it to discuss a project we're working on and needed an update. After that, I worked in my office for a while and then went home. When I left his apartment, he was still alive."

"OK. Do you know anyone that would want to hurt Mr. Lopez?"

"No. Not at all. I mean, I hadn't talked to him in several years, but when I worked for him, everyone liked him. I doubt that had changed."

"And do you think Mr. Lopez would hurt himself? Suicide?"

"No, absolutely not. He was always a cheerful guy. He never really let anything bother him."

"And did Mr. Lopez have any next of kin, or someone in his life?"

"No, not that I know of. Like I said, it's been several years."

"One last thing, Mr. Stone. Why does, or rather did, Mr. Lopez call you 'Stookie'?"

"When I first worked for him, I discovered that Golden Gate Park had a lot of old statues, but they were all buried behind bushes and plants. When I asked Javier about it, he told me that McLaren, the original park superintendent, despised statues and made sure that after installation, he planted shrubs around them to hide them from view. He felt monuments to people were intrusions in his park. Plants are beautiful, statues aren't. McLaren called the statues 'Stookies'. I guess it's an old Scottish word meaning plaster cast, or something like that."

"But why call you Stookie?"

"Because, back then, I was really obsessed with them. I was going all over the park, looking for them, studying them. Youthful hobby. So, he nick-named me 'Stookie'. Look, Detective, I hate to cut this short, but I need to be down in the lab to give the demonstration to my board. I'm sorry... I'm still in shock. Javier. Dead."

Stone got up from his desk and walked around to escort Eckhart and Fowler out of his office. Eckhart thanked him for his time and let him know he may need to ask him some further questions. Stone agreed and closed the door behind the detective.

Stone went back to his desk and slumped into the large leather recliner. He thought, 'This is the last thing I need right now. I'm too close and I don't need both the board and now the cops sniffing around.' He spun around in his chair and peered out the 3rd story window at the assorted pines and small sequoia that dotted the hillside down to the valley below. Silicon Valley. What used to be orchards that produced prunes were now companies that produced millionaires. Before that, just oak-strewn rolling hills inhabited by Native Americans, hunters, and gathers, living as simple a life as you could imagine. How did things become so complicated?

He spun around in his chair and looked at the time on his watch. Nine forty-five. Nearly time for the demonstration. The demonstration that he hoped would placate his board of directors, so they continued to fund his project. Of course, the project he was showing to the board wasn't the one he was most concerned with. Yes, this would make the company and its investors a lot of money. It would make David and the rest of the board rich beyond their dreams. But that wasn't enough for David. The project he was showing today used only a fraction of the money David was asking for in funding. He knew the board would never approve of what he was really working on. They were so short-sighted. What was the point of making all this money if you couldn't enjoy it?

Enough procrastinating. David got up from his desk and left his office. He walked down the hall to the elevator, pushed the down button, and the doors immediately opened. He stepped inside and pressed the button for the first floor, where the labs were. As the elevator descended, David thought he would check on his other project before going to the lab. The project where most of his funding was going. When the elevator reached the first floor and the doors opened, he stepped out and made a quick turn to his left to the door marked "Authorized Personnel Only". He looked around and, seeing no one in the halls, he quickly swiped his key card and punched in his code to gain access. The familiar sound of the beep and heavy 'thunk' sounded and David swiftly opened the door, stepped inside, and closed it behind him.

Inside was dark until he felt to his right on the wall and found the light switch. No motion-activated lights in this area. Once illuminated, David turned to the stairs to his left and quickly descended. The elevator didn't reach this area of the building. This was by design. David's design when he was first working with the architect to plan the company's new headquarters over a decade ago.

At first, they used the area for document archive storage, but as the company grew and the amount and importance of the data grew with it, they moved document storage off-site. After David contracted with a company that specialized in document storage and retention, the basement went unused for several years. Until David started working on his pet project. He needed the privacy that the basement provided. Benton and he were the only two with access to this area, and Benton hadn't been in there for years. Most of the employees never gave it a second thought, if they thought of it at all.

When David reached the bottom of the stairs, he hit the bank of switches on the wall with the side of his hand, flipping all three toggles on. One by one, the fluorescent lights came to life. Several workbenches filled the room, the kind you would see in a medical lab. Dozens of beakers covered their surfaces, along with test tube racks, Bunsen burners, and an array of notepads and other lab paraphernalia.

In the middle of the room stood a large contraption that resembled a still, the kind you'd see in the backwoods of Tennessee. Unlike one of those, medical-grade stainless steel made up this still. A stainless-steel boiler that sat on top of a radiant heat cooktop, a glass swan's neck coming out of the boiler, leading to another stainless-steel pre-heater, and then a curled glass worm pipe leading into the condenser. A tap protruded out of the bottom of the condenser and a large glass jar was collecting the small amount of moisture that dripped from the tap.

What also made this setup different from your common still were the high-end gauges that provided the various temperatures of the three components. There was also a small indicator on the tap. David walked over to the gauges, looked at each one, and then went to the nearest table and grabbed a notebook to jot down the various numbers. He went back over to the gauges and took one last look before turning the lights off and heading back up the stairs. When he reached the top, he turned off the entry lights and exited the door, making sure it latched and locked before walking away.

Stone headed to the main lab, the one where the demonstration would take place. It was on the main floor, next to the lab where he had just shown the detective their work. It was a little before ten when he opened the door to the lab and walked in. Empty still. Good, time to set up and get this over with. Of course, what he was going to show the board wasn't the full-scale project they were working on. This was a smaller version meant to fit in the small area this lab provided. Once they had perfected the process, they would build a manufacturing plant that could handle the quantities and provided the needed security.

The wall next to the security door had a rack of several white lab coats. Stone grabbed one and slipped it on. Not that this lab was the kind where you could get your street clothes dirty or there was any danger of chemical spills. It was just a tradition in labs, especially those in Silicon Valley, that companies provided their lab workers with the traditional white lab coats. Stone was used to wearing them ever since his days in the chemistry department at Stanford. It was a force of habit.

Stone walked over to the small version he would use today. In basic terms, it was a tabletop nuclear reactor. The process is necessary to remove the required number of protons and electrons from a lead atom and convert it to an atom of gold. Of course, he hadn't successfully accomplished this yet, but he knew he was close. He had been successful in removing the electrons, but all that created was an ion of lead. Not what he or the investors wanted. The problem was removing the protons. He was close.

But that wasn't the plan for today. Today was going to be more of a magic trick. Sleight of hand. Something to keep the board and specifically Benton, happy and continuing to sign those checks. Today the atom of gold was already going to be in the reactor and other than some noise and lights, nothing was really going to happen. He could have built a complex plating device, something to plate a bar of lead with gold, but in the end, he truly believed that eventually he could make this process work. There had to be some level of truth to the documents he found. It was just a matter of cracking the code.

The day he found those notebooks, he knew they were important, and he was just as confident that they were accurate and had been actually used to transform lead into gold. When he eventually showed them to his college friend Alex Benton, along with the proposal for starting this business, Benton was just as confident. Benton had been a classmate of David's at Stanford. Stone majoring in biochemistry and Benton in finance. They both minored in business, and that's where their friendship developed. When Stone approached Benton about his idea for starting Stone Technologies, they became inseparable. Benton had been part of the company from the start, first as the COO and now as the chairman. Until a week ago, he had supported Stone and his project.

Stone assembled the board a year ago to prepare for the IPO. He had just assumed he would be both the CEO and the Chairman of the board. That didn't happen and the last twelve months had been a struggle between him and the board over the amount of money being spent on his pet project. The project that Stone was confident would make them all rich and change the world of technology. You had to spend money to make money, right?

But now Benton was even questioning the viability of this project. With very little to show for it, Stone understood the concern. He just always felt he would have his friend in his corner. With the impending IPO, it was obvious his friend was thinking more about short-term gains. Like a true numbers guy. It really wasn't that big of a surprise to Stone. His friend had always been concerned more with the bottom line than the potential of the idea. He thought Benton never really believed in the project. He just went along with the idea, since the company had potential in other areas for a constant stream of money. It still made the IPO viable, but that wasn't what they were selling to their potential investors.

The familiar sound of the beep and thunk of the security door unlatching snapped Stone out of his thoughts. It was time for his performance. The board slowly filed in, one by one, with Benton bringing up the rear. Stone busied himself, ignoring the board members until Benton spoke first.

"Are we ready for the demonstration?"

"Yes, just a few last-minute adjustments," Stone said, without looking up and acknowledging the group that now stood around the lab bench where the small but sophisticated device sat. He was still upset by the emergency board meeting last night and the board questioning his progress. This was his company, goddamn it! But if the Apple board could kick out Steve Jobs, his board could certainly do the same to him.

"Gentleman, as you know, our Project Alchemy's mission is to find a more reliable and cost-effective method to replace selective plating of printed circuits. In our current manufacturing process, a tin-nickel amalgam is used to protect the copper-clad printed circuits from corrosion. This works relatively well, but it has known deficiencies. Over time, the coating or plating can break down, especially in the presence of moisture and heat. In the past, we selectively gold-plated portions of a printed circuit for its conductivity qualities and its resistance to corrosion and durability. But gold was and is expensive. The industry moved to our current process and accepted the deficiencies. With Project Alchemy, we eliminate those costs and inadequacies. The upside for us is tremendous! By manufacturing our own gold out of cheap lead, our product will surpass all of our competition, keeping our manufacturing costs down and profit margins high."

Stone looked around the room at the board members. Instead of seeing a look of interest, he saw the blank stares of men that were promised progress and yet shown none. He turned back to the large tabletop reactor and donned a pair of thick safety glasses. Grabbing a box full of the same glasses and handing it back to Benton, Stone asked everyone to take one and then stand behind the two-inch plexiglass wall at the end of the lab.

"David, this is all well and good. We know the basics of the project. What we're here for is to see what progress you've made. We've included this in the prospectus for the IPO tomorrow and we better have something to show in order to make the IPO successful," said Benton.

Stone continued to make sure the reactor was ready to fire, not turning to face his friend and the board. When he was sure everything was ready, he picked up a handheld actuator with a long cord attached to the finely machined apparatus. Walking towards the glass partition, he addressed the board one last time.

"In just a few minutes, I'll show you exactly that. But there is one more thing I think you should all consider. If it hasn't already become apparent to you, there is a significant upside to this project. One that only myself and you, the members of the board, will have knowledge of and benefit from. In developing this process, I also explored the possibility of transforming these metals strictly for monetary gains."

Without waiting for a reply, he turned back to face the reactor, raised the hand holding the actuator, and pressed slowly down on the button. The lab floor began a deep vibration along with a low hum. A strange burning smell could be detected. He released his finger and as quickly as it started; the vibration stopped, and the hum subsided. After a brief pause, Stone stepped around the divider and walked towards the small reactor. He picked up a large crescent wrench and unbolted the back end of the device. Removing the 6 large nuts holding the casement to the reactor, he slowly removed the cover and carefully slid a screened tray out of the device. Walking back to the board, he held it up and displayed its contents.

The members of the board leaned forward in unison to see what was on the small tray. As they got close enough, the fluorescent lights of the lab glinted off the small flecks of material in the mesh tray's bottom. Gold!

CHAPTER FIFTEEN

The board of directors of StoneTech continued to look on in amazement at the small, yet very real collection of gold flecks in the bottom of the screen tray David Stone was holding. He had accomplished what he had set out to do, albeit on a much smaller scale than they expected. But the possibilities of what this could mean financially for their company, and ultimately for them, were astounding. He handed them the tray, and they passed it around, gazing at the results, and then at each other, huge smiles appearing on their faces. Several of the board members actually reached into the tray and touched the small gold flecks.

"Oh, they're real, touch them. Better yet, each of you should take a small bit with you. Something you can remember this day by."

Each member of the board reached into the tray and snatched a small fleck of gold out. The tray quickly made the rounds, and the tray was nearly empty when it was passed to the last board member. Although the flecks were no bigger than the tip of a pencil eraser and paper thin, each board member had a huge smile on their face, like small children given a shiny new penny.

"So, gentlemen. As I promised you, the process works. Of course, this reactor can only transform small amounts of lead at a time. My request for increased funding is necessary to build a large enough device so we can go into production. I'm assuming I can count on you to not only continue my funding for this project, but to increase it to the requested level that will allow me to build a full-scale reactor?"

The board, all of them smiling, looked at each other and then at Alex Benton, the Chairman of the Board. Finally, one of them spoke.

"I think I speak for all of us when I say this demonstration has been quite impressive. I think with some further discussion, we should be able to come to a consensus on your funding. Gentlemen, let's all regroup in the conference room in an hour."

Benton looked from the board back to Stone and then walked over to the table-top reactor. Without touching it, he inspected it, walking around the large, heavy metal work bench to get a better look. When he got to the side of the bench where the tray had been removed from the reactor, he reached out to touch the reactor.

"Please don't touch that, Alex," Stone ordered.

"You all go ahead. I'll be right up. I just need a few minutes with David," Benton replied, looking directly at Stone. He walked them to the lab door and closed it after they had all filtered out.

"What the hell are you trying to pull?" Benton screamed at David Stone. "We both know what you showed them was some sort of trick. How did you do it?"

"I'm warning you, don't push me. I'll do whatever it takes to keep funding this project. Your only job at this point is to convince the board to do just that." Stone responded without turning to face Benton.

"What happened to you? This isn't the guy I went into business with. You used to be focused on building this company. Now, all you think about is this crazy idea and you're acting irrational. If it's not working, why are you so intent on continuing to throw money at it?"

Stone felt himself raging. His heartbeat quickened and his muscles tensed. He towered over the bespectacled Benton by a good six inches, his mass nearly double that of the thin money man. Had he wanted to, he could make quick work of Benton. Not yet.

"Look, before you head upstairs to discuss this with the board, I want to show you something. Something that will change your mind. Follow me."

Without waiting for Benton to answer, Stone strode out of the lab and headed down the hall towards the elevator. He couldn't keep this to himself any longer. Maybe if Benton saw what he was really spending the funding on, he would realize how important this was. Stone hadn't wanted to share this with anyone, but it felt like the only choice he had. He needed Benton in order to convince the board not to cut his R&D budget.

"Where are we going?" Benton asked in confusion but followed Stone down the hall.

When they came to the elevator, instead of pushing the button to go back up to his office, Stone swiped his keycard to open the door to the storage room downstairs. After keying in his code and the door unlocked with its familiar clunk, he held it open for Benton and gestured him in. Once they were both in, Stone hit the switch to light up the stairwell and quickly and silently descended the steps and into what used to be the documentation storage area. He then flicked the switch to illuminate the entire area and turned to Benton.

"I didn't want to show you this until I had perfected it, but I guess I need to, so you'll understand why we need that funding."

"What the... What happened to all our archives? When did this lab get built?" Benton slowly surveyed the room, stunned.

"I've moved them all to an off-site location. Earlier this year, it was almost at capacity. I could have spent money to have it all digitized and reduce the space, or just paid for it to be stored elsewhere. Once the room was clear, I put it to better use."

"But, what? Why?"

"Look, remember why we started this company? The information I found? Well, there was more that I kept to myself. I didn't understand it at first either, but over time I came to understand. This is all part of Alchemy and our project upstairs. That can make us and the board money. But this? This is what will allow us to spend it."

"I don't understand."

"The philosopher's stone. It's what all Alchemists were searching for. But even they misunderstood what that was. They thought it was some mystical element found in nature that helped transform base metals like lead into noble metals such as gold. They believed all metals were essentially the same, they just transformed over time from one stage to another, finally reaching the ultimate purity of gold. Except they were wrong. In more ways than one."

"Of course, they were wrong. We know that metals and other natural elements are unique unto themselves. They don't change mystically."

"Yes, and they were also wrong about the philosopher's stone. What it was and what its intended use was. In the research I did, there was mention of the stone and what it could provide for true believers. Alchemists spoke of it in esoteric terms and most researchers believed that this was the agent of change mentioned in their ancient texts."

Stone explained that the terms philosopher's stone and elixir were often found together in ancient writings. That this information was in multiple texts dating back to ancient

Mesopotamia. There were references to it found in several cultures, across several hundreds of years.

Stories regarding the philosopher's stone and this mysterious elixir were in ancient documents from China, India, Europe, and Japan. The one commonality between them all? The documents, although found in these various countries, spanning hundreds of years, were all written in Arabic. Some researchers first thought because of this, the concept must have originated in Arabia. But Stone had wondered if that was just because they were first documented by the Arabians. Because of his love for the Rosicrucian Society and the research of their members going back thousands of years, Stone believed that Alchemy was actually born in Egypt and that the Egyptians, believers in the afterlife, had actually perfected the process. They believed that the philosopher's stone was actually the elixir of immortality and used this to extend life.

Benton listened quietly as Stone outlined his theory. He wasn't sure if this was the same guy he had gone to college with. That person was highly intelligent and not given to flights of fancy. Or at least that's what he thought. After the last few days, he wasn't sure of anything anymore. He certainly wasn't sure of Stone's mental state, given his actions and now what he was hearing.

When he finished, Stone turned to the contraption in the middle of the room, the condenser, and removed the small glass jar from where the tap was slowly dripping a clear fluid. He held it up to the light and swirled it around, like a wine connoisseur examining an expensive Bordeaux. A grin formed on his face. His eyes opened strangely wide as he continued to look at his creation. Benton felt like Stone was in his own little world now, lost in the wonder of his creation. Just when he thought Stone had forgotten he was even there, he turned to Benton, still holding the glass at eye level, and offered it to Benton.

"So, these past several months, I've developed a process for creating this elixir. In simplest terms, it's a distillation process. Extracting the active agents from the various elements into a very refined and potent elixir. That's why I need you to head back up to that board room and convince them to continue funding our Alchemy project. Considering how excited they were when they left, you won't have to do much convincing. They look like they're ready to give me anything I ask for."

"And what happens when they find out that little demonstration was all a fake? And they will find out."

"Is it though? It's possible I can make that process work. And even if I can't, the only way they find out is if you tell them. And that will not happen. Will it?"

Stone continued to hold the glass up, his eyes never leaving it. Slowly swirling the liquid in the glass, his gaze unwavering.

"Take it," Stone said in a voice that made Benton uneasy.

"What do you mean, 'take it'?"

"Drink it. I'm offering you a chance of a lifetime. No, that's not exactly true. I'm offering you a lifetime, the time to do whatever you want, to have whatever you want."

"You're crazy. Even if what you said is true, and I'm not saying I believe it is, this would need extensive testing. Trials, blind tests, the whole shot before we even consider human trials."

"I've already started human trials."

"Me. I've been taking limited doses for 6 months now. Before starting, I took blood and several DNA and cell swabs and recorded everything for future comparisons. The samples are in deep cold storage. I've been taking monthly samples and comparing them to the originals. I think you'll be amazed at the results. Of course, I started treating rats with the liquid to observe any negative side effects. There were none. But I can tell you, the positive effects have been astounding! Older rats showed an increase in vitality and alertness, as well as the ability to solve complex maze problems with acuity."

Benton stared at Stone, trying to assess if what he was hearing was true or if his friend had gone mad. Perhaps both. Six months. That was just about the time that Stone isolated himself, his behaviors becoming different. Of course, the isolation could relate to the secret project and all the time he'd obviously been spending down in the basement lab. But it could also result from whatever was in this liquid.

"Stone, let me ask you, what specifically is in the distillation? What are you distilling?"

Stone, thinking that Benton was suddenly interested in the project, excitedly replied, "That's just it. Nothing special. Just a combination of different elemental metals, heated to a liquid state and then slowly distilled into this liquid."

"How did you know what to use? I just don't understand."

"It was all in those notebooks I told you about. At first, I thought they were about transforming base metals into rare metals. You know, the ancient Alchemy idea. But when analyzing them against findings from other scientists of the time, I discovered that what they were all trying to discover, or create, was the process that makes metals transform."

"Stone, we know that's not true, because —"

Stone cut him off. "Yes, I know, they were wrong, but they were on to something else. They thought the philosopher's stone was the mystical compound or nature's elixir that transformed metals to their highest state. But in reality, the philosopher's stone was just a metaphor for their ultimate discovery. The elixir of immortality!"

"Ok, say I believe you. How do you know this elixir is doing what you say it is?"

"Great question! So, you know from your studies that as people age, their cells become rather sticky. They collapse on themselves and aren't as robust, let's say. Well, my initial cell analysis showed just that. But after several months of intake, my cells plumped up and looked like the cells of a much younger man."

"That really proves nothing. You'd have to do years of trials and do more than just look at your cells in a microscope. This is nuts."

"Try it. Join me. We can live longer than anyone has ever imagined. Time to spend the millions, no, billions, we will make."

"Hell no. You're crazy. I know you think that charade would convince the board to continue your funding, but I'm ending that. I'm going to the board and telling them to cut the funding. Not only that, I'm recommending that you're removed as CEO of this company."

Benton turned away from Stone and left the lab. Stone still fuming from what his old friend had told him. There is no way I'm letting him end this!

CHAPTER SIXTEEN

After regaining his composure, Stone climbed the stairs to leave the lab. He couldn't understand how Benton didn't understand the potential of what he was working on. Stone always was the one with vision. Benton was just the numbers guy and could never see beyond the bottom line. He knew what he had to do, and he had so little time to handle the issue. As he opened the door to the hall and turn to take the elevator to his office, a voice from behind startled him.

"Mr. Stone, the detective is still here. He says he has a couple more questions for you. He's in the lobby," the pretty young blond receptionist said, waiting for a response from Stone.

"Tell him I'll be right there. I just need to run to my office."

"Yes sir", she spun around and started walking back to the reception area, just as the doors to the elevator opened. Stone stepped in and punched the 3rd floor button hard enough to break it. Still seething from his confrontation with Benton, and worried about what he might, well probably, say to the board of directors. Stone knew what he had to do. The elevator reached the third floor, the doors opened, and he stepped out and headed to his office.

Once inside, he slid behind his desk and opened each drawer, frantically searching for something. His thoughts were torn between what he was looking for and what had just happened in the lab, and the ramifications of that meeting. He still couldn't completely understand why his old friend, someone he had started the company with, could not see the awesome possibilities of what he was doing. Of what they were doing. But it didn't surprise him. There were two kinds of people in the world. Leaders and followers. Innovators and non-believers. And now he had these detectives poking around. None of this would be good for the IPO. He had to get rid of all these problems. And he had to do it now.

He continued to rummage through the drawers, pulling them open, flipping through papers, push pins, paper clips, old badges, and key cards. Finally reaching the bottom side drawer with a handful of hanging files in it. Mostly reports and statistics of the latest sales reports and project updates provided by the department heads. He pushed the files against the back of the drawer, exposing the bottom. And there it was. His old Blackberry, the one he used in college, was still in its original holster case with the magnetized flip cover. He grabbed it, opened the flip cover, and pulled the phone out, checking for a charge. Dead. He looked back into the bottom drawer and saw it was empty. Damn it! He pushed the row of files and bit harder and saw the end of the charging cable. Stone reached under the files and removed it, got up, and walked across the office to an available wall outlet. He plugged in the charger and then attached the old Blackberry to it and saw the small charging indicator light up. Great!

Stone slammed the drawers shut, stood up, and adjusted his coat and tie. He took a deep breath and calmed his nerves. He needed to present a calm, businesslike demeanor to the detectives. Stone needed to put all this to rest. Once and for all. He needed to keep this project alive and make sure the IPO on Wednesday was successful. If he could hold it together for just one more day, this would all be worth it. The board would finally be on his side and they would all be rich!

Stone left his office, locking the door behind him and went back to the elevator. He took it down to the first floor, again adjusted his tie, and strode confidently towards the lobby and the waiting detectives. He made the short walk, his mind still playing over what he needed to do. What he had to do. His friend and chairman of the board was about to expose him to the board of directors, his project was going to be stopped, and he was going to lose his company. Yes, this had to be done.

"Detectives, what else can I help you with?"

"Well, we got a few blocks away and realized that you might help us with some information regarding your old boss since he doesn't have any next of kin," Eckhart spoke first.

"You had said that you don't know anyone or any reason that someone would hurt Mr. Lopez, correct?" Fowler asked.

"That's right."

"Is there anything you know about Javier Lopez that would put him in any danger from anyone? Any activities he has, addictions, bad habits, hobbies, anything that could help us?" Fowler continued.

"Look, Mr. Stone, we know you were in a hurry earlier, but we really could use any information you may have about your old boss. With no relatives or other friends to speak to, we are kind of at a roadblock. Anything. Anything at all might help." Eckhart implored.

"I honestly can't think of anything. Like I told you earlier, Javier was a really easy-going guy. He was almost always happy, loved his job, and loved plants. He was just… happy."

"And was there anything about this thing he found, this notebook, that would be a reason to hurt him?"

"Not that I know of, no. It was just some old notebook. He called me because he thought I could help him figure out what it all meant. All I could tell him is it looked like a lot of chemistry formulas, but I didn't know what they meant. That wasn't my area of study at Stanford."

"And what happened to the notebook?" Fowler asked.

"What do you mean?"

"Well, we didn't find it at the scene. Did you take it with you?"

"Why would I take it with me?"

"I don't know. That's why I'm asking." Fowler kept pressing.

"No. No, I didn't take it. It must have burned in the fire."

"Or whoever killed Mr. Lopez took it." Eckhart offered.

Stone was spinning now. Did they know he had taken the notebook when he left Javi's apartment? He needed to deal with that. Just like he needed to deal with Benton. And he had to deal with both soon. Before they wanted to search through his company.

Stone could feel himself tensing up, his heartbeat speeding up. He hoped that this minor change wasn't noticeable to the detectives. He knew they looked for things like that, things that would turn someone into a suspect, and that was the last thing he needed. Not now. Not when he was so close.

"Honestly, I just can't imagine someone wanting to kill him. Really, I just can't. Javier was like a second father to me. I loved working for him. With him. I learned a lot from him. Are you sure that it was a murder? That it wasn't an accident?"

"Well, no, we aren't sure. But we need to explore every possibility," Fowler responded. "We'll know more when we get the M.E.'s report."

"Ok. Well, I'd like to know when you find out. And since Javier didn't have any next of kin, I'd like to take care of the arrangements when the time comes."

"We'll be in touch, Mr. Stone. Thanks for your time. If you think of anything else, you know where to reach us," Eckhart said as the two detectives turned to leave. They had nearly gotten to the exit doors when Stone called out after them.

"Detectives? I loved him. Like a father." And Stone turned away and went through the door, back to the hallway leading to the labs and the elevator.

When he got to the elevator, he pressed the Up button, and the doors immediately opened. He got in and pressed the button for the third floor. It felt like an eternity, but in a matter of seconds, he was on the third floor and heading back to his office. The phone only needed a small charge to get what he needed. He used his key card and swiped to get into his office. Stone quickly walked over to where he left the charging phone on the windowsill. He picked it up and noticed it already had a ten percent charge. That's enough, he thought. He pressed the power button and the familiar Blackberry logo flashed on the screen and then the small screen populated with the ancient-looking icons.

Stone smiled to himself as he looked at the phone. Only ten years old and the thing in his hand felt like an ancient artifact, something so old that was so cutting edge at one time. He shook himself out of the daydream and quickly reacquainted himself with the technology. Using the scroll button and making a few clicks here and there, he found what he was looking for. A few more clicks and keystrokes and the task was done. It was just a matter of time now. He unplugged the phone from the charger and the charger from the wall, wrapped them up together and returned to his desk. He pulled open the bottom drawer, pushed the files to the back, and dropped them both into the drawer, pulling the files back to cover them up again.

He sat down at his desk, slumped back into his chair, and calmed himself. Stone had some time before he had to meet with the board of directors and Benton. He felt more confident now that he'd be able to convince them that the project deserved the continuation of funding he was requesting. Regardless of what Benton felt, Stone was still the CEO of his company, and he planned on keeping it that way. Tonight would also be a good time to get them focused on the IPO and what that would mean for all of them and their investors. It was time to flip the script with them, redirect their focus, and return to the original path his company was on. Stone felt himself nodding off. It had already been a long day, and he still had a lot of work to do, but giving himself twenty minutes to catch his breath before dealing with the board was something he deserved. He let his head go back against the headrest of his chair and closed his eyes.

After Stone left them in the lobby, Eckhart and Fowler looked at each other and went through the door, heading back to the car. They walked in silence until they reached the car and Eckhart spoke.

"What do you think?"

"Not sure, but he seemed a bit nervous about some of the questions, specifically the notebook."

"Yeah, I think we need to keep him on the list of possible suspects."

They got into the car and left the parking lot, heading back to the Taraval station. As Fowler drove, Eckhart went over Stone's answers to their questions. He knew more about the notebook than he was letting on, but Eckhart couldn't quite put his finger on what that might be. This was the point that both he and Fowler agreed on. Stone was holding back on information related to the notebook.

As far as Javier's death, Eckhart couldn't be sure, but Stone seemed genuinely upset about it and that he possibly had nothing to do with it. That part neither of them could be sure until the M.E.'s report came out, and they confirmed whether he was dead before the fire. And if the SFFD could determine with any certainty if the fire was accidental or purposely set, would go a long way towards motive and suspects. For that, they would have to wait.

Even with a cause of death, it would be hard to pin it on Stone unless they found evidence at the scene beyond him being there. He admits to seeing Lopez and discussing his find, but other than that, Eckhart had nothing. If Stone were innocent and did take the notebook, why deny it? More questions than answers at this point.

CHAPTER SEVENTEEN

Benton left the lab, angry and upset at what just transpired with his college friend and the company's CEO. How could this intelligent man he had known all these years think what he was doing was safe? And it wasn't just the safety issue. That he could believe in such a preposterous idea as immortality troubled Benton. Although he didn't want to, the actions of Stone and the drastic changes to his personality over the last few months were enough to justify removing him from his position as CEO. Benton had been noting those instances where Stone's actions ran afoul of the board of directors and compromised the integrity of the company. During that same time frame, he had printed out emails and other documents and removed them from his office, just in case they were needed. Now was that time.

Instead of taking the elevator to the third floor and the board of directors waiting for him in the conference room, he went to his car and retrieve the evidence so he could present it to them now and start the process of Stone's removal. He honestly never thought it would come to this, and he worried what Stone would do in his obviously altered state of mind. But he also had to think of the employees, the company's investors, and the upcoming IPO. When he first started printing the emails and other project status reports and documents, he really never thought he would have to use them. He did it more as a precautionary step, thinking he would just destroy them later when they weren't needed. But after the encounter with Stone today, he knew he was past the point of no return.

He walked across the large lobby of StoneTech and approached the automatic sliding doors. They opened, and he passed through, making a left towards the employee parking lot. The sun was just setting in the hills to the west of Palo Alto and the sodium lights of the parking lot were flickering into action. The large native pines and tall redwoods dotting the lot cast long shadows that the lights struggled to remove. Benton enjoyed this time of the evening. On a better night, he would head to his large home in Los Altos, to enjoy a glass of very expensive wine and watch the sunset. Instead, he was dealing with this mess and trying to hold the company together through the IPO.

Benton's car was at the far end of the parking lot. Although the lot rarely filled, having more spaces than employees, he had a habit of parking as far away from everyone as possible. Mainly to protect his $100k car, but also to get exercise every chance he could. Since graduating college and helping to start Stone Technologies, any time left for exercise was very limited. He was halfway across the lot and the shadows from the trees nearly covered the lot now. The sodium lights created small yellow iridescent circles on the ground that helped illuminate the path to the car but did nothing to light up the entire lot. The figure lurking in one of those dark shadows was counting on that to conceal his location until the time was right.

Benton was so focused on Stone and what he was going to do, no, what he needed to do, that he didn't notice someone was following him to his car. He knew that something had changed in Stone the past several months, and now he had reason to believe that Stone's obsession with this project was probably the cause. Although, after seeing what he had been doing, experimenting with this concoction on his own body for six months might have as much to do with his mental stability as anything. It didn't matter to Benton what the reason was. For the success of the company and the

IPO, Stone needed to be removed from making any decisions that could adversely affect that success.

Benton and Stone were fast friends at Stanford and to see him decline to this level was scary. How could someone so smart, so talented just throw it all away on something that obviously had no chance of working? It had the same feeling as the gold miners that rushed to California in the 1850s. Visions of getting rich quickly clouded their better judgment. They called it gold fever. More likely caused by the mercury they used in the mining process to remove the gold from quartz ore. The only people that got rich during the gold rush were the entrepreneurs that were smart enough to get into the business that provided supplies to all those seeking gold. Shovels, pickaxes, food and alcohol. Prices for some that were higher than they are today.

It felt like Stone was heading down that same delusional path. But worse yet, he was possibly killing himself in seeking immortality. Benton thought about the distilled drink that Stone had offered him. He should probably get that analyzed. Everything aside, he still cared about his friend and once he got the company stabilized and the IPO rolled out, he wanted to make sure that Stone wasn't doing irreparable harm to his body. Once he spoke with the board, he'd return to the lab and get a sample for evaluation.

He wondered if Stone had planned this all along, even going back to their college days. Stone's plan for developing a better printed circuit processing method came after a couple summers interning with a local high-tech firm. The intern jobs were posted at Stanford and a majority of them were offered by past graduates that started and ran businesses after their college days. Encouraged by professors and enabled by the vast landholdings of the university, some of the largest firms in the world were only several city blocks from each other. All on land leased from the university. It was a very incestuous business model.

Looking back, when Stone approached Benton about his idea of becoming the largest and most profitable circuit processing facility, the business plan sold him. He was a quick learner and adept at finding cost-saving measures and streamlining techniques that Benton thought were brilliant. It took a little convincing, and the two quickly pulled together a core team of grads to make their stake. But looking back, Benton now realized that Stone always had other ideas. He remembered that one day when Stone had a few too many beers at a campus party; he blurted out something about finding some ancient clues. He had reached into his pocket and pulled out a folded-up sheet of paper containing what looked like chemical formulas. The paper looked to be a copy of an older document, and when Benton had reached out to take it for a closer look, Stone had snapped. At the time, Benton figured he was just drunk and never thought of it again. But now, perhaps that paper was the clue he spoke of. Perhaps it was what started Stone down this path of absurdity.

Benton snapped out of his thoughts as he approached his car. He fumbled in his pockets for the fob that unlocked the Mercedes S-Class sedan. He opened the driver's side door and then realized that the documents he was looking for were in the trunk. Benton closed the door and headed around to the rear of the car. It was at this point that he finally sensed something was amiss, that he wasn't alone. He turned around quickly just as the stalking figure got within a few feet of him. The long shadows of dusk swept across the stranger's face. He took a step closer, and a filtered ray of sun illuminated his face. Benton squinted, and then a sudden look of familiarity came across his face. He smiled.

"You, you startled me, what are____"

Before he could get the full sentence out, Benton saw the flash of shiny metal reflecting the last light of the setting sun. The assailant, in a swift and deliberate motion, sliced open Benton's neck. He felt it before he could come to grips with what was happening. The front of his shirt became wet and warm and he felt himself unable to catch his breath, although he could hear breathing. He instinctively tried to raise his hands in a defensive move, but also to grip his neck and somehow stop the bleeding. He could do neither. His assailant had dropped his weapon and grabbed both of Benton's arms in order to hold him steady against his car. He was becoming lightheaded, and he felt himself slipping when two large hands moved up and gripped his shoulders and held him upright. His eyes were fluttering, and he was still trying to comprehend what had just happened. How could he have done this and why? He tried to speak, but all he could muster were some gurgling noises. His voice box had been severed along with his throat and jugular vein in his neck.

Benton had been murdered, and he was still alive to feel and see it happening. To himself. He tried to push the two enormous arms away, to raise them to his throat to somehow stop the bleeding. To stop it before it was too late. Was it too late? He again tried to speak, this time mouthing the word exaggeratedly. "Why?"

"Why? I'll tell you why. I can't let you ruin my investment in this company. I've waited far too long for this opportunity, and I will not let some petty pencil pusher keep me from acquiring what I deserve. You were never that smart at Stanford. You were just lucky. Lucky to connect with someone smarter than you. Someone who could actually make things happen. Why? Guys like you come along every year and stumble into millions. I will not let you keep me from mine, that's why!"

Benton felt his body slowly slipping away. He reached out and tried to grab at his assailant's face, his hands flailing at the killer's jacket, scratching, clawing. His assailant stared at him, watching him. The blood still pumping from the large gash in his neck, fast at first, now slowing to a smaller stream. The vision of his assailant slipped in and out of focus as he lost consciousness. Benton made one last attempt to fight back. With his last ounce of energy, he swung his right arm at his attacker, catching him on the shoulder with a weak slap.

His hand continued across the attacker's chest, his fingers catching the jacket pocket and ripping it off.

"Relax, my friend. Your heart is beating faster than normal. You're losing a lot of blood and becoming faint and feeling weak. It's called hypovolemic shock. Blood helps regulate the body's temperature. Losing this much so quickly, I'm sure you're feeling colder. Yes, I can feel your body shaking. It won't be long now."

Dusk had turned ominously darker, the shadows completely concealing the scene at the edge of the employee parking lot. To anyone driving by or looking on from a distance, it appeared to be two people, sex undetermined, talking and possibly hugging. Nothing to see here, move along. The reality of the situation was much worse as one man held the other, watching the life slowly slip out of him.

As Benton's eyes finally fluttered and closed for the last time, the blood slowed to a trickle and the gurgling stopped. His assailant pushed him back against his expensive German car and, holding him up with one hand, reached for the key fob with the other. Benton's head snapped back in a grotesque motion that opened the gash in his neck even further. The assailant found the keys and quickly activated the trunk lock. He heard the thunk of the lock disengaging and the lid of the trunk pop open a crack. He grabbed Benton by both hands and led him to the rear of the car, once again propping him up so he could open the trunk fully. Once open, he let Benton fall backward into the trunk and quickly closed it. He wasn't dead yet, but he knew there was no coming back from this. The trunk lid closed, and he was left to bleed to death in the dark.

"I'll be back later to take care of you. Well, your body."

The last thing he heard before consciousness finally slipped away was the familiar beep his fob made when he locked his car and the loud thunk of the locks engaging.

CHAPTER EIGHTEEN

Stone woke up from his brief nap without the help of any alarm clock or reminder from his watch. He had been taking 'power naps' since his days in college. When he read about entrepreneurs and people with high IQs and how they accomplished so much on so little sleep, he made of point of training his body to do the same. While going to college, he would set his alarm to wake himself after only six hours of sleep each night. Each month, he would shave another fifteen minutes off of that time until he was down to four hours. He had continued that same regimen of only four hours of sleep each night, and allowed himself a couple of twenty-minute naps during the day as 'boosters'. Over time, he would fight taking the daytime naps as being weak and lately, he felt like he didn't need them. That was until this week and the pressure of the IPO, the push back from Benton and the board's scrutiny of the company's finances and requests for more project spending.

He looked at his watch and realized he had actually slept twice as long as he wanted, nearly an hour. It still left him time to gather his thoughts and pull himself together for the meeting with the board. After the successful demonstration earlier today, he felt confident that they would green-light the increase in spending he had requested. There were no guarantees, so he was ready to convince them if he had to. Announcing the new process for manufacturing printed circuit boards on the same day as the IPO was certain to get an influx of much-needed cash, and convince the board to loosen the purse strings and allow the spending now.

Stone got up from his chair and left his office, heading to the boardroom. Board meetings used to be something Stone looked forward to, even enjoyed. It was his opportunity to dazzle the older executives on his board with his technical expertise. That was until the last few weeks. The pressure of the upcoming IPO, along with their scrutiny of the money he was spending on his special project, had taken their toll. Benton was no help. Instead of providing a supporting role, Benton had been siding with the board regarding his spending and project management. What bothered Stone more was Benton questioning his ability to run the company. That was something Stone wouldn't stand for.

As he made his way towards the boardroom, Stone could see that several of the board members had just arrived and were entering the large room. Stone ignored them and walked confidently into the room and took his seat at one end of the large oval table. The rest of the board members were seated, or getting coffee and Danish from the side table, prepped by Stone's assistant. The last stragglers wandered in and took their seats. While he waited for them to all take their seats, Stone gathered his thoughts and decided to regain the control and power he once had over the board.

"Gentlemen, thank you for meeting with me. As you requested last evening, I provided the demonstration of my new project to reduce costs and increase profits. I'm sure you were all satisfied, if not amazed, based on the looks of several of your faces. Now that you've seen the project and had time to discuss it among yourselves, I'm confident that I can count on your continued support…. and increase in funding."

"I think we should wait for Benton," one of the board members said.

"Where is he?" asked another.

Stone looked around at the members, who were staring back at him.

"I'm not sure, but we have the IPO tomorrow and I need to know whether you're going to support this project through to production. It's one of the big selling points for any of our products listed in the prospectus and it's what our investors are counting on to make them money."

"We should have never agreed to have that publicized until we saw the demonstration and were sure it was viable."

"So, you saw it in action today, with your own eyes. I don't understand your reluctance now."

"It's not reluctance. But we will not agree to anything until Benton is here and we discuss this as a board."

"Whether or not Benton is here, you vote as a board. His vote doesn't count any more than any of yours. You voiced your concerns about the viability of this project. It's not the main thing that investors are looking for when buying our stock. But it is the thing that will make all of you and me a lot of money. You asked for a demonstration and I gave it to you. You all saw that what I have been telling you for months is now a reality. This is something that I have been researching and dreaming about for years. And now, here we are, on the eve of going public and you still have reservations? What the hell are you still concerned about? Our core business is providing a state-of-the-art printed circuit manufacturing process, one that has captured nearly 70% of the Valley's business. I have consistently delivered for this company and this board. To be honest, I'm tired of constantly being second-guessed by a group of suits that have no clue about the potential I am offering you."

Stone rose from his chair and paced around the room, his thoughts gathering momentum, his anger rising. He was no longer waiting for a response from the board members. He had spent too much time, too many years to get to this point, only to be asked again to provide more or wait. They had asked for a demonstration and he provided that. He had shown him that what he was working on could be successful. That he could not only deliver the returns they had asked for, but more. Much more. His pacing slowed as he calmed his nerves. Getting angry would only make matters worse, but he was tired of this constant micromanaging. And Benton was to blame for most of this. His best friend, the man he started this company with should be here as his ally. But that was over as well, wasn't it? No, this was all on him now and that's just the way he liked it.

"Gentleman, you called me in here yesterday because you were concerned with the direction the company was taking and that we were spending too much for a project you all deemed a failure. Even my chairman, the man who helped me start this company, questioned my methods and motivations. The board asked me to prove this project was fiscally viable. I delivered that proof. You saw it for yourself. Benton, not bothering to be here for the meeting, should tell you something. I believe he has wasted the board's and my time with these frivolous accusations. Especially now, when we are so close to going public when this new project is so close to becoming a reality. This should be grounds for his removal from his position, not me. Yes, that's right, I know what this has all been about. To remove me from my company. Why do you think he was trying to do that? Because he was jealous, he's always been jealous of me, of my success with this company. In fact, right after our meeting the other night, he followed me to my office and threatened me."

A shocked look crossed the faces of the board members. Several turned to each other in hushed conversations. Stone watched them and the hint of a smirk appeared. He once again felt he had retaken control of the situation and especially the board.

"Look, I'm not suggesting that you remove Alex Benton as chairman of the Board. Far from it. But I expect you all to at least put him on notice that we will not tolerate this sort of activity. He could have very well jeopardized our ability to have a successful IPO. I also expect you all to take a vote regarding my request for additional funding. If the vote is close and we need Benton's vote in order to break the tie, fine, I'll wait. But if not, then being able to make an announcement regarding the potential this project provides to our investors when we go public tomorrow, well, I don't need to tell you what that means to all those stock options you all hold."

Stone scanned the room one more time and made his way back to his seat. He looked across the table at all of them. They all stared back. All he could think about was the funding he needed to continue his project. To build the larger reactor needed to produce gold at the level he wanted to. And not just for himself, although there was a level of greed that was creeping in. He truly believed that being able to produce a rare metal, one that improved the performance and reliability of the circuits they manufactured for their clients, at such a reduced cost, would make his company profitable for years to come. With the funding he was requesting, he could make that a reality.

"Look, you've seen the potential this project has in terms of profits. That alone should be enough to justify my request for the additional funding I am asking for. But there are also the technical and long-term reliability aspects of what this project can deliver. Our customers will be delivered a product that will enable them to save money in support costs and additional manufacturing because they will reduce replacement numbers exponentially. We will essentially be creating our own resources, reducing our costs, increasing our profits, and putting us ahead of the curve against all our competitors."

Stone looked for any signs from the board that they were ready to approve his request. There wasn't any. Instead, what he saw were mostly bored and disinterested looks.

"I know a lot of this technical information is beyond all of you. Your only concern is the bottom line. I get that. And with the IPO just around the corner, that's understandable. Your concern for our potential investors is noted. And like you, they will be concerned only about the return on their investment. All true. But think about this. In this day and age, with so many concerned about the environment and limited resources, we are at the forefront of being part of the solution and not contributing to the problem. That puts us in the unique position of actually enticing investors that are more altruistic. They will want to invest in us, not for the bottom line, but because it fills a need for them that other companies ignore. That, gentlemen, is something that should make you proud to be involved in our company. That feeds your soul. That allows you to sleep better at night."

Stone had been walking around the room, circling the large conference table as he spoke. He had reached his own chair as he finished and slowly pulled it back from the table and sat. As he did, his face scanned each member of the board. He held his gaze with each before moving on to the next. Trying to use his powers of suggestion to influence the decision he sought. He was hoping this would be enough. That they could finally see the benefit of approving his request. He had appealed to both their financial well-being and their humanity. The only question now was which side was more important to them. Stone didn't care one way or another. He just wanted to wrap this up and move forward on his plans. He felt his time was running short.

"So, can I rely on you all to take that vote tonight?"

CHAPTER NINETEEN

Once the company parking lot was in total darkness, aside from the small spots created by the sodium lights, he returned to the car, used the fob to unlock it, and slid behind the wheel. The Mercedes eight-cylinder diesel engine roared to life, and he put the car in drive and pulled out of the lot and turned right on Page Mill, and headed down the hill towards 101 and San Francisco. He knew what he had to do and where the body needed to be left. He just needed to make one stop first.

At this time of the evening, the drive across Palo Alto did not take long. The car turned onto Bell Avenue and pulled up to the neatly manicured bungalow. The driver got out and looked around to make sure no one was watching. Seeing no one, he went to the side of the yard and opened the gate leading to the backyard. He opened the side door with the single key in his pocket and entered the garage. He immediately went to the row of cabinets containing the usual garage items. Opening the first cabinet and moving the stored suitcases to the side, he found what he was looking for. The notebooks. He quickly grabbed them and left the garage the same way he came in. He opened the gate a crack and peeked out to make sure the street was still deserted. Seeing it was, he quickly left the backyard and made his way to the driver's side of the Mercedes, getting in and starting the car.

He pulled out, went to the end of the block, and made a U-turn, leaving the subdivision and heading to 101 and the City. He looked down at the two notebooks he had tossed on the passenger seat. It was time to return them to their original location. He couldn't have these around any longer, and they were no longer needed to achieve what was rightfully his.

Benton's Mercedes made the trip from Palo Alto to San Francisco in forty minutes. At this time of night, and with the limited traffic on Highway 280, the trip could have been much shorter. The driver knew this, but carrying a dead body in the car's trunk tends to make you follow the speed limit a bit more judiciously. Once he hit 19th Avenue he relaxed a bit, knowing that his destination was just blocks away. He hit every intersection just as the timed traffic lights turned green. He wasn't sure when or how he learned about them, but tonight he didn't care.

Nothing really prepares you for carrying a dead body in your car. And television shows that make it look so easy are just wrong. Every bump in the road, every sound you hear, becomes that much louder, that much more suspicious. You check your rearview mirrors a lot more. You look up and down every side street looking for that black and white with the Christmas light bar on top. Random people on the street are now witnesses, watching your every move, filing away every detail of how you look, the car you're driving, and the exact time of night they see you.

And of course, none of this is true. People are creatures of habit. Most remember nothing past the last five minutes. Someone passes them on the street? You'd be lucky if they could remember if it was a man or woman, old or young. No one can tell you the model of a car that's parked on the side of the street, let alone one driving past them in the darkness of night. Describing a driver? Forget it. All of this was just paranoia brought on by a heinous act of greed and selfishness.

He continued on 19th Ave and followed it through The Avenues until he reached Lincoln Way on the southern border of the park. He followed 19th through the park and then turned east on Fulton until he reached 8th and the entrance to the park on the North side, closest to the

McLaren statue. As he pulled Benton's car to the edge of the JFK drive, the sun had completely set and there were no other cars in this area of the park.

At night, most traffic simply passed through the park, workers heading home, either from The Peninsula to the Richmond District or from downtown to the Sunset. Either way, the only people in the park after dark were the homeless and dog walkers. He sat in the car waiting, making sure the street was empty and calming his nerves for the next step. When an hour had passed and no one had driven or walked by, he got out of the car and popped the trunk.

Looking around one last time, he bent into the trunk and grabbed Benton under his arms and pulled his body over the rim of the trunk. Unable to hold his entire weight, the body slipped from his grip and hit the ground with a sickening thud. Quickly looking around, he bent over, got a better grip on the body's upper torso, and dragged it across the sidewalk and toward its final destination. At least final as far as he was concerned. Once past the sidewalk, he relaxed a bit, as now his activities were covered by the heavy foliage on each side of the path he was dragging Benton's body on. He stopped and took a breath. There were still 30 feet to go. He continued to drag the heavy body until he was completely out of the area, covered by the streetlight. He stopped and caught his breath, relaxing a bit more. In complete darkness now, the rest of his path would be out of anyone's view. He started pulling again and finally reached the small rock wall at the base of where John McLaren's statue was standing. He dragged Benton around the short wall and up the gentle slope to the base of the statue.

Once he was at the statue, he propped Benton's body up against the side of it, away from the street. He walked back to the car and looked towards the statue. From where he was standing, there was no way to see what was behind the cast iron replica of the park's original superintendent. Perfect!

He opened up the door to the front passenger side and pulled out the two notebook boxes. As he was heading back to the statue, he stopped in his tracks, frozen with fear. "Shit! I knew I forgot something. A damn shovel". He stayed motionless, his mind racing for an answer. "Can't stop now."

He continued to the statue, dropped the boxes, and headed back to the car in a hurry. He ransacked the front and back seats, under the seats, looking for something, anything he could use as a shovel. Nothing! Kneeling on the back seat, exhausted, afraid he wouldn't be able to complete his task tonight, his head dipped to the seat. Suddenly, a huge smile filled his face. He rushed around to the back of the car and popped the truck again. Damn it, nothing. Wait. He lifted the carpet covering the trunk and found the space-saver spare tire. Yes, it had to be there, usually under the tire.

He spun the large plastic nut that holds the spare in and lifted it out of its concave perch. Yes! The tire iron was right where he thought it would be. Not exactly a shovel, but tonight it will have to do. He pulled it out, slammed the trunk shut, and jogged back to where he left the boxes.

Using the flat end of the tire iron, he worked at the earth behind the statue. He dug behind the statue for close to an hour, something that would have taken a far shorter time with a proper shovel. No matter, he was nearly there. With the full concrete cover exposed, he'd be able to slide it to the side and return the boxes to their cubby. As he dug with the tire iron, he could see the cover move slightly. Loosening the compacted dirt relieved the pressure on the side cover.

He slid the inch-thick slab to the side. Grabbing one box at a time, he placed them reverently back into their crypt. He leaned back and rested on his knees, looking at this treasure one last time. With a sigh, he pulled the concrete cover back over the opening and filled the hole back in. This part went faster, as he could use his feet to kick a majority of the dirt back into the hole. He tromped on the loose dirt, compacting it as best he could. He then gathered handfuls of leaves and twigs and spread them over the freshly moved earth, trying his best to hide the activity.

Satisfied, he walked around the entire scene, making sure that nothing would rouse any suspicions. Well, except for the dead chairman of the board, everything looked wonderful. Reaching into his pocket, he retrieved Benton's cell phone, wiped it clean of fingerprints, and slid it into the inside pocket of his suit coat. He then grabbed the car keys and was about to do the same when he thought better of it. Instead, he headed back to the car, got in, and started the car. Taking one last look back at the scene, he pulled away from the curb. Just as he did, he remembered the tire iron. He stopped the car, got out, and ran back to the scene. He looked around until he found it. Covered in dirt, he thought better of returning it to the car. Instead, he looked around and, with one swift motion, flung it into the bushes about twenty yards away. Satisfied, he returned to the running car.

He swung the car around and exited the park. Heading back down Fulton, he drove a couple of blocks and then pulled down a random block and parked the car in an open spot in the residential neighborhood. He stopped the engine and left the keys in the ignition. He got out, left it unlocked, and walked away, back towards the park.

As he walked, he pulled out his phone, found the Lift app and scheduled a pickup back to StoneTech so he could retrieve his car. He gave the address of the coffee shop at the corner of Fulton and 8th as the pickup location, but given his disheveled and dirt-caked look, he thought it best to wait outside. He looked at his reflection in the shop's window and wasn't sure he recognized who he saw. How did he get to this point in his life? The last couple of hours were a blur, but now that it was done, he went over every moment and it shocked him what he was capable of. He justified it to himself as something that needed to be done, to protect his investment, that he deserved this after everything he had been through.

As he was staring at himself, his phone vibrated with a notification that his ride was here. He turned and saw a small and silent electric car idling at the curb. He opened the back door and hopped in. The driver confirmed his destination and then pulled away. He really wasn't in the mood for chitchat, and was hoping he could make the drive in silence. No such luck.

"So... looks like you're having a bit of a day, huh?"

"What do you mean?"

The driver looked at him through the rear-view mirror, calculating his next comment. "I mean, looks like you might have had some car trouble or something?"

"Yeah, or something. Look. I've had a long day. I just want to get to my office, and then get home. No offense, but we can we just make the drive in quiet?"

"Sure. Sure thing, man." He looked at the disheveled passenger one last time through the mirror and then focused his eyes straight ahead.

The passenger felt himself dozing off and figured he'd close his eyes for just a second to catch a breath. The next thing he knows, the driver is waking him up in the parking lot of StoneTech. "Man, you were really out. I was getting worried you kicked it. The last thing I need is a dead guy in my car."

Looking at him with a weird smile, he replied, "Yeah, yeah, the last thing you need." He got out of the car and walked away without saying another word. He could barely hear the Lift driver thank him as he approached his car, pulled out his keys, and slipped behind the wheel. He could feel himself going again, giving into sleep. Thankfully, it was a short ride home.

Driving on autopilot, he made the short drive across town in a haze. He was exhausted and needed to crash. He pulled into his driveway and got out of his car. Feeling like an old man, his body ached from carrying Benton and all the digging tonight. He got inside his home and went straight to the master, disrobing as he went. He dumped his suit jacket and pants, along with the rest of sweat-stained clothes in a heap on the floor, walked into the en suite, and turned the shower on full blast. As he waited for the water to heat, he stared at himself in the mirror. *What did I just do?*

CHAPTER TWENTY

Eckhart and Fowler both got an early start at the office the day after the explosion on 22nd that killed the gardener and bank teller. The lab had no luck recovering anything beyond what they had yesterday, and both detectives were a bit frustrated with what little they had to go on. So far, the lab had been unsuccessful at restoring anything from Miss Quinn's phone, and it didn't look like they would be. As of late last night, the only thing they had from Mr. Lopez's phone was a few texts and a handful of pics.

"I wish we had more of the notebook, so we could confirm its purpose. Maybe Miles Ward is having some luck." Eckhart said.

"Yeah, well, if we find it, we'll find Javier's murderer."

The watch commander popped his head into the detective's office and yelled, "Eck, Fowler, we got a stiff in the park. Off of 8th at JFK Drive. An officer has secured the scene for you guys."

"Thanks, Harry. Fowler, take a ride?"

They made the short drive from the Taraval station, taking the same route the killer did the night before. When they pulled up to the scene, there was a single patrol car and several looky loos standing by. Patrol had the area taped off to protect any evidence. Eckhart and Fowler got out of the car and walked up to the officer. He gave them a brief update on what they had and then pointed out the woman who found the body.

Fowler walked over to where she was standing, holding the leash of a small yipping dog. "Hi, I'm Detective Fowler. So, you found the body?"

"Well, I take Percy out for his morning walk every day at 7:30. We always loop through this part of the park. There's less homeless and I feel safer. So does Percy. He really doesn't like the homeless, you know? And it's a better walk for me than going the other way to JFK, because that just leads to 19th and there's too many cars. Percy doesn't like the cars either. He just barks and barks. You know?"

"Yes ma'am. But could you tell me how you found the body? Did you touch anything?"

"Oh, well, so we were just starting our walk, see. And I let Percy off his leash. I know I'm not supposed to, but there's no one else around and he likes to explore, you know. Anyway, he runs ahead, and he's right at the statue and he's about to do his business, you know. And he stops and starts barking. So I figure there's a homeless guy sleeping against the statue and call for Percy, see. But he doesn't come, so's I walk over and see this guy laying there, up against the statue like he's sleeping. But I could tell he ain't sleeping. I seen enough SVU to know a dead guy when I see one. So's I call 911 and here we are."

"And did you see anyone else on your walk? Anyone suspicious?"

"Well, there's the guy that stands on the corner of 9th every friggen mornin, yelling at the cars. That's why we avoid that way. But if you mean around the body, no, didn't see anyone, suspicious or not."

Fowler jotted down some notes from the witness and then looked over in the body's direction. Eckhart was squatting down, examining the surrounding ground. Fowler thanked the witness and walked towards the scene. He lifted the crime tape and bent under it to join Eckhart.

"Find anything?"

"Well, he wasn't killed here and whoever did this wasn't a pro. I'm sure the M.E. can confirm the cause of death, but at first glance, I'd say it was this gash to the neck. Wherever he was killed, there's gotta be a lot of blood."

Looking back towards the street, Fowler noticed a pair of very slight grooves in the lawn. "Looks like he was probably drug from a vehicle to here." They both looked back towards JFK Drive and could barely make out the parallel grooves, probably made by the victim's heels as he was drug to his resting place. The M.E.'s vehicle pulled up and broke their train of thought. Brian Hackman, who Eckhart thought looked like a blond version of that TV medical examiner, slash, serial killer, got out of his vehicle and approached both him and Fowler.

"Another morning, another stiff."

"Living the dream", Eckhart replied sarcastically. Hackman was an appropriate name for the M.E. Terry thought. Not only did he remind him of Dexter, but sometimes he gave off the same creepy vibe. I guess when your co-workers are stiffs instead of live bodies, your social skills are affected.

"So, any idea what happened?"

"No, but it looks like he was killed somewhere else. Of course, you're the expert."

"Well, let's see what we have."

Hackman examined the area around the body and then raised the victim's head to get a better look at the wound. He lifted the body away from the statue and moved his jacket to get a better look at his back. He then checked the liver temp and looked for lividity. Two necessary checks for time of death, and whether the body had been moved from where it passed.

"Well, based on a quick look, and I'll confirm back in the lab, I think you're right. First, the body was definitely moved. He was lying flat on his back when he died based on lividity. The blood, what's left of it, pooled all along his back. Someone placed him in a sitting position here. Liver temp says time of death sometime around five to seven yesterday evening."

"Thanks, Brian. While you're digging around in there, can you check his pockets for anything? Wallet, ID, keys, anything."

"Sure." Hackman checked the victim's coat and pants pocket. "Couple of things. Wallet and what looks like a security access card. Name on it is Alex Benton. Stone Technologies Corp. Nothing else. No keys."

"Seriously? What the hell is going on here? Fowler and I were just down at Stone Technologies yesterday talking to the CEO. He had worked for the gardener killed in the house fire yesterday. Is it OK to move the body so we can have a look at the scene and get the crime guys in here to do a thorough once-over?"

"Sure. Let me get a bag and the gurney, and I'll get him back in the lab on a table."

Once the body was tagged and bagged, Eckhart and Fowler started surveying the scene for anything out of the ordinary. Once they saw the area behind the statue had been disturbed and then attempted to hide it, they called over the crime guys and let them do their thing. In less than an hour, they had the area completely cleared, and the hole opened back up. Fowler and Eckhart had been watching as they did their job, and moved in when one of the team waved them over.

"Looks like we have something here at the base of the statue. Loose panel."

"OK, be careful opening it. We don't want to disturb anything inside."

Both of the crime scene techs looked up at the same time with a look of derision. "Really? Would you like to do this?"

"Sorry guys. Didn't sleep well last night."

They both turned back to their work and slowly slid the concrete lid to the side. "Theres something inside." Donning gloves, they carefully removed the first one, then the second box, placing them both on a tarp that was laid out next to the hole.

Eckhart, seeing both, turned to Fowler and said, "That looks like the same box we saw in the gardener's pic. And there are two of them. Either this is a hell of a coincidence, or we have enough to tie these two cases together."

"So, he's killed somewhere else. The killer dumps the body here. Why here? And then he leaves."

"If I had a guess, I would say it has something to do with the notebooks, and why they were hidden here. The ground looked freshly disturbed. I'd say the killer brought the body and the notebooks. Dumped the body and hid the notebooks. But he, and I say he since the body was dragged all this distance, had to have known there was a hidden compartment in the statue. Otherwise, it's just a coincidence.

And we know someone who has worked in the park and was obsessed with the statues. Mr. Stone."

"Are these worth killing over, or is there something else?"

As they were about to leave the scene and head back to the station, Eckhart's cell vibrated from an incoming call. He pulled his phone out and saw it was from the watch commander, Harry Dawson.

"What's up Harry?"

"Just got a call looking for you. From Palo Alto PD. They say they have something they think may be related to the case you're working. They're waiting for you two in the StoneTech parking lot."

"Did they say exactly what?"

"Not really. Something about some evidence you might want to look at."

"OK, we're on our way. Thanks, Harry." Eckhart hung up and turned to Fowler. "Looks like we're going back to Palo Alto."

They walked back to where Fowler had parked the car and got in. Fowler started the car but before he could pull away, Eckhart stopped him.

"Fowler, Hackman said he didn't find any keys on the vic. You find that strange?"

"Not really. Why?"

"Not sure. Just a feeling I have. Give me a minute."

Eckhart got out of the car and walked back to the scene. He approached the cop that was first to the scene. Fowler watched as Eckhart had a brief conversation with him and then returned to the car. He got back in and closed the door.

"Ok, let's go."

"What was that about?"

"Just a feeling I have. The keys. Unless I'm home, my car keys are always in my pocket. Since they weren't on Benton, I'm having him get the address for Benton and we can have a patrol check on his house for his car. If it's not there, then it's where Benton got murdered, or the killer used it to dump the body and then dumped the car somewhere. Close to here, I suspect. He's checking registration for the make and model and then I told him to do a three or four-block radius search of the area for it. If my gut is right, it's around here. Considering Benton's wound, there's gotta be a lot of blood where he was killed and in the car that transported him here. The killer wouldn't have used his own car for that reason. Use the vic's, dump it, leave the keys so some schmuck steals it. Hopefully, he can locate it before any evidence is compromised."

"And you got all that from 'no keys'?"

"Just a hunch. Now let's head to StoneTech and see what PAPD has for us."

They made the drive to the company in thirty minutes. The morning commute to the south bay was over and the freeway was virtually empty this time of morning. They exited 280 onto Page Mill and drove a couple of blocks before pulling into the employee parking. There was one PAPD patrol car there with the misery lights flashing, and a small portion of the parking lot roped off. They pulled up behind the patrol car and got out.

"Officer, this is Fowler. I'm Eckhart. Thanks for the call. What's going on?"

"The security guard noticed it this morning when he arrived at work. He called us and also mentioned that two SF detectives were down here yesterday interviewing Mr. Stone about something. We called SF headquarters to see what cases involved a Palo Alto company and came up with your names. We didn't want to alert anyone inside until you've looked at this. Although by now most of the employees have arrived, so I'm sure word has spread about us in the parking lot."

"Yeah, doesn't help you got the lights going. How about cutting those? I don't think you'll need em. Why don't you show us what you found? Also, where's the security guard now?"

"He's over there." The cop gestured to the guard that Eckhart recognized as the same one working the front desk yesterday when they were there to speak to Stone.

They led Fowler and Eckhart under the police tape and over to a spot on the asphalt parking lot that had a couple of numbered plastic 'tents' that marked potential evidence. The patrol cop told them both that they hadn't touched anything and were fairly certain no one else had either, since the security guard was usually the first to arrive. They pointed to where the guard usually parks and mentioned that he noticed the evidence when he walked by on the way inside.

Eckhart took a pair of gloves out of his pocket, put them on, and walked over to the first numbered tent. Before he got too close, he could see what it was. He'd seen enough dried blood on asphalt to know that's what was marked by the evidence tag. There were several small pooled drops on the ground and a larger one in the middle. He pulled his phone out and took several pics of the blood. He squatted down closer, and without touching anything, tried to determine if the blood was still wet or mostly dry.

He looked up at the second evidence tag, which was close to the first, perhaps a couple of feet away. It was near what appeared to be a bit of torn cloth, covered in the same blood. He took some pics of that as well. He called to Fowler to get an evidence kit from the car. When Fowler returned with it, he told him to get a plastic evidence bag out and to bag the piece of cloth. He also had him get a couple of swabs of the blood and bag them as well. As he watched Fowler, he could see that the blood hadn't completely dried yet.

When they finished bagging the evidence, they returned to where the patrol car was and approached the security guard. Eckhart asked him the obvious questions. When did you arrive? How did you discover the scene? Did you touch anything? Did you notify anyone else? And then he asked the less obvious question. Did he contact Mr. Stone, the CEO? The security guard said no, he contacted the police first and stayed in the parking lot to make sure no one disturbed the scene. He had called the guard that does the night shift to let him know he was going to be late relieving him and why.

"Have you seen Mr. Stone arrive for work yet? Is his car in the parking lot?"

"I haven't seen him, and his spot is empty. He usually parks over there." The guard said, pointing to a spot at the far end of the lot. "He doesn't like to park his Beemer near any of the other cars, or under the trees."

"And who parks here?" Eckhart asked, gesturing to the spot next to the pool of blood.

"Mr. Benton, the chairman of the board."

CHAPTER TWENTY-ONE

Eckhart wasn't sure they had enough evidence for a warrant, but he felt he should start the process. He and Fowler make the cross-town drive to 16th and Rhode Island Street to meet with Ally Wilder, the Assistant District Attorney of San Francisco. Eckhart and Ally have known each other since he was a beat cop and she worked for the public defender's office. In those roles, they had mostly adversarial confrontations. Wilder had questioned Eckhart on the stand more than a few times. Since Wilder had become the ADA and Eckhart moved to detective, that relationship shifted to more of a cooperative one. There were still times when Eckhart felt she was questioning his methods, but they were less often than they had been.

When they arrived at the DA's office, Fowler pulled up in front and let Eckhart out of the car. Eckhart turned and leaned in through the open passenger window. "Not coming in with me?"

"I'll stay in the car. Bad part of town, you know?"

"Right."

Eckhart smiled, knowing Fowler had seen a few confrontations between him and the ADA and he wasn't in the mood to watch another one. He turned and climbed the steps to the entrance of the District Attorney's offices. He opened the glass door and took the elevator to the second floor. Ally's receptionist smiled when she saw Eckhart approach the desk. She was in her late sixties and had been sitting at the same desk for over twenty years. The DAs came and went, but Ginny was the one constant.

"How are the grandkids?"

"Ones in college and the other two are in high school. Thanks for asking Terry."

"Wow, you're making me feel old! Is Ally available?"

"She's expecting you. Go right in."

Eckhart thought it was strange that Ally Wilder would expect him. Neither he nor Fowler had called over to let her know they were coming, and what the visit would be about. He wondered if Captain Jordan had jumped the gun on him. Something he had a habit of doing when he was expecting quicker results.

"How did she know I was coming over?"

"I left a message for you at the station. Miss Wilder wanted to go over your testimony for the trial. I assumed that's why you're here."

"Ah, ok. No, I haven't been at the station, so haven't gotten your message. Thanks, beautiful."

"Sweet talker," Ginny replied and laughed as Terry walked into Ally Wilder's office.

Ally was seated at her desk. The top of which was covered in case folders. She was flipping through one and looked up and over the top of her glasses as Eckhart walked through her office door. Her raven hair was in a makeshift bun, several tendrils of silky hair hung down, framing her olive-skinned face. Her full red lips broke into a smile as she closed the file and stood to greet him.

"Hi Terry, thanks for coming over. I'd ask how things are, but based on your last case, I know you took that one personal. I thought it would be good if we could spend a little time going over your testimony for the case."

Eckhart found something in her eyes that hadn't been there in the past. He had always found her to be an attractive woman, but because of their professional relationships, he had never looked at her as anything more than the ADA. But that smile had him feeling something, and it made him happy.

"Ginny mentioned that, but that's not why I'm here. Fowler and I caught a couple of murders. Well, definitely one murder and a suspicious death. The chairman of the board for StoneTech in Palo Alto was found dead in the park. Wasn't killed there, dumped. Looks like he was done in the parking lot of his company. Yesterday a house on 22nd exploded, gas leak, two dead. Definitely suspicious. What evidence we have is pointing to the CEO over at StoneTech. A David Stone. We think he's good for it and need a search warrant for the company headquarters and his home."

"What evidence do you have that links the two?"

"The CEO used to work for the parks department and reported to the head gardener. The gardener, Javier Lopez, died in the house explosion. Stone was the last person to speak to him. There were pictures on Lopez's phone of this old notebook that he found in the park. We discovered that notebook and a second buried in a statue where the stiff was dumped today."

"Seems more than coincidental. But why the CEO?"

"Fowler and I interviewed him yesterday. He seemed like he was holding some information back. Gut feeling."

"The judge is going to need more than gut feeling. You know that, Terry."

"Fowler and I are working on it. We're just concerned that he might try to dispose of any evidence linking him to either victim. I also have a feeling that he's holding back information on what his company is doing. Can't prove anything yet, but there are definitely a couple of areas that I'd like to get a look at. Once the evidence from the parking lot and Golden Gate Park are analyzed, I'll probably have more for you. The lab is trying to pull prints from the notebooks and the boxes they were stored in. If we can get a match on any prints other than Lopez's, that will go a long way toward involvement. My money is on Stone's prints being all over this."

"Anything that puts him at either scene or at least enough circumstantial evidence that supports him being the prime suspect. You're right, prints would be good. Do you have a motive yet?"

"Not sure. The company has an IPO coming up, so I'm assuming there is a lot of financial pressure. The CEO claims they have a proprietary manufacturing process that a lot of companies in the valley could benefit from. And then there are the notebooks."

"Notebooks?"

"Yeah. The gardener had some pictures on his phone of these old-looking notebooks. He had texted the pictures over to Mr. Stone. Stone had worked for Lopez at the park years ago, putting himself through college. When we spoke with Stone about them, he acknowledged seeing them at Lopez's but denied taking them. Then they turn up in the park, hidden in the statue next to where we found Benton's body."

Ally was taking notes as Eckhart laid out his suspicions and what little evidence he had. When he stopped, she continued writing in one of the many yellow legal pads on her desk. When she was done, she started clicking her pen open and closed but continued to look down at the pad and her notes. Eckhart was watching her and just as he was going to ask her a question, she finally looked up and spoke.

"Terry, based on what you've told me, there seems to be circumstantial evidence that supports the allegation of guilt for Mr. Stone. Unfortunately, it also could be used to find any number of other people guilty. Without an obvious motive, we really have nothing to warrant a search. Are these notebooks worth killing over? And if they are, why would the killer leave them in such an obvious and easy place for them to be found?"

"We're not sure what the notebooks have to do with this or if they're worth anything. You're right. It makes little sense that they were left near Benton's body. But as far as we can tell, they were the start of it. Maybe Fowler and I should pay Stone another visit, see if we can shake him. You remember my old partner? Miles Ward? I have him looking at the notebooks to see if he can shed some light on what they contain and if they would be a reason to kill anyone."

"Of course, I remember him. I haven't heard that name in a long time. How's he doing?"

"Fine, professor of chemistry at Stanford now. Fowler and I had already dropped off the few pics we originally had of the notebooks. Now that we have the actual thing, I'd like to see what he can come up with, after the lab is done with them, of course. Listen, I'm sorry I came in and just jumped into this like I did. Still feeling the blow-back from that last case and not looking to add to it with this one."

Eckhart saw the compassion in her eyes. She had some idea what he was going through, at least what he was feeling after the kid killer case. Eckhart will have to face a defense attorney that will look for any mistake to get their client off. This could also involve questioning his methods. The methods he used to solve one of the more heinous crimes San Francisco had seen since the Zodiac killings. As the lead detective on the case, it wasn't a great place to be in.

He liked where their working relationship was, now that they were on the same side of law enforcement. It obviously made working together easier, although there were still times when the DA's office and LE disagreed on the approach and method. Eckhart didn't feel that applied to the previous case. In fact, he felt Ally was on his side. That she understood the pressure he and Fowler were under to catch Jim Pascal before he killed another kid. He was looking at her in a different light. And it surprised him.

"Terry, I'm sure it will be fine. No matter how bad you think it went, or what mistakes you think were made, I'm sure we'll get a conviction. We can go over your testimony and make sure you're prepared for whatever his defense attorney throws at you."

Eckhart smiled, and for the first time in a long time, saw Ally as more than just a DA. He thought he detected something more. He wondered if she might be feeling the same vibes he was feeling. Terry always found her attractive, even when she was grilling him during a trial. The timing was never right between them for anything other than a working relationship. He wondered if that timing might change now.

"If you're free later this evening, we could meet at Joes, I'll buy you dinner and we can go over some trial prep. I might have enough evidence in the StoneTech case by then, so you can get me that warrant."

"Hmmm, are you asking me out on a date, or is this just work?" she asked with a coy smile.

"Both? Work first, then date."

"That actually sounds nice. Can I let you know later this afternoon? We can agree on a time, then."

"Sounds good, counselor. Ok, I gotta run. Fowler is probably circling the block and pissed at me. We'll talk this afternoon."

Eckhart left Ally's office hoping she would call later and agree to meet for dinner. Yes, he needed to convince her to get Fowler and him a warrant so they could find evidence on

Stone. And he wanted to make sure he was ready to answer questions at the kid killer trial. But he hoped to explore his feelings for her. He went back down the elevator and left the building. Once outside, Eckhart looked down the street in both directions for Fowler's car. Not seeing him, he pulled out his phone and dialed his number. Just as he was about to hit send, Fowler pulled up and yelled out the rolled-down passenger window, "The lab just called. They got the results back from both crime scenes."

CHAPTER TWENTY-TWO

When they arrived back at the Taraval station, Eckhart hoped that whatever evidence the lab had for them would be enough to get a warrant for Stone's home and business. They parked and went into the station house, heading straight for the lab.

"So, what have you got for us?" Eckhart asked.

Tim was looking at the computer monitor at his desk. He spun around when he heard Eckhart's question and motioned him over to the computer screen. He shut down what he was doing and opened another window, showing the results of the blood and cloth evidence from the parking lot at StoneTech. Fowler and Eckhart joined him, standing behind the seated tech as he explained what he had so far.

"So, what you see here are the blood analysis results from the swabs taken at the StoneTech parking lot. And here is the analysis of the blood taken from the body at Golden Gate Park. It's an identical match. The blood in the parking lot definitely came from the victim in the park. The amount of blood spilled in that parking lot, along with the lividity tests, shows the victim died there and then transported to the park at a later time. Lividity shows that he was laying down for at least two to three hours before he was left by the statue in the park. You can see from the picture here that the blood pooled in his back. If he was still alive at the park, it would have pooled at his lower extremities. Liver temp confirms the time of death to be sometime last evening, between five and eight. "

"Killed, then dumped in the trunk of his car. Car left in the parking lot until later that evening so the killer could leave without being noticed and dump the body in the park. Fowler, have we located the car yet?"

"Not sure. There was a stack of messages on my desk. Let me go check."

"What else Tim?"

"Well, back to the blood. An incision that size would have drained the guy fairly rapidly. The possibility that the killer has Mr. Benton's blood on him is quite high. Unless he was wearing a hazmat suit, there would have to be splatter. Oh, and he also has blood on his right shoe."

"Right shoe? How would you know that?"

"Look at this photo from the crime scene. Notice anything about that pool of blood on the ground? The irregular shape? It's not uncommon for blood to be everywhere, and for it to pool on the ground as it drips from a victim, especially that much blood. However irregular, the edges of any liquid will have a soft, rounded edge to it, where it contacts with a different material. Like the inside of a glass, the water forms a slightly concave shape, with a meniscus where it touches the glass. The reverse is true for a liquid on the ground. You would see a curved edge where it contacts the asphalt. Since blood is thicker than water, that edge would be more defined. As you can see in this picture, it is. Except for there." Tim pointed to a spot on the photo that had an indented, rounded shape.

"It looks like the toe of a shoe."

"Exactly. And in this photo taken a few feet away, you can see the slight hint of a shoe print, as if some of the blood seeped under the shoe, and then as the killer walked away, the shoe left that imprint on the asphalt."

"Can you tell from that what kind of shoe we should look for?"

"Not at the moment. I'm going to enhance the photo and run it against the database and see what comes up.

Should take a few hours and then I might have something for you."

Fowler had returned and let Eckhart know he had spoken to the beat cop at the GGP scene and he, in fact, had located Benton's car a few blocks from the scene. The keys were still in the ignition and the car was unlocked. The officer inspected the vehicle and found small traces of blood on the driver's side floor mat and a large amount in the car's trunk. They were having it towed to the evidence lot, where they would take samples of the blood and have then analyzed to confirm they came from Benton. Fowler also asked them to dust for prints.

"Just like you thought, Terry."

"Like I said, just a hunch. Glad it panned out. Tim, anything else?"

"Yes, the piece of cloth you found at the scene. It was covered in blood. We took a sample, and it also matches the blood of the vic. However, the cloth did not come from him. If I had to guess, I'd say in the struggle to defend himself, he probably tore it from the killer's jacket."

"Why do you say jacket? How can you tell?"

"Well, for one, the back stitching tells us it's a pocket. See there, how the edges are all folded over and stitched down? Then there is the shape of the pocket. Definitely not a suit jacket. The upper pockets on suits are sewn inside. This came from a casual jacket, one where stitching isn't as important as a formal suit jacket. And the material. Definitely from an expensive yet casual jacket. I'd say herringbone tweed."

"OK, thanks, Tim. Have you pulled any prints yet? Matches?"

"Just doing that now. I was able to make a suitable set of elimination prints from Lopez."

"Thanks. Let us know when you have something."

They both left the lab, and they made their way back to the detective's office. As they passed Frank Jordan's office, he yelled out at Eckhart, "Terry, get in here!"

"What's up, Captain?"

"What's up? I'll tell you what's up. I asked you to keep me updated on this case and I haven't heard anything from you all day. I'm getting heat from downtown and now that Palo Alto PD is involved? Why wasn't I informed of this? Now I have two police chiefs wondering what the heck is going on and what progress there is in finding out who did this. And when my boss gets edgy, I get edgy. Where are we?"

"The body discovered in the park this morning was the chairman of the board of Stone Technologies. The same company whose CEO is our suspect in the Javier Lopez and Mary Quinn deaths. Right now, we don't have any evidence that Stone is involved, but I'm not ruling it out. Looks like Alex Benton, the chairman, was killed in the parking lot of StoneTech in Palo Alto and then later dumped in the Park. The killer used Benton's car and then dumped it in The Avenues a few blocks from the scene."

"Fowler found the car and we have the techs going over it now for any potential evidence. Looks like the footprint in the parking lot may come from a unique style of shoe, which may narrow down our suspect list. Also, a piece of fabric the lab thinks came from a jacket. If I had to guess, Captain, I'd say Stone killed Lopez for the notebook he found in the park and Quinn was just collateral damage. Stone used to work for Lopez at the park and may have found the notebook at another time and then hid it where Lopez found it a couple of days ago. We're not sure what the significance of the notebook is, and why Stone would hide it there, but it's one of the things we're working on."

"Ok, this is good. Anyway, we can find out what's in the notebook and if it's valuable enough to kill over?" Captain Jordan asked.

"Way ahead of you. Not sure if you remember a beat cop named Miles Ward. He was my partner when he first joined the force and I was still on the street. Anyway, he left the force and became a teacher down at Stanford. I showed him the pictures we got off of Lopez's phone. He thinks it's some sort of chemical formula but needs more time to look at it. Should have checked with you first, Cap, but I thought since he used to be on the job, it would be fine."

"You're right. You should have checked with me first. Used to be on the job or not, we shouldn't be involving civilians in our cases. We don't have any idea what the fuck this Miles is doing now, old partner or not. Eckhart, you fucking know better than that."

"Settle down. I only gave him a few shots of the notebook and I have a feeling he'll be able to let us know what they are and if they would be a reason to kill someone. Fowler and I are going to follow up with him later and see what he has for us. It's not compromising the case in the least, and there's no break in the chain of evidence. The original pics are intact on the victim's phone, and the phone is safely stored in the lab with the rest of the evidence."

"Settle down? There are procedures to follow here, Eckhart. You get my nuts in a vice because you just want to go rogue, and I'll make sure you feel the same pain I do. To be honest, I'm still surprised you have Fowler as a partner. You go through them faster than a baby goes through diapers. I've warned you before that if you lose another partner, it will be you moving, not the partner."

"Unless you've heard differently, Fowler and I are good. He's a good detective. He learns fast and listens, unlike some of the boots you've assigned to me."

"I haven't heard anything from him. It's just a preemptive warning to you. I spend more time policing you than I do the rest of the department."

"Well, there's a solution for that. Stop micro-managing good cops. Look, I'd love to stay and debate this with you, but Fowler and I need to head back down to PA to question the Stone Technology board of directors. I'm also trying to figure out if there is anything on site that could implicate

Stone. Later this afternoon, I'm meeting with the ADA and hopefully have enough evidence to get a warrant so we can search the company and his home. There's something hinky about this guy. I can just feel it. We're also going to go over trial prep for the Pascal case. I'm supposed to be in court tomorrow. So, if it's alright with you, I'd like to get back to my job and this case."

Without responding, Eckhart turned and left Jordan's office.

"Fine, get back to work. But Terry, you make sure you're prepared for that trial. I don't need that blowing up in our faces if you screwed the pooch, you hear me?"

Without turning back around, Eckhart responded, "Loud and clear."

CHAPTER TWENTY-THREE

The Shadowy Figure made his usual rounds. Breakfast on Geary at a small coffee shop, then a slow walk towards the beach to the west. Some days he would make it all the way to the great highway and the expansive sand of Ocean Beach. Other days, just a few blocks before his thoughts made him turn around and head back to his car.

He had heard on the radio that the police discovered a body in Golden Gate Park. The news reporter said that the police were still gathering evidence and so far, there was nothing to connect the murder with the explosion on 22nd Avenue. She interviewed the Taraval station captain, Frank Jordan, but he wasn't giving the media any information. The victim's names hadn't been released, pending notification of the next of kin. She finished the story with the statement that Terry Eckhart was the detective in charge of both cases, and Captain Jordan would brief the media if there were any breaks in the cases.

He was feeling like this might be one of those 'all the way to the beach' walks. He laughed to himself again about how the police department worked and their general ineptitude when it came to murder. They were pretty good at solving them when the doer was a family member, husband killing his wife, that sort of thing. But random was tough. There was the motive issue, the why. Then there was the list of suspects depending on the victim. So many people to rule out and there were usually no prime suspects until they gathered enough evidence and some sort of timeline was created. But even that only helped if the vic and the suspect had some prior relationship or contact. Even then, it took longer than normal to put a case together, and he relied on that.

For years, he relied on the fact that nearly sixty percent of all murders go unsolved. Or rather, unresolved. What most people don't realize is, the police can clear a murder case if they make an arrest. That doesn't translate to a conviction. So, if a suspect is identified, the case can be considered resolved. And when the murderer is a stranger, the percentage of unresolved cases is closer to eighty percent. Detectives rely on several factors when investigating a murder case. First, most murders are committed by a person known to the victim. And of those, most are crimes of passion, spur-of-the-moment incidents. This creates lots of mistakes. Lots of evidence. But even with all that going for law enforcement, it's still difficult to gather enough conclusive evidence to not only tie a suspect to the crime, but to get a conviction.

The Shadowy Figure relied on that historical data, along with his unique ability to manage every detail, every aspect of his acts. That, and the fact that in every case, he was a complete stranger to the victim. Well, almost every case. At least as far as witnesses were concerned. He was a ghost to most people. The unnoticed, every man, the person you passed on the street and never gave a second thought to.

When he was younger, it used to bother him. Now, he reveled in it. You don't want to notice me? You ignore me? Fine. You pay the ultimate price. And that went for the cops, as well.

Unfortunately, this all came at a cost. As his visions grew stronger and more frequent, his confidence grew. As his confidence grew, he found his planning and execution became sloppy. Well, sloppy for him. He was still far more skilled and exacting than some common street scum. And it certainly wasn't the sort of thing the average detective would ever notice. But it bothered him. It was like staring at a group of items, all lined up and symmetrical, except one was just askew. Not enough that the average person would notice. But for him, it was as if someone had thrown a bucket of black paint on a white canvas. Obvious and annoying. Something that had to be fixed. And he would fix it. Pay more attention to it. Or it would be time to stop it all. But he would need help if he decided that was the path to take.

He returned from his thoughts and realized he had walked several blocks. More than he planned, but he obviously needed the distraction to think. It wasn't a huge thing, but these 'blackouts' had become more frequent and longer lasting. They used to only happen when he was sitting or lying on his bed. Several minutes passing by with little or no recognition of what had just happened. They gradually became longer, some lasting as much as an hour or more. Now they were occurring on his walks. He'd find himself blocks, even miles from where he started, with no memory of what he had passed or saw. The interesting thing was, they never happened when he was with one of his 'subjects'. At those times, he was as awake and attentive as he ever was. His biggest fear was if one of his 'blackouts' happened when he was driving. For that reason, he tried to avoid daydreaming when driving. But he knew it was just a matter of time before he had one of his 'waking dream' moments when he was driving.

His walk had taken him past the businesses on Geary and he was now in a mostly residential neighborhood. He must have walked a couple of blocks over from Geary by habit. Sometimes he would cross over a block and be entirely in the residential area of the outer Richmond district of San Francisco. Older homes that were built in the 20s and 30s, now housing multi-generational families. Instead of the busy lives, workers, shoppers, diners, just one block over and the Richmond was very quiet. There really were no front gardens, so not a lot of residents spent time in front of their homes. Most of them were at work at this time of day, and if grandma lived with them, they were generally inside babysitting or down at the corner park. If he were into B&E, the Richmond and Sunset were perfect. Hardly anyone paid attention to what was happening to their next-door neighbor. You could stroll by a couple times and get the lay of the land, case the homes to make sure they were empty during the day. Using a sham like a repairman or delivery guy, and even if someone saw you, they assumed you were legit. The mistake most of these rookies made was they just looked guilty. You've got to just walk right up and in, like you own the place. That kind of attitude worked for almost any crime.

But that wasn't his gig. Too petty, and he didn't get the rush. Plus, those visions. The visions told him what he needed to do. The how and the when. Sometimes he just had to pick the who. Sometimes he didn't. When he was younger, there was a lot of guesswork trying to figure out the visions, trying to put some sense to them. But as he grew older, they became more defined, more exact. A lot less was left to the imagination or to interpret.

And those visions were very narrow in their focus.

CHAPTER TWENTY-FOUR

Eckhart and Fowler both left the station house on Taraval, but this time, heading in different directions. Fowler to the M.E. to meet with Ms. Quinn's parents, and Eckhart back to Palo Alto to clear up some questions with David Stone. Eckhart wasn't sure which task was least desirable. It was always difficult to speak with the relatives of a victim. Especially parents who never planned to bury one of their kids. It never got easy, no matter how many times you had to do it. Fowler was good at it. It came naturally to him. Not that speaking to relatives of a dead vic is something natural. But Fowler had a built-in empathy and inherent compassion that Eckhart lacked. For all his experience, Eckhart found he needed to work harder to exhibit those emotions and feelings that came naturally to others. For that reason, today he felt better about interviewing Stone, then having to meet grieving parents.

The drive wasn't as quick or traffic-free for him. 280, which runs along a ridge top that separates The Peninsula valley from the Pacific Ocean, had patches of traffic all the way to Palo Alto. Not that you could see the ocean from the highway. There was another range of mountains between the ocean and here, but the drive was far more scenic than taking 101, the main freeway from San Francisco to Silicon Valley. Crystal Springs reservoir to the west of 280 was the end point of all the water captured in the Sierras and transferred by viaduct to provide the drinking water San Francisco and much of the valley used.

Eckhart made it to StoneTech forty-five minutes after he left the station house. He was hoping to catch Stone before he left for lunch, but today that would not be an issue. As he pulled into the parking lot on Page Mill, there was a lot of activity, with several news vans camped out, their portable satellite dishes extended and cameramen and reporters milling about, hoping to catch one of the executives as they came or left the building. Because of this, all the employees were hiding out inside. Even though they had gathered all the evidence, they thought they could from the parking lot, Eckhart saw the PAPD still had that section roped off. Probably a good idea. Didn't need the media taking pics of bloody concrete and splashing it on the news.

With crime scenes like this that happened on private property, the owners typically pestered the police to let them clean it up as soon as possible. Since this was in the PAPD's jurisdiction, they would be the ones to release the site back to the owners for clean-up. Eckhart wondered if any calls had been made to the PD to move the process along. Knowing that Stone Technologies was on the verge of its IPO, he was certain their executives wouldn't want any evidence of a crime when hosting potential investors. Depending on how PAPD handled the situation, there was a decent chance that the crime scene would remain that way for at least a day or two longer. It wasn't out of the question to keep a scene sealed for more than a week, but those were typically homes or apartments where it took far longer to collect any potential evidence.

Eckhart parked and navigated the various news vans with their talking heads until he reached the entrance. Although he was in plain clothes, he had the look of authority and it didn't take long for them to decide he was with the department. Once one reporter started yelling questions at him, they all joined in. Trying to get any breadcrumb of info for their nightly news. The murder of a Silicon Valley chairman of the board was big news. He headed straight to the lobby desk manned by the same security guard that was here yesterday.

"Pretty busy out there. Has anyone from the company been out there to make a statement?"

"Not that I'm aware. Those sorts of things were usually handled by Mr. Benton, so maybe no one really knows what to do. And most of the executives have been upstairs since they got in."

"And is Mr. Stone in? Can I see him?"

"Sure. Let me call him, but let me tell you, he's not too happy today."

"I can't imagine. His best friend murdered and all."

The guard made the call and within minutes, Stone walked through the double doors that led back to the offices. The guard was right. He looked pissed. Not the usual look of someone who just lost a good friend, one that had been murdered in your company's parking lot. No, this was a look of a man whose world was closing in on him. He looked stressed.

"Detective. Follow me. Any leads on who killed Benton?" Stone didn't wait for a response from Eckhart, spinning and going back through the same doors he had just come through.

"No. No leads. We're still gathering evidence. Waiting for the lab to run their tests. You know, that sort of stuff. Quite the scene out there. I'm sure this is upsetting to many of the employees, and especially you. Being Benton was an old friend and all."

"What do you want, detective? I really don't have time to deal with this right now."

"Kind of a coincidence, don't you think?"

"What?"

"Two people close to you murdered the past couple of days. I mean, that's got to be shocking. Even concerning that you might be next."

Stone stopped and spun around to face Eckhart. Terry couldn't decide if the look on his face was concern that he might be the next victim, or that he might be a suspect.

"It hadn't even crossed my mind. I'm focused on our IPO. I'm sorry if I don't come across as sympathetic to the death of my friend. Of course, I am. But I have a business to run. Alex was a good friend. He helped me start this company. He would want me to continue what we started.

And I see nothing that links these two deaths. They didn't know each other, and you even said you weren't sure that Javier was murdered. That it could have been an accident."

Stone turned back around and continued walking down the hall towards the elevators.

"Yes, I did. But Mr. Benton certainly wasn't. Why do you suppose he was murdered, then dumped all the way in San Francisco in the park? Next to these notebooks that your old boss had just texted you about not two days earlier? I find that enough to connect the two deaths and to consider Mr. Lopez's death a murder and not a suicide. And right now, the only thing I have linking both of those events is you."

They reached the elevators, and Stone punched the up button. The doors opened, as if the elevator was just waiting for Stone, Eckhart thought. Or that he had just come down the elevator to greet him and no one else had used it in that short period of time. Most likely, employees hunkered down at their desks, anything to avoid both Stone and the press. Stone stepped in and punched the button for the third floor, again, not waiting for Eckhart to step in after him.

"I told you before, I know nothing about those notebooks other than what Javier showed me. And as far as

Benton's murder, I was with the board of directors at the time he was murdered. In fact, we were all waiting for him in the boardroom and he never showed. Feel free to corroborate that with any of the board members. They are here today planning for the IPO."

"I will, thank you. How do you know when Mr. Benton was murdered? And that you were with the board at the same time? We haven't even gotten a time of death from the M.E. yet."

"Well, the security cameras, of course. I had our guard review the tapes to see if we could see anything. The time stamp put the murder at the same time I was with the board discussing our funding. Have a look for yourself."

"I will. Would you mind getting me a copy of those tapes? Who knows, there may be something on them that helps us identify the killer."

"Sure. I'll have the security department make a copy for you. You can pick them up on your way out."

"Great. Now, if you don't mind, I'd like to speak with your board of directors."

"Down the end of the hall. Large double doors. Can't miss it."

Eckhart watched as Stone stepped into his office and closed the door behind him without another word to the detective. He was exhibiting all the behaviors of someone running scared. He had seen it before. Many times. From suspects that took matters into their own hands in the spur of the moment. When they did, they left evidence that would link them to that crime. Spur of the moment acts weren't clean. They weren't planned, and they certainly weren't well thought out. Because of that, suspects made mistakes and they started acting paranoid. Stone was in that mode now, and Eckhart could sense it.

Of course, none of that mattered if he couldn't find the evidence he needed to make an arrest. Until he did, he needed to keep the pressure on Stone without letting on that he was Eckhart's prime suspect. Give him enough rope, as the saying goes. And he could sense that Stone was on the verge. It might have something to do with the company's coming IPO, but Eckhart felt that a majority of Stone's angst was from his guilt. He made a mental note to call Fowler when he was done with questioning the board. Fowler should be done with Mary Quinn's parents by then and back at the station. He wanted the lab to check for any prints on the notebooks and boxes they came in. He was hoping any prints they could pull would match Javier Lopez and Stone. At least confirm that Stone handled both. Not that he was denying it, but it would help to build his case. But he also wanted them to run any other prints through AFIS, the Automated Fingerprint Information System, and see if they get any hits. It was a long shot, but you never know.

Sometimes you needed a long shot.

CHAPTER TWENTY-FIVE

The SF Medical Examiner's office is at One Newhall Street just north of Hunters Point and a short drive from City Hall. Fowler made the drive from the Taraval station in a little over thirty minutes. This time of the morning there was very little cross-town traffic. Most commuters were already at their offices and it was still too early for lunch. Even though the Quinns hadn't arrived yet, Fowler wanted to make sure he was there when they did. Making parents wait when they are there to identify a dead child's body isn't a good move.

Miss Quinn's parents, coming from Sacramento, would arrive on 80 via the Bay Bridge, which would let them off right at the Medical Examiner's office. It had only been an hour since Fowler spoke to them, so he knew he had some time to meet with Hackman alone and see what he might have come up with. Fowler made his way to the M.E.'s office and knocked on the outer door. Brian Hackman looked up from his desk and gestured Fowler into the office.

"What can I do for you, detective?"

"Eckhart and I wanted to see if you had any of the labs back on the Quinn woman. Just wanted to confirm cause and time of death. I also wanted to be here when the parents came to identify the body and make their arrangements. Is she respectable enough for them?"

"When a body goes through a tragic or catastrophic accident and identification is necessary, most medical examiners do their best to prepare the upper body, especially the face, for the next of kin. Sometimes it's almost impossible to spare them the pain. In those cases, we can use photographs of specific body parts or markings that can be used to positively identify the body. Here, the body was so badly burned, it was impossible to tell if she had any tattoos or other body markings. I did my best to clean up her face, removed most of the burned skin, but it's still going to be difficult to see. Dental records are also useful as long as there have been procedures done and local. In Miss. Quinn's case, it wasn't possible to determine where dental procedures were done, so we're going to have to rely on the parents' ID and maybe they can tell us if they know what dentist she used."

"Ok, well, I have several questions for them if they are up to it."

"To answer your other question, yes, we could determine cause and time of death. Based on our findings and the time of the explosion, I would put her time of death at about 4:20am. The cause of death was asphyxiation, but there was a significant bump on her head. The blast probably sent her against the wall where we found her. Probably out cold, but still breathing. We also got a tox screen back and there was nothing remarkable on it. Small traces of alcohol, but no drugs of any kind."

"What about Javier Lopez? Same cause of death?"

"Unfortunately for him, no. Since he was upstairs and closest to the source of gas, I would guess the apartment filled significantly before leaking to the downstairs apartment. Because of that, when ignited, the upper floor became a fireball. I'm sure he was consumed immediately by flames. It happened fast, so it's difficult to tell if the cause of death was the explosion and fire or asphyxiation."

Fowler thanked Hackman and left the morgue to wait for Miss Quinn's parents in the waiting room. He didn't have long to wait. Just as he got seated and flipped through the old magazines, the administrative assistant came in and notified him that Mr. and Mrs. Quinn were in the lobby. He left the waiting room and saw them standing there. He could tell the mother had been crying, probably the whole ride down. Her eyes were red and her face was puffy. The father looked a bit more composed, but still ragged, as if neither had slept much in the last twenty-four hours, which was understandable. Fowler had no idea what it felt like to lose a child, and he didn't want to either.

He walked over and introduced himself as one of the investigating officers, extended his condolences to them, and asked if he might ask a few questions after they identified the body. Mrs. Quinn broke down and cried, and Mr. Quinn consoled her and said, yes, they would answer questions, especially if it helped them catch whoever did this.

Fowler led them to the viewing room and left to let the M.E. know. He came back in the viewing room to be with the Quinns just as Brian Hackman rolled the gurney in with the body of Mary Quinn on it, covered in a crisp white sheet. Fowler asked them both if they were ready. They both slowly nodded, and Hackman lowered the sheet from around her head. Mrs. Quinn began sobbing again and Mr. Quinn fought back tears and confirmed the body to be that of Mary Quinn, their daughter. Fowler signaled to Hackman to cover the body, and he closed the shades to the room. He sat quietly for a few moments to let them catch their breath and compose themselves, then asked,

"Can I get either of you anything? Water, coffee? Perhaps we should go back out to the waiting room, where it's more comfortable."

Without saying a word, they followed Fowler to the waiting room. He got them seated and then asked the admin to get a couple of cups of water. She returned shortly with two bottled waters and left. They both sat there in silence, not touching the water. After what seemed like an appropriate amount of time, Fowler asked them if he could ask a few questions. They both nodded yes.

"So, how long had your daughter been in San Francisco?"

"A little over a year." Mr. Quinn responded.

"And prior to that, she lived in Sacramento? With you two, or on her own?"

"Yes, in Sacramento with us. She lived at home while she went to Davis to get her accounting degree. She had graduated a couple of years ago and got a job with a local branch of B of A. After being there for less than a year she came home and told us she was thinking of moving to San

Francisco and had applied at a couple banks down there. I mean here."

"Was she in any relationships while she lived with you? Anyone that might have been upset with her?"

"You mean anyone that would want to hurt her? No. Everyone loved Mary. She was a sweet girl, and got along with everyone. Of course, she dated, but nothing ever serious. Although she had told us recently, she was seeing a man at the bank where she worked. She seemed thrilled. Wanted us to meet him."

"So, you haven't met Mr. Dillon yet?"

"Is that his name? No. She was planning a trip back home in a couple of weeks to bring him with her to have dinner with us. Is HE responsible for this?"

"No, we don't think so, Mr. Quinn. He seemed genuinely upset about her death, and his alibi was solid. Did she ever mention anyone or anything that she was worried about, scared of? You know, threats of any kind?"

"No, of course not. Like I said, everyone loved her."

"How about at her first job in Sacramento, or in college, anyone she mentioned that she might have issues with? Anyone follow her or just show up at work?"

"No. What are you getting at, detective?"

"Just standard questions. Jilted lover, maybe someone asked her out, and she said no, he didn't take it well. That sort of thing."

"No, not that we know of."

"Well, there was that one guy, Maurie. The one that always waited for her when he was making a deposit. Remember? She told us he was kind of... special."

"What do you mean 'special' Mrs. Quinn?"

"You know, not playing with a full deck. We used to call it retarded. I know we can't say that anymore. But Mary said this older guy would come in maybe twice a week. He would stand in the queue but would always let others go ahead of him until her window was open. Wouldn't say a word, just pass his deposit slip and paycheck over to her and just stare. Mary said she thought he was harmless. That was towards the end of her stay at B of A. She moved to San Francisco, and never spoke of him again. I assume she never saw him again. I mean, how would he know where she moved to or worked now?"

"Probably nothing, but you don't happen to remember his name?"

"I don't. I remember Mary saying it was one of those names that sound the same, you know, rhyming? Like his first and last name sounded the same."

"Alliterative? OK, well if you remember, you'll call me, ok?" Fowler handed her his business card.

"I still can't get over that she's gone." She put her head into her husband's chest and sobbed again.

"I think that's all for now. You can go to the front desk and make the necessary arrangements. Thank you and again, I'm sorry for your loss."

Fowler left the visitor's room and walked down to the front desk to let the admin know the Quinns would be out in a few minutes to make arrangements for the body of their daughter.

CHAPTER TWENTY-SIX

While David Stone was back in his office, Eckhart spoke with the board of directors alone. He wasn't sure what he was looking for, and couldn't be sure that anyone else on the board might be involved, but he had to take that chance. At first, his questions involved the IPO, how it worked, and trying to gain an understanding of the impact it can have on a company. The pressure to raise the funds necessary to grow a business must have been enormous. But would that pressure be enough to make someone kill? Wasn't that always the question?

Eckhart interviewed the board, more like a reporter than a cop, relaxing them into explaining the details of their business, the finances behind it, and the direction they were going. Each had their own reasons for joining the board when asked by Stone. Typically, being a member of a board was a mutually beneficial relationship. The CEO or president gained years of business experience, typically in areas where the CEO or founder of the company lacked. That wealth of knowledge gave a company the leverage to grow faster than its competition.

Board members were influential business executives or venture capitalists that wanted a say in the company's direction that they were providing significant funding for. They help the company grow and increase profits, and they put those profits straight into their pockets. The board explained this all to Eckhart, along with their belief in the product and projects that Stone was working on.

The board explained what an IPO is and how it affected current investors and the company itself. An IPO transfers a private company into a public company. It allows the current investors, mostly those on the board, to realize gains from their initial investment in the company. Those gains typically came from a share premium for the current private investors. It also allowed public investors to take part in the offering of the new stock. This influx of capital allows a company to grow and expand. Along with this new capital comes new transparency and regulations. The company is no longer privately owned and must adhere to SEC regulations and the responsibility of its public investors. The board explained that this additional public and SEC scrutiny was why Stone and the board were so concerned with the current events and how it might affect their IPO.

"Of course, the death of Benton puts us in a rather sticky situation. Going forward with the IPO makes us look like unfeeling, money-hungry businessmen. Delaying it has the potential to cost the employees here a chance at a vast amount of personal wealth. A lot of the upper management were convinced to join the company for less salary, compensated with a large amount of stock options. Those options are worthless until the company goes public. And only if that public offering is successful. So, this IPO isn't just about us and the company, it's important for the employees here as well." Leonard Atwater finished explaining to Eckhart, trying not to sound greedy as he did. He wasn't that successful.

"I think I understand, Mr. Atwater. But aren't there considerations for delaying the IPO given the death of your chairman? I mean, it sounds as if Stone and Benson were friends since college. I would think that would take priority over your IPO."

"Detective, we've considered all that and assure you, the death of Alex Benson is not being taken lightly. We are all deeply saddened by his brutal murder. None of us can comprehend why anyone would want to hurt him.

Unfortunately, people in our position have to make hard and sometimes unfavorable decisions."

"I think I understand and I wasn't implying that you didn't care about Mr. Benton. I was just curious. So, as far as the IPO was concerned, all of you are confident with the direction the company is going? With how Benton and Stone were running it?"

"Mostly. We had our concerns. Still do. Mr. Stone has been, how do I say, acting different lately. Raising some concerns. Eventually, even his friend Benton was concerned. We were discussing his potential removal from the company. Something no board looks at lightly. We don't want to create another Steve Jobs situation. Not that this company is anything like Apple, but you know what I mean."

"I'm afraid I don't."

"Well, when a small company starts out, key employees are hired directly by the founder. It's like a family. There is a certain amount of loyalty to that person. And there is a level of trust in that person's decisions, even if they seem odd or out of the norm. The employees trust that person with their financial livelihood. They're invested, shall we say? The board of directors, although primarily selected by that same person, aren't looked upon as kindly. So, you could see that if the board removed Mr. Stone, the concern would be the mood of the employees and potentially losing key staff. It can ruin a company, especially in Silicon Valley, where any of these employees can walk down the street and get offered a similar, if not better, position. It's the nature of the high-tech industry. With Apple, removing Jobs seemed like the financially prudent thing to do. And initially, it was. But long-term fallout and losing key staff can do more damage. Apple found out the hard way and eventually hired Jobs back. And now we all have iPhones, iPads, i everything, and Apple profits are through the roof."

"I see, so you hadn't actually agreed to get rid of Mr. Stone yet then? Is there any possibility it may have leaked that you were considering it? Who, other than the board, knew about this?"

"No, we haven't decided yet. In fact, after yesterday's demonstration, we were considering tabling it. But Mr. Benton was still quite adamant that something needed to be done. He was to meet with us last night and never showed. Now we know why. But to your question of any leaks. Well, only the board, including Mr. Benton, knew of our discussions. Of course, I can only speak for myself, but I'm confident that none of us would have leaked that information prior to the IPO. We ARE invested, detective."

"And you don't know what Mr. Benton wanted to discuss with you last night?"

"No idea. We all assumed it was the same that we had been discussing. That Stone was overspending on his special project, with little to no results. Benton was concerned that not only was it taking away from the core business plan of the company, but that Stone was almost obsessed with it and failing to manage the rest of the business. Which would be a financial concern for the board. However, after the demonstration, it convinced us that the project was making progress. The only thing left was Stone's management of the rest of the company. Benson never came out and said it, but most of us felt he was concerned with Stone's mental state. As I mentioned earlier, there were signs. But most of us on the board have sat on other high-tech boards, and some of us still do. And if there is one constant in the valley, detective, it's that most of these companies are started by, how do I say it, unique individuals."

"What was the project about? What was the demonstration of?"

"Sorry, detective. Unless you have a warrant, we really can't discuss that."

"Let me ask you one last question. Do you think Stone is capable of murder? That he could have murdered his friend Benton because he got wind of what you were planning to do?"

"Honestly, detective. I'm not sure of anything anymore. I wish to believe that he didn't, couldn't do that. But who knows? But there was one thing that continually bothered the board." Atwater looked around the room and several of the board members began nodding as if they knew exactly what he was about to say.

"And what was that?"

"One thing that troubled the board was the fact that both Stone and Benton continued to take advice from a third party that wasn't on the board and wasn't an employee. None of us thought that was a good idea. But of course, it's not unheard of."

"That doesn't seem to be a big deal. Why was it such an issue for the board?"

"Because neither of them would disclose who this person was. That would make any of us uneasy."

"I'm not sure I understand."

"Well, we have invested a large amount of money in this company. One benefit of that investment is the ability, no, the right, to advise the principals of the direction of that company. That direction affects all of us, and the financial success of this company depends on the advice we give, and that advice is given the weight it deserves. To have an anonymous third-party providing advice or counsel that is given more weight than ours is distressing. Plus, we'd like to know what interests or investment this other party has in the company."

Eckhart nodded in understanding as Atwater finished speaking. He thanked the board members for their time and advised them all that he may need to speak with them in the future. Eckhart left the boardroom and took the elevator to the first floor. He thought for a moment of going back up and poking Stone one more time, but thought better of it. Instead, he left the building and got into his car. He pulled out his phone and dialed Fowler's number.

"You back at the station yet? If so, can you go to the lab and see if Tim has gotten any prints off the notebooks or boxes they came in? If he has, see if he has found any prints other than Lopez's or Stone's. If he did, make sure he runs them through AFIS. I'm curious if he gets a hit."

"You got it, Terry. How did it go with Stone and the board?"

"About what we expected, but there's a possible wild card. I'm on my way back. Fill you in when I get there."

Eckhart started his car and made his way out of the parking lot and west onto 280. The drive back to San Francisco and the Taraval station didn't take long. It was late enough that the lunchtime traffic was over and early enough that the evening commute home hadn't started yet.

He pulled into the parking lot in front of the station and went straight to the detective's room. Fowler wasn't there, so he figured he was in the lab with Tim. Eckhart thought about stopping by the captain's office first and giving him an update on his interviews in Palo Alto, but figured he would play it dangerously and ignore him until after he found out if there were any prints pulled from the notebooks and boxes.

"Were you able to pull any prints off the notebooks?"

"Terry, yes I was. Actually, still in the process. There are several prints, some obviously newer than others. I'm in the process of isolating Stone's and Lopez's. Those two left the larger amount of prints, and the cleanest. Getting prints off of paper isn't as hard as some people think. The oils from your skin get into the porous surface of the paper and really stick. Of course, older prints don't hold up as well. The oil eventually dries, but I'm pulling a lot of partials. A lot of different prints. These notebooks have been handled by a lot of people."

"What about off the boxes? Anything jump out?"

"Not really. A lot of partials. The wood has so many uneven surfaces and depending on how someone touched them or held them, I'm only getting very small bits. Nothing with enough to conclusively say who's print it is. I think I'll eventually have more luck with the actual pages of the notebooks. Some of the pages obviously have more prints than the others. Once I have enough full prints, I can run them through the spectrometer and determine the age of the print. In other words, newest from older. Of course, anything older than a couple weeks will be hard to determine how old the print is. But at least we'll have a timeline of who held them last."

"Based on first glance, would you guess Stone touched them last?"

"Actually, I'm not able to at this point. His are some of the latest prints, but there are partials that don't match Stone or Lopez that could be newer. So far, the best one I've pulled off isn't large enough to give us 8 or more points of comparison. But it is enough to know it's neither of their prints. So, I can say that you have a third person who could have held these books last. But there is one interesting aspect of that."

"And what's that?"

"These third sets of prints? None of them are on the inside pages. I'm not done going over all of them, but so far, not a single partial match for the third person. Whoever this is, never opened the books. They just handled them on the outside. As if they just carried them."

CHAPTER TWENTY-SEVEN

Eckhart left the lab and returned to the detective's room. Fowler was on the phone and giving someone an update on the case. It wasn't much of an update, but whoever he was speaking with was satisfied, as the call ended quickly.

"Who was that?"

"Kevin Dillon, the boyfriend. He was just wondering where we were with his girlfriend's death. He also asked about her parents and how they were doing."

"Careful. We haven't ruled him out entirely. So, I'm clocked out and gonna head over to Joe's to meet with Ally. But before I do, let's take a walk so I can update you on what I got from the board at Stone Tech."

They left the station house and headed south on 24th towards Taraval Street. It was less than a half block and when they got to Taraval; they turned left and headed up the street to 19th.

"Let me buy you a beer at the Arms."

"Sounds good. So, what did you find out from the board? And what's with this wild card?"

"Let's get that beer first."

The walk was short, and they went through the old entrance to Shannon Arms, an Irish pub that had been in the Sunset for many years. More years than Eckhart could remember. When he started on the force, his first partner introduced him to the Arms. It was a typical Irish pub, dark, with the smell of 100 years of spilled beer and Irish tears. It catered to locals, specifically Irish locals, though others weren't turned away. They were just looked upon with a wary eye by whoever was tending bar that day. Eckhart knew this and although it wasn't his go-to place, he stopped in a time or two to wash down the foul taste of a brutal day.

There were a couple of older men sitting in the middle of the long bar. Eckhart guessed them to be in their seventies by the way they were dressed. One had a worn green herringbone flat cap and zippered cardigan sweater. Both looked like they had been worn daily. The other had on a San Francisco Glens soccer jersey that probably was his when he played. They spoke to each other in strong Irish accents, nursing the pints in front of them. They were both intently watching the soccer match playing on the TV hanging at the end of the bar. On the other TV, near the entrance, the Giants game was on with no sound.

Eckhart and Fowler walked past them in the narrow pub and took a seat at the end of the bar, facing out. The two drinkers acknowledged them with a slight nod of their heads and went back to their conversation. The bartender, an elderly, gray-headed woman who might have been older than the two patrons, looked up from her Chronicle and asked what they'd have.

"Harp", replied Eckhart.

"Same. So, are you gonna tell me what you found out? And what's with this wild card?"

The bartender poured a couple of pints from the tap and brought them over. No cocktail napkins were used at a place like the Arms.

Eckhart nodded thanks to her, took a sip of the cold beer, and turned to Fowler.

"When I first joined the force, my first partner would take me here every once in a while. Usually after a bad day. When things went sideways, or to total shit. He would sit here, slowly downing a beer or two, enlightening me on the ways of the force, imparting his experience to me. One thing I'll always remember him telling me, and have used to this day, is the idea that the simplest solution to a problem is usually the right solution. And that applied to solving crimes, too. That's how I have approached every case since becoming a detective. Mostly, he was right."

"But after one of those cases where things didn't go as planned, he mentioned the exception to that rule. That sometimes nothing was as it seemed. Where the facts would lead you down a path, only to hit a dead end and then lead somewhere else. After speaking with the board, I'm thinking this might be one of those cases."

"So, the wild card."

"The wild card. According to the board, Benton and Stone have, or had, been getting advice on running their company from an outside source. When they confronted Stone about it, he wouldn't answer. Same with Benton. Of course, it's not that uncommon, to get advice from someone outside of the board and investors. But what is, is keeping it secret. That worried the board because of any financial implications it may have, and combined with his other actions, was why the board was considering having Stone step down."

"And they had no idea who this secret adviser is?"

"I don't think so. At least they didn't allude to anything. But I think we should look into the finances and see if there is anything that jumps out. Large payments to shell corporations, strange assets coming in. Anything that looks like it's coming or going on a regular basis. Can you take care of that?"

"Sure. Let me see what I can do without a warrant."

They finished their beers, and Eckhart ordered another round. He wasn't meeting Ally at Joe's for another hour, and he had something else he needed to discuss with Fowler.

As the bartender was putting their beers down, two twenty-somethings walked into the Arms. They were both wearing Carhartt pants and vests over long-sleeved plaid shirts. Both were covered in a layer of sawdust and Eckhart figured they were just getting off from some local construction job. They took seats at the opposite end of the bar, near the entrance. They both had beards. One looked like he just started a week ago, and the other had several years into his.

Long beard yelled down to the bartender standing next to where Eckhart and Fowler were seated and ordered a couple of Buds. His tone and volume were enough to get the two old Irishmen in the middle of the bar to look over at him. Long beard saw this, stared them both down until they returned to their beers.

The bartender took a couple of bottles of Budweiser from the cooler under the bar, opened them, and delivered them to the two men. They both took long draws from the bottles.

"Hey, can we get the game on that TV?" long beard said, pointing at the one currently tuned to the soccer match.

Again, the two old Irishmen looked back towards the young men, this time with a little more annoyed look. The bartender walked down towards the two newer drinkers and said they could move to a spot at the other end of the bar or a booth so they could see the other TV.

Eckhart could feel the possibility this was going to escalate and nudged Fowler with his knee under the bar. Of course, this wasn't necessary, as Fowler was already tensed and ready.

"We don't want to move and we want to watch a real sport. Not that foreign crap."

"Real sport, right" said Glen jersey-wearing Irishman under his breath.

"What did you say, old man?" short beard said.

Unfazed, Glen jersey-wearing turned and faced the two directly. He slowly took a sip of his beer and said in a thick Irish accent, "What I said was, you two wouldn't know a real sport if it slapped ya on the beck."

The two young men started laughing and long beard started to get up from his stool. Eckhart and Fowler both slid their hands down to their holsters, just in case. The bartender had moved to the furthest end of the bar. Both old Irishmen had swung their stools around to face the two young men. The Irishman with the herringbone flat cap spoke next.

"I'd watch yourselves, boys, unless you be liking hospital food. Now, sit down and let us finish watching our match."

The two young men broke out in an even louder laugh and both of them got up and walked towards the older men. Eckhart had seen enough and got up, Fowler following him.

"Stay out of this. This is between us and the two old micks."

Eckhart continued walking toward the two and pulled the edge of his jacket aside, revealing his detective's badge. Fowler did the same, also showing his shoulder holster.

The two young men stopped in their tracks as Eckhart and Fowler passed the two older men and moved between them and the young men.

"Hey, we don't want any trouble, just wanted to drink our beers and watch the game."

"Then I suggest you finish them and watch the game somewhere else," Eckhart said.

The two returned to their beers, downed them and short beard pulled out a credit card to pay for them. The bartender yelled from the other end of the bar, "Cash only."

"Fuck this," long beard said. Both started rifling through their pockets for cash.

"They're on me boys, you can just leave. And find another bar to frequent from now on." Eckhart took out a ten-dollar bill and put it on the bar next to their empties. The two left, and Eckhart and Fowler turned to go back to their seats.

"We could have taken them, you know," Glen jersey said.

Without turning around, Eckhart said, "Undoubtedly, but then we'd have all this paperwork to do, and we really don't have the time for it."

CHAPTER TWENTY-EIGHT

Eckhart walked into Joe's of Westlake and saw George, the bartender, hanging a picture behind the bar. Instead of the usual news clipping of the latest Giant's, Niner's, or Warrior's win, this was a framed picture of a man in his fifties. He was dressed in all white, holding a large bowl with the words, "Tom and Jerry" in gold script on the side. Eckhart took a seat at the bar, facing the door. It was a cop thing, eyes on the entrance and exit sort of thing.

"What's with the picture?"

"Adam Richey passed. He was a legend around here. I got my training from him at Tadich Grill."

"Oh, man. Sorry to hear that. Now that you mention it, I might have met him at MoMo's in the Financial District."

"Probably. He's tended a lot of places around town. I feel bad for his wife and kids. He was too young to go. The usual?"

Eckhart nodded, and George produced a Manhattan in a matter of minutes. He swirled the maraschino cherry around in the glass as he waited for Ally. Eckhart was just about to take his first sip when he glimpsed her walking in.

He watched her as she looked around the crowded bar for him. He could have waved her down, but he enjoyed watching her. Unlike earlier today, her hair was down and she had added a touch of makeup.

She finally saw him and started the long walk to where he was seated. Eckhart could feel that he wasn't the only one in the bar watching her path. She was wearing the same clothes she had on at work. The long gray skirt hugged her ample hips, the white blouse and matching gray coat did little to hide the bounce of her bosom, and her high heels accentuated the entire package. Eckhart was watching her the whole way, with a fresh set of eyes.

When she finally made it to his side, Eckhart stood and pulled out the stool next to him so she could slide in and sit. Through all the years they had known each other, worked together. This was the first time he was seeing her as more than just a colleague. Even though he had asked her here to discuss the case, he knew in the back of his mind that there was something else there.

Eckhart took another long sip of his Manhattan and then waved George over. When he finally made it to their end of the bar, Eckhart asked for another Manhattan and turned to Ally to place her order.

"I'll have a Macallan, up."

"Impressive. I wouldn't have taken you as a scotch drinker."

"I'm sure there are a lot of things about me that might surprise you."

"Well, the night is young."

"And are you both having dinner tonight?" George asked as he poured Ally her scotch and made Eckhart his Manhattan.

"The chicken parm is the best. Or the ravs. Or both." Eckhart offered, and the bartender smiled and agreed.

"I'll just have the Caesar salad and a side of the ravioli." Ally said.

"George, I'll have the parm, side of ravs, and bring us some sourdough too."

"You got it, Terry."

"So, Terry, I'll be honest with you. We don't have enough to issue the warrant you want. And even if we did, what little evidence you have is so circumstantial I wouldn't be able to make it stick. Think about it. So, the guy worked in the park years ago for the gardener. You even said he looked distraught when you told him Javier was dead. And now Benton is dead, but all that says is there may be a connection between both deaths and the company, not specifically the CEO. That's a stretch."

"Maybe, but I've been doing this long enough to see the connections, and it's a feeling that I get. Hard to describe. It's like when you first meet someone and you just don't like them. They don't even have to open their mouths. It's just that vibe. That's what I get from this guy. Yes, he was genuinely upset when he heard about Javier's death, but he's hiding something. I know it. And I think whatever it is, it's at StoneTech or his house. I could just come out and ask him if he'll let me have a look around, but I'm not sure he'd actually show me everything. And guys like this. They think they're smarter than everyone else. I can just sense that with him. So smart he thinks he has us all fooled."

They both took another sip of their drinks before either spoke. Eckhart looked around, doing a once over of everyone there. It was a force of habit, being a cop and protecting his turf. His bar. For as long as he had been coming here, there had been no problems, other than the occasion drunk that he helped usher out to a cab. But it was his nature to be on point, watchful. The place was always busy, but it was mostly locals, mostly family or friends after work. It wasn't your typical dive bar since there was a full restaurant that had been here since they developed the area in the 50s. It was regulars, people that lived or had once lived in the neighborhood.

"Look, I understand where you're coming from. Fowler and I are still gathering evidence. I just met with Stone again and evidently, their security tapes caught the murder in progress. Of course, they aren't clear enough to determine the identity of the killer, but I have the lab analyzing them. Hopefully, they can enhance the video and we can get a clearer picture. According to Stone, he was with the board of directors at the time it happened, but I want to make sure they haven't doctored the tapes. I just don't want this guy slipping away from us or getting rid of anything that can pin him to the murders. Putting those notebooks back into the statue is the first step. If they were still with him or whoever did this, it would be a tremendous step towards motive. There is something this guy is hiding and I believe it's somewhere in his corporate headquarters."

"Terry, you get me that evidence, and I'll be able to go to the judge for the warrant. Until then, my hands are tied. You know that."

Just then, George, dressed in the tuxedo that all the wait staff wore, delivered their meals. The conversation shifted to trial prep and going over the questions the defense might ask. Specifically, Ally covered the decision to proceed without a warrant, what was behind that decision, and how best to answer questions regarding it. As they were finishing their meals, the conversation smoothly shifted to a more personal note. Terry opened up about how cases like the kid killer tore at him. How it consumed his life and affected what little personal life he had. That led to him opening up about his marriage and divorce and how being married to a cop meant being married to the job. Something Eckhart's wife just couldn't deal with.

"Do you think you could ever get married again?" Ally's interest peaked.

"I'm not sure. Maybe. How about you? What's your story?"

"Similar to you. I was a defense attorney for a while, but you know that. At some point, I decided I was tired of defending mostly guilty clients. An opportunity came up in the DA's office and I took it. Been there ever since and love it. I'd rather be on the same side as you guys, instead of constantly battling against you."

Eckhart felt things shifting between them. There seemed to be a warmth from her he was just noticing. And his interest in her went beyond the job. He was looking at her in a completely new light, and he liked how it made him feel.

It was getting late, and they both had to be in court tomorrow. Eckhart paid the bill, and they left Joe's. As he walked her to her car, Ally gently took his hand and said she wasn't ready to go home yet. Terry took the queue and offered to have her come back to his place for a nightcap. She agreed, and minutes later, they were in front of Eckhart's home in Westlake. He got out and opened the door for Ally.

"Such a gentleman."

"I try."

They walked up the path to the front door and Terry opened it for her and let her enter first.

"You always leave your door unlocked? Do you think that's safe?"

"Sure, I think there's a cop that lives around here." He said with a smirk on his face. "Make yourself comfortable. What can I get you? Beer, scotch?"

"How about a scotch? Beer's too heavy at night."

"You got it." Terry went into the kitchen and poured a couple of glasses of scotch. He returned to the living room and Ally's back was to him. She was looking at Eckhart's overly stuffed bookcases of mostly crime fiction with a few true crime novels thrown in.

"You like to read?"

"When I have the time" Terry walked over to her and handed her a glass. He held his up to her and said, "May the best day of your past be the worst day of your future." He clinked his glass to hers and took a small sip.

"Interesting toast."

"My first partner out of the academy was Scottish. He'd been on the job a long time, and I learned a lot from him. Any time we had a bad day, had to deal with anything ugly, he'd take me for a shot to forget the day. He loved that toast."

"Nice. Thanks for dinner tonight."

They sat on the couch and sipped their drinks. They both put their glasses down on the coffee table and an uncomfortable silence hung in the air. Just as it appeared Ally was going to say something, Terry blurted out, "Let me check the guest room and make sure there are clean sheets and towels for you in the morning. The cleaning lady is so unreliable."

Before Ally could respond, Eckhart was up off the couch and walking down the hall. Passing the linen closet, he grabbed a couple of clean, white towels and entered the guest room, just opposite the hall from the guest bath. He busied himself with making sure the sheets were clean and the room was tidy. It was an act of stalling. No one had spent the night at Eckhart's in years, at least not guests that would use this room. The room itself only had a bed, a nightstand, and a chest of drawers. There was really nothing to check. He took one more scan of the room, left the towels on the bed, and then went back down the hall to the living room.

"OK, the room is the first door on your right. I left some clean towels on the bed and you can use the guest bath right across the hall."

"Thanks, Terry." Ally wasn't sure what to make of this. Any other guy would have been going pretty hard to the basket to get her in bed. She'd been there before, most of the time fighting them off, seldom letting anyone in. Tonight, she was ready to let that happen. She liked Terry. She always had, even during their adversarial days as public defender and cop. Underneath that gruff, business-like exterior, she knew he was a sweet, caring gentleman. Someone she could trust. And wasn't that exactly what he was doing now? Caring for her, being the gentleman, someone she could trust.

"Well, I've got to meet Fowler early tomorrow. We need to get that evidence so you can get us the warrant. I'll see you in the morning?"

"Sure, Terry. I have an early morning too. And thanks again for taking care of me."

Eckhart made his way back down to the end of the hall where the master bedroom was. He went in and closed the door. He could hear Ally get up and head down the hall as well, then heard the door to the bathroom open and close and water running. Eckhart laid down on his bed, fully dressed, listening, making sure she was Ok. He finally heard the door open again and the light padding of her feet on the hardwood of the hall, making her way into the guest bedroom. The door closed and then silence. After a time had passed, he turned over and tried to sleep. The case re-entered his train of thought and he ended up staying awake for the next hour or so going over what he had so far. It wasn't much, but he still thought there was something up with Stone and his company. How many were involved and what was with those notebooks? Now that they had them in their possession, he could have the professor analyze them and see if he could come up with anything.

Eckhart slowly drifted off to sleep, the case bouncing around in his head. The next thing he knew, he woke up to the rich smell of coffee and the sound of the shower in the guest bath. He looked at his watch and saw it was six-thirty. The morning light was breaking through the bedroom window. He realized he had slept in his clothes and got up to take a quick shower and put some fresh clothes on. By the time he left his bedroom, Ally was already in the kitchen with a cup of coffee.

"Morning sleepy head."

"It's not even seven yet. How'd you sleep?"

"Great, thanks. Maybe we can have another sleepover soon." She smiled and turned her back to him to refill her cup.

"I'd like that." Deciding to take advantage of the situation, Terry stepped in, spun Ally around and gave her a quick kiss. As he pulled away, she grabbed him by the shoulders and pulled him back for a longer kiss.

"I was hoping for that last night."

"I was too."

"Then why did you wait until this morning?"

"I'm not sure. Probably didn't want to mess up a good thing."

"I don't want to mess it up either, Terry."

CHAPTER TWENTY-NINE

Thoughts of Ally were still in his head as Eckhart headed into the station to meet Fowler. Nothing had happened, and yet something happened. It had been a while for Terry, and being a cop did not make for a suitable partner in a relationship. His marriage failed because his job consumed him. It had to in order for him to do it right. She just never got it. And worrying that he may not come home, that he spent more time working or with work on his mind than with her. It was eventually a deal breaker.

But this felt different. Ally knew what being a cop was about, and Terry felt like this might work. He got the impression that she thought it could work as well. He was glad he took it slow last night. As much as he was tempted, he thought restraint was the best plan of action.

He made the drive to Taraval station, alternating thoughts between the two murder cases and the time he just spent with Ally. One leaving him confused and frustrated, the other warm and comfortable. But deep in the recesses of his mind, the impending testimony in the child killer case later today was taking his thoughts hostage. Fowler and Eckhart did everything by the book, except waiting for a warrant before breaking down Jim Pascal's door. He knew they had enough evidence to make a case stick, and he was more concerned with stopping a second killing than just standing by while he waited for a judge to agree.

Ally had convinced him they had enough evidence to convict. She needed Eckhart to be one-dimensional in his answers to the defense's questions. She had told Eckhart that there was evidence they may have overlooked in the disclosures she had sent over. If that were the case, she had an idea that she could spring it on the jury and the defense, leaving them flailing for cover. She told him they would go over it just before the trial, leaving enough time for the defense to change their plea or move to have the evidence dismissed. If neither happened, she was confident they had missed it in disclosure. He hoped she was right.

Eckhart arrived at the station and saw Fowler's car already in the lot. He went straight to Captain Jordan's office so he could pro-actively get him off his back for the rest of the day. He would touch base with Fowler as soon as he was done.

"Captain, just wanted to give you an update on where we are with the StoneTech case. Spoke with the DA yesterday and she thinks we have enough to get a warrant, as long as we get what I'm hoping from the lab today. I'm heading down to the company later to serve it and gather the evidence we need to make an arrest. Everything points to Stone offing them both, the gardener and Benton."

"Thanks, detective. See, that wasn't too hard."

"No sir. Also, I'll be giving testimony today. Pascal kid killer case. Shouldn't be more than a couple of hours gone. Meeting with the ADA first to go over testimony."

"Right. Make sure you say nothing that fucks this up."

"That's the plan."

Eckhart left Jordan's office mumbling under his breath about what a waste of oxygen his boss was. As soon as he entered the detective's office, Fowler looked up and could see the look of frustration on his face. He took his seat and waited for Fowler to make a comment. None came. He picked up his messages and quickly flipped through them to see if there was anything dealing with the current case or the testimony later today.

"How did it go with Quinn's parents?"

"OK. Of course, they are taking it pretty hard. They confirmed most of what Kevin Dillon told us about Mary Quinn. She had moved from Sac about a year ago. Worked at a bank there before getting the job at Community. Nothing really enlightening. They mentioned the same incident that Dillon mentioned. About the older guy that was bothering her when she worked in Sac. They didn't think much of it either, but I'm going to see what I can dig up about it. Just to close the loop on that."

"Sounds good. Might be difficult since there was no restraining order, but see what you can find out. Have you heard anything from the lab?"

"Sorry Terry, I haven't had time to check yet this morning."

"OK, let me run back there."

Eckhart left the detective's room and headed back to the lab. Tim was busy running fingerprints through the police database. The computer screen looked just like what you would imagine, or see on one of the many late-night cop shows. The suspect print on one side of the screen, while thousands of other prints flashed by, the program comparing the eight or more points of reference between the two. Unlike cop shows, the search took longer than a couple of seconds, and the case was unlikely to be solved in an hour, including commercials.

"Any more on my murders?"

"Not much. I recovered the rest of the gardener's phone data. Nothing really there. Very few calls. Even fewer texts. Only other pictures look like they are of plants in the park. According to the fire department, the fire and explosion were definitely caused by gas leaking from the stove. Probably built up in the apartment, and when Miss Quinn came in and flicked the light switch, it ignited. They said one burner being left on could be considered an accident, but all of them make it look intentional."

"As far as the Benton murder. I've confirmed the time of death between five and eight that evening, which means he was most likely dead when he was placed in the car's trunk. He was probably in that trunk for a good three or four hours. And yes, the blood in the trunk matches Benton's. We couldn't pull any other samples than his. We found one interesting thing. On the driver's side of the car, the floor mat had a faint blood impression. Looks like it matches the impression at the scene. Same shoes. Just confirms that it's likely the murderer is also the person who drove the vehicle to dump the body."

"The security tapes you dropped off look legit, and the timestamps match my findings on the time of death. I'm still running them through our analyzer to see if there have been any attempts to alter them, but given the consistency with time of death, I'd agree they are original."

"What's going on with the fingerprints?"

"Well, not much more. I could eliminate a lot of the prints on both the notebooks and boxes as Stone's and Lopez's. That left several partials that I gathered from the outside. Like I said earlier, I did not find this third set of prints inside on the papers, which is a problem. If they were, the oils from the skin would have saturated into the porous fibers of the paper and I would have been able to get a suitable set or two. Instead, I had to pull them off the cover and the wooden boxes. The cover is leather, so at least what prints I could get are in good shape. Unfortunately, the person they belong to was holding the notebooks in such a way that his or her palm touched the cover, and the fingertips wrapped around the spine and only partially touched the back. So, I pulled half a dozen prints with about a third of the finger. Not really enough to make a match that would hold up in a court, but possibly enough to get us a match."

"How long do you think it will take?"

"Hard to say. I'm running it against pretty much everything. This is running against AFIS right now. I contacted a buddy over at the FBI and asked if I could borrow some time to run it against their database as well. If the person has a driver's license, has a record, or been scanned for any kind of clearance for employment, they'll eventually show up."

"OK, what we have so far might be enough. Let me know if anything else turns up."

Eckhart went back to the detective's room and gave Fowler the same update.

"Do you think that's enough for a warrant?"

"It has to be. I'd like to wait for the prints, just in case. I'll call Ally and see if she agrees."

"You got something going on there? First name and all."

"It's a work in progress. I'll let you know."

"Good for you, partner."

CHAPTER THIRTY

Eckhart left the Taraval station house and made his way to the criminal courts on Bryant Street. As much as he was regretting having to testify, he was looking forward to seeing Ally. It had been a long time since he felt this way about a woman. And it was a pleasant distraction from the case he was working on and the testimony he was about to face. He knew he wanted to see her again, and not just at the trial.

He parked his car and entered the courthouse from the back where cops and defendants made their way in, alone from the media and distraught family members. He knew both sets of parents would be there. The parents of the child that was killed and the parents of the one that they saved. Eckhart and Fowler had worked the case as hard as they did for both of them, to gain justice for the grieving family and to spare the other from having to plan a funeral. He couldn't face either at this point.

Eckhart made his way through the metal detectors and checkpoints and then to the stairs that led to CR12. As he rounded the marble staircase, he saw Ally standing at the top, waiting for him. A smile immediately appeared on his face, and she returned the same emotion. When he reached the top step, it took a great deal of willpower not to embrace her.

Ally took Eckhart into a room usually reserved for defense attorneys to get their clients' lies straight before going into court. She wanted to make sure Eckhart just answered the questions and not offer any more information than the defense required. Sometimes when cops get on the stand, they get wordy and end up saying something the defense can use against them. Eckhart had been through this before. It wasn't his first rodeo, and he wasn't about to give the defense anything. He thought Ally just wanted to be alone with him. He wasn't altogether wrong.

As soon as both of them were in the room and the door closed, Eckhart could hold back no longer. They embraced and kissed, the tension from the night before spilling over. Terry could feel the passion in her kiss and figured it had been as long for her as it was for him.

"I'd like to have dinner again with you tonight. The guest room isn't clean though, so…"

"I'd like that, too Terry. But let's focus on this right now."

Ally detached herself from Eckhart's embrace, reluctantly. The smile was still on her face, and a rosy glow on her cheeks now accompanied it. Eckhart could see she was struggling to compose herself.

"Look, the main thing he's going to try is to create a scenario where you didn't have probable cause to enter. That there was no immediate danger."

"That's bullshit. He had a kid. When we entered, he had a gun to the kid's head. If that's not immediate danger, I don't know what is."

"Terry, I'm on your side. I'm just preparing you for what the defense might say. He's going to try to rattle you, get you to say something you shouldn't. Keep your cool, answer yes and no if possible. If he asks any open-ended questions, keep it short and to the point. Nothing extra."

"I got it, counselor."

They left the conference room and headed into CR12. Eckhart took a seat in the back row and Ally proceeded to the prosecution's table. The defense attorney and his client, Jim Pascal, the kid killer, were seated at the defense table. Eckhart almost didn't recognize him. The defense team had transformed his look. Pascal could pass for any white-collar employee at some hi-tech firm. Gone was his foot-long beard, he was now clean-shaven. He had an expensive-looking haircut. He was wearing an off-the-rack suit instead of the military fatigues he was wearing when arrested.

The judge entered and both the defense and prosecution entered several pleas and once they were disposed of, the trial continued. Several other witnesses were called and after an hour, it was Eckhart's turn. The defense attorney called him to the stand. He took his oath and then looked over at Ally Wilder before staring at Pascal and then at the attorney. After the obligatory questions confirming his name, rank, and assigned station house, the questions began.

He ran Eckhart through the basic questions of what led him to suspect his client, why he hadn't gotten a warrant before arresting him, and the list of evidence that the prosecution had on the case. Eckhart answered the defense's questions with yes and no answers, only expanding when necessary to judicially brief responses. At several points during the questioning, Eckhart looked over at Ally with a slight smirk, acknowledging her pretrial prep. But he was no stranger to the stand or a defense attorney's questioning. He knew better than to provide even the hint of an opening.

The defense objected several times to Eckhart's responses, wanting him to provide more detail or answer with something more than just acknowledging a yes or no. The judge upheld his objections a few times and Eckhart would have some fun with the response, expanding a yes answer to 'yes, I did' or 'yes, that's true'. After more than an hour on the stand, the defense finished questioning Eckhart and turned him over to the prosecution and Ally.

"Detective, do you need a break before we continue?"

"No, I'm good."

"Detective Eckhart, what evidence did you have that linked the suspect to this case?"

"My partner and I obtained the CCTV footage of the arcade where the first victim was abducted. Time stamps show when the victim entered the arcade and when the suspect entered. We also have traffic cam footage of the suspect's vehicle in the area just prior to him arriving at the arcade and the same cams showing his car leaving approximately twenty minutes later. We have witnesses that picked Mr. Pascal out of a lineup confirming his whereabouts in the arcade during that window of time when the first victim was abducted. Witnesses place the same vehicle in the schoolyard's vicinity where the second child was abducted, around the same time as that abduction."

"When you say you have footage of Mr. Pascal entering the arcade, isn't it true that there is no actual facial ID in that CCTV footage?"

"That's true, but we have witnesses that confirm he was in there during that time."

"Detective, isn't it true that witness corroboration is very unreliable? And isn't it possible that just because we see his vehicle on traffic cam footage in the area, there's no way to know whether the vehicle went anywhere near the arcade?"

"These witnesses picked Pascal out of a lineup."

"As far as the schoolyard, there is no video footage available near the schoolyard, is there?"

"No, unfortunately, the school's security cameras were down for repair during that time frame."

"So, really, all you have is the traffic footage from a few blocks away from the schoolyard. Nothing more that puts Mr. Pascal there at the time the child was abducted."

"Yes." Eckhart looked over at Ally, then back at Pascal as he smirked at the detective.

"And of the traffic cam footage of both abductions, did you get clear pictures of the license plates of the vehicle in question?"

"No, just partials from both cameras."

"Well, then, how did you arrive at the vehicle belonging to the suspect?"

"The camera near the arcade showed the first two digits and the one near the park showed the last three of a commercial plate. Combining the two, plus the type and color of the van, resulted in thirty-three matches in the DMV database. We eliminated twenty-five by interviewing the owners and confirming their alibis. That left eight. Five were owned by businesses that had graphics painted on the sides, which the traffic cams confirmed could not have been the same vehicle. Of the remaining three, one has a broken headlight, one had a dent in the driver's door, both eliminated when comparing to the footage. That left Mr. Pascal's."

"And did you verify that no work had recently been performed on the suspect's vehicle?"

"Yes, we did."

"Detective, this all sounds quite circumstantial. Was this the only evidence you had that tied the suspect to the abductions?"

"No."

"No? Then what conclusive evidence did you have in order to single out Pascal as the only suspect?"

"Fingerprints."

"Fingerprints? Well, of course, the suspect's fingerprints would be in the van. It was his van."

"No, in the arcade. Once the abduction was reported, and we confirmed the child's last whereabouts was the arcade, we closed it off and looked for any evidence. Security cameras in the arcade showed the video games he played and when we dusted for prints, we found the child's along with a dozen or more we had to go through to eliminate them as suspects. Most were other kids, except one we couldn't eliminate. Mr. Pascal's."

"Detective, is it possible that Mr. Pascal had been there earlier or even another day?"

"Unlikely. Our lab could verify that the suspect's prints were on top of the abducted child's prints, meaning he was at the video game after the child. Based on this and the CCTV footage, as well as those 'unreliable' witnesses, this puts Pascal in the arcade at the same time as the child and the same time as the reported abduction."

"Detective, wouldn't the police still consider this circumstantial?"

"Maybe so, but the other fingerprints pretty much locked it."

"What other fingerprints?"

"The ones in Pascal's van."

"I object! We've gone over this, your honor. Of course, my client's fingerprints would be in his van."

"Detective, can you explain what you mean?" The judge asked.

"Sure. We found the suspect's fingerprints in the van, which we expected. It was the other sets of prints we found that linked the suspect to the two abducted children. Even though the van was completely sanitized by the suspect, using bleach and water to remove any blood evidence, he didn't do a thorough enough job. Behind the support posts in the back of the van, where it looks like someone was handcuffed, we found two sets of prints, as if they were gripping the post. The suspect failed to wipe those clean. Both sets of prints matched the murdered child and the second child we rescued."

Ally Wilder finished her questioning and returned to the prosecution table. She looked over at the defense attorney and his client, James Pascal. Pascal's once cynical expression had changed. He had a pale, waxen look now. His smile was gone and a deep, furrowed look now covered his face. Before sitting down, she turned to the judge and stated, "That's all, your honor."

When the judge called a recess and the courtroom was cleared, Eckhart joined Ally at the prosecution's table. She confirmed that his testimony was good, and that, combined with the evidence, meant he probably wouldn't be needed at any further point during the trial.

"But, you know, don't leave town… just in case we need you again."

"I'm not planning on that anytime soon, counselor."

"So, dinner tonight?"

"Sure. I need to get back to the station and see if the lab has anything more on the StoneTech case. Call you?"

Ally smiled, and they parted ways. Eckhart to the elevators leading to the parking area and she to her office next door. As he rode the elevator down, he went over the testimony in his head. He thought what he had to say, and the evidence, should be enough to put Pascal away for a long time, if not a reservation for the chair at Q.

His thoughts then returned to Ally and the feelings he hadn't felt in some time, probably since he was married.

CHAPTER THIRTY-ONE

Eckhart left the courthouse and headed back to the Taraval station. His thoughts went from his testimony, which he felt went pretty well, to Ally and where he thought this relationship was going. The drive back to the west side of the city and the Sunset was quick during this time of day and he pulled up just a little after two in the afternoon.

He parked his sedan in one of the empty stalls across the street, facing the playground. It was empty today except for one older gentleman sitting on one of the old wrought iron benches feeding a small group of pigeons. An occasional seagull tried to interrupt the feeding pigeons, but they stood their ground and quickly grabbed every morsel of stale bread the old man fed them. Eckhart smiled to himself. This scene had been played over and over for as long as he could remember, at various locations throughout the city. He watched as the man went from reading his newspaper to feeding the pigeons. As Eckhart watched him, the old man noticed him watching, and he slowly raised his hand and waved.

He got out of his car and walked up the steps and into Taraval. Once inside, Frank Jordan yelled from his office for Eckhart to join him. He knew what he wanted. It was always the same thing. Jordan needed updates as soon as his detectives walked in the station house door. He did it with all his reports, and Eckhart figured it was as much about control as it was about being kept abreast of any ongoing investigations. Most of the time he could blow him off or just feed him enough to get him off Eckhart's back and let him do his job.

Eckhart went straight to Captain Jordan's office and before he could ask, Eckhart dumped as much data on him as he could.

"Captain, just wanted to give you an update on the testimony I gave today. Seems like it went well, but you could speak to the ADA and get her input on it. She thinks they'll be able to get a conviction based on the testimony I provided, along with the defense attorney's lack of preparation. Miss Wilder caught them off guard. But that's just my opinion."

"As far as the Lopez/Benton murders, I was just about to see if the lab had any further evidence for me. I discussed the warrant with the ADA today as well. She agrees we'll need something more than just circumstantial. Depending on if Tim has anything new, and what it might be, I think we should have enough to get a warrant to search the StoneTech company headquarters and the CEO's residence."

Captain Jordan listened intently as Eckhart rattled off his update, his mouth slightly agape. More information than he needs, Terry thought. Best approach yet. Since Jordan hadn't replied yet to his update, Eckhart turned and left the office, announcing over his shoulder, "I'll let you know if the lab has anything."

Instead of heading straight to the lab, Eckhart stopped at the detective's office to see if he had any messages. He saw he had one from Ally and one from Kevin Dillon, Mary Quinn's boyfriend and co-worker at the bank. He had a pretty good idea of what Ally wanted but was curious about what Dillon would want. Maybe some information he forgot to tell us? He'd call him back as soon as he was done with the lab. Fowler was just hanging up the phone and turned to Eckhart.

"That was the Quinn's. They wanted to be kept up to date on our investigation, specifically if it ended up not being an accident. Nice people. Really felt sorry for them."

"Did they have anyone they thought might want to hurt their daughter?"

"Not really. All the regular answers. Everyone loved her. She was happy with her new boyfriend. No stalkers or anything. Although, they mentioned one customer when she worked at the bank in Sac. Mother called him 'special'. He always asked for her. Never said much, according to the daughter. Just a strange old guy. Says Mary never mentioned him again once she moved to The City."

"Well, check it out just in case. See if anyone at her old bank remembers the guy and maybe we can get some contact information. Probably nothing, but follow it up. And Fowler, can you give Mr. Dillon a call and see what he wants? He left me a message. I'm gonna see if Tim has anything else from either scene."

Eckhart left the detective's office and headed back to the lab. When he entered, Tim was on the computer and Eckhart could see a picture of the notebook on his screen. Tim was sifting through several pictures, mostly of the notebook, or different pages from it. Then occasionally a picture of the box it supposedly came in popped on the screen.

"Looks like you have more from the gardener's phone?"

"Yes. It isn't much, though. As we suspected from the call and text logs, Mr. Lopez didn't use his phone very much, if at all. However, I recovered all the jpegs from the phone, as well as the complete call and text history. Looks like he used it more for pictures of the work he did around the park. Lots of shots of different plants, close-ups. Almost amateur photographer-like. There are more of the notebook, various pages, and several of all sides of the box. A couple of texts were sent to Stookie the day the photos of the notebook and box were taken, and a 6-minute phone call preceded the text. Probably called him and Mr. Stone asked him to text over a pic. So, not much else to go on connecting David Stone to the explosion, or the missing notebook. But nothing to exclude him, either. It actually confirms what you already know from your interview with Mr. Stone, correct? I mean, he admitted to meeting with Lopez, just no evidence that he caused the explosion or took the notebook."

"That's right. I know that he's involved. I just need to find the evidence to prove it. Anything else from the murder scene at StoneTech or the dump site?"

"Not really. Blood analysis confirmed it was the victim's. Tox screen was negative, no drugs or alcohol in his system, so he wasn't compromised."

"Tim, how close does someone have to get to make that kind of wound?"

"Pretty close. I'd say within a couple of feet."

"I think Benton knew his murderer, or at least felt safe enough for this person to approach him that closely. Wouldn't you agree?"

"Yeah, I'd have to say so."

"And a wound like that, blood all over the place. The suspect would have gotten Benton's blood on his clothes. It would be impossible to avoid it. So that patch of material you recovered at the scene, the jacket it came from, would have blood on it, as well as the deck shoes. Correct?"

"Unless they were wearing a hazmat suit, I would have to agree. Of course, he, and I'm assuming a male, could have just disposed of the clothes anywhere."

"Maybe. Maybe not. Murderers don't plan crimes of passion or opportunity. They make mistakes. They don't notice details. He might have washed them, thinking that all the evidence would be gone. And I agree this suspect is male.

The force it would have taken to make that deep cut, as well as the strength to move the body, and place it like he did. I'm thinking of a taller, younger male. The jacket is out of place for me. David Stone wears very expensive, finely tailored suits. Not tweed jackets. I still think Stone is good for the Lopez/Quinn murders, but he may have a partner that took care of Benton. But who? Who else would benefit from Benton's death? The board of Stone Technologies mentioned that Stone and Benton were in contact with someone that wasn't an employee or a board member and possibly taking advice from them. Maybe that person didn't agree with Benton's idea to remove Stone as CEO of the company."

Eckhart left the lab and went back to the detective's office and sat down. He went through his notes one more time and closed his eyes for a few seconds as he thought. Going over everything in his head. Two murders on 22nd and a murder at a tech firm in the Valley. How and why are they connected? The only common denominator was Stone. But there was this other mysterious person they both were getting advice from. What kind of advice and what was their stake in this? Eckhart opened his eyes and looked over at Fowler.

"Fowler, can you get a list of all the shareholders of StoneTech, specifically ones that aren't on the board or employees there? I want the entire list, but let's focus on anyone that's not a board member or employee."

"We may need the warrant for that, but let me see if I can sweet talk their HR department into providing a list. Since they are going public, their prospectus might have the information we need too."

"Not sure what any of that means, but get whatever you can. I want to see a list of investors or people that stand to make a profit that aren't employees."

Fowler got on the phone and made the call to StoneTech. He asked for the head of HR and identified himself as a detective investigating the murder of Alex Benton. As part of that investigation, they would like to know all investors, silent and active partners, and anyone else that might be listed in the IPO prospectus that has an interest in the company. Eckhart listened as Fowler made his request and then watched a smile form on his partner's face. He provided his department email address and thanked whoever he was speaking with and hung up. He swung his chair around towards Eckhart and held his hand up for a high five.

"And that's how it's done. She'll be emailing me a contact list and the preliminary prospectus for our review."

"You're the man." Eckhart smirked at Fowler and slapped his hand. "Let me know when you get it."

Eckhart picked up his phone and dialed the number for Ally Wilder's office. He let it ring a few times and then the answering system picked up. Eckhart left a message regarding the updated lab findings and then offered to meet her for dinner at Joe's later that evening. He hung the phone up just as Fowler was turning to tell him he received an email from StoneTech's HR department.

"It's quite a list. Looks like there are a couple hundred names on the list, separated by board members, employees, and those listed as 'other'. Let me print it out."

Fowler sent the file to the common printer in the office. It took a few seconds and then the printer came to life and it started spitting out several pages. When it was complete, Eckhart walked over and retrieved the prints. He started quickly flipping through the list. The list was broken down as Fowler said. Board of Directors first, along with their previous corporate association and current number of stock options. Most were in the six figures except Benton and Stone who had a majority of shares in the seven figures which would keep them as majority holders. Well, at least Stone would. Eckhart wasn't sure what happened to a person's options when they passed before a company went public. Did they go to heirs or get redistributed to other shareholders?

He flipped to the next sheet, and this one listed all the employees. Or at least those that had stock options with the company. Listed alphabetically, along with their title at the company and then number of shares. Since the options were used to attract employees that were in demand in the valley, most of the positions were engineers and scientists and they all had somewhere between fifty and seventy-five thousand shares each. There was also a smattering of other positions listed, even down to the rent a cop, but most of their shares were in the hundreds to a few thousand. Eckhart did some quick calculations in his head and even if the IPO was mildly successful, everyone would stand to have a nice chunk of cash out of the deal. Some in the millions.

He continued to scan the names and finally got to the last page. The one that contained those people with stock options that weren't employed by StoneTech. It was only a single page, but it had around thirty names on it. Based on the designation next to their names it appeared most were friends or relatives of Stone and Benton, probably a way to pay them back for being in their lives. As Eckhart scanned down the list, he saw Javier Lopez's name along with the designation 'Friend' and the number of options listed as twenty thousand. Eckhart thought that despite his feelings towards Stone, the man had a soft spot for Lopez and really cared about him. Too bad he would never benefit from that generosity.

Eckhart continued to scan down. And then. There it was.

"Fowler. Let's go, we need to get to StoneTech, but we have to make a stop first."

CHAPTER THIRTY-TWO

Eckhart and Fowler left the Taraval station house and got into Fowler's vehicle. Eckhart hadn't explained the urgency to Fowler, but he didn't have to. He could tell Fowler felt him and just instinctively got into the driver's side. As they pulled out of the lot, Fowler finally asked Eckhart where to.

"Stanford. I need to see Miles before we head to StoneTech. I think he can help us, or at least I hope he can."

It seemed like the drive to Stanford took forever, but since it was the middle of the day, they made the drive in a little under forty-five minutes. Eckhart would occasionally flip through the list of stock option holders and then look out through the window in deep thought. Fowler knew best not to bother him when he got this way. He felt like a chess master, but instead of thinking through future moves, Eckhart was busy piecing the whole thing together in reverse, trying to understand how they got to where they are and explain the whys of the case.

When they finally pulled into the same parking lot they were in yesterday, Fowler had to wake Eckhart from his deep thoughts. They left the car, with Eckhart taking the lead and Fowler following behind. Into the building and bounding up the steps to Professor Ward's classroom. This time, he hadn't bothered to call first to make sure he was free. He felt he needed to interrupt him, no matter what he was doing. He was the only one who could answer these questions.

When they finally reached the outer door to his classroom, Eckhart looked in and saw that, in fact, there was a class in session, Miles Ward pacing in front of the class, lecturing them on something that he barely comprehended. Eckhart kept his face in the glass opening of the door until Ward had turned and started pacing back towards them. He looked up and saw Eckhart's face in the window. He kept lecturing but signaled to Eckhart that he would be just a few moments as he looked up at the clock. Looking at his watch and seeing it was almost two, Eckhart assumed the class was about to end.

He stepped back from the door and in a matter of seconds it swung open and the students streamed out, groups going in varying directions depending on their next class location and time. Eckhart and Fowler waited until the room had emptied and then entered. Miles Ward was still standing by his desk, a smile on his face.

"This is a surprise, Terry. I haven't had time to really look over those pictures yet, so I'm not sure that I can help you much more than I already have."

"Actually Miles, I think you can."

Eckhart explained about the body they recovered in Golden Gate Park and the evidence found at the scene. He detailed why he thought this latest murder was tied to the explosion at 22nd Ave. And that meant the police were now treating 22nd Ave as a homicide and not an accident. He laid out Stone's connection to both and that he suspected the IPO and some project Stone was working on led to all three murders. Eckhart explained his theory about how the notebooks were involved in the murders and whatever Stone was hiding at his company. When he finished, Miles Ward still wasn't sure why Eckhart thought he could help.

"Because you had Stone in your class. You know him better than us, and whatever he is doing there at StoneTech is beyond my technical expertise. I brought the original notebooks with me so you could have a look at them and hopefully tell us what this all means."

"Notebooks? You have two of them?"

"Yes, recovered from the scene where Benton's body was dumped. We're not sure if the killer wanted us to find them or not, but it was a pretty sloppy job of hiding them." Eckhart handed the two notebooks over to Ward and asked him to have a look.

Miles Ward sat at his desk and slowly flipped through the notebooks. First the one that Eckhart had given him pictures of and then the second one that they had just recovered from the dump scene. Eckhart and Fowler watched him, hoping to see some sort of facial expression that might explain what it was all about. Professor Ward finally looked up from the notebooks and sighed.

"Terry, I can't be sure, but I think Stone might be building or has already built a nuclear reactor at StoneTech. I can explain on the way, but I think it's imperative that we get to StoneTech as soon as possible. This is not something a novice should toy with. Regardless of what he learned in school, or what he thinks he may know, handling a nuclear reaction, even a small one, can be a tricky thing. And it's not just about building the reactor. Handling the fissionable material, the safety of the rest of the employees, let alone the neighborhood, and being prepared if something were to go wrong. All of this takes more than just googling answers. You need experienced experts, people that have spent years studying, training, and learning from others. I can guarantee you Stone does not have that knowledge or experience. I can explain more on the way there, but we need to go. Now!"

The three of them left the classroom, jogging down the hall to the staircase, taking them two steps at a time, and then out the main door to Fowler's sedan. They jumped in, Fowler behind the wheel, Eckhart in the passenger seat, and Miles Ward in the back.

"So, Miles, why are we in such a hurry?" Eckhart said as they pulled out of the Stanford parking lot.

"Terry, what time I did have, I discovered that the pictures you showed me came from the first notebook. They appear to be chemical formulas from what's called alchemy. In basic terms, alchemy is the forerunner of today's science. After a quick glance, I'd say these chemical formulas are what Alchemists thought were the way to transfer basic metals to noble metals. Iron to gold. But of course, today, we know none of this is possible. It's not as simple as applying the philosopher's stone to each element and transforming it to a higher level. You're talking about an atomic alteration. Stripping electrons and protons out of an atom to form a completely different atom. We can create isotopes and ions of distinct elements by removing an electron or more, but have been unable to alter the nucleus of those elements."

"Ok, I get that, but why the urgency?"

"It's the second notebook, Terry. I'm concerned that Stone doesn't fully understand what he found and how to use it. Or worse, that he DOES know. And if I'm right, we may be too late."

"Can you explain it in terms I can understand?" Eckhart said, flustered.

"Sure, sorry. The idea of changing one base element to another has been something scientists have been trying for centuries. Each element has an atomic number, and that number corresponds to the number of protons in that element. Well, also the number of electrons because there needs to be a balance in order for the atom to not have an electrical charge. So, for example, lead has an atomic number of 82. This means there are 82 protons and 82 electrons in every atom of iron. If the atom only had 81 protons and 81 electrons, it would be thallium."

"I said in terms I can understand!"

"Right. So, the Alchemy theory is by removing some protons and electrons from lead, you would theoretically create gold. The first notebook is the chemical formulas and process to remove the electrons necessary to change one element to another. It's the second notebook that is extremely dangerous. It outlines the theoretical process for removing the needed protons. The dangerous part is the amount of energy needed to accomplish that. Loosely translated, it discusses the power of the sun needed to complete the task. And as you know, the sun is a giant nuclear reactor."

"Ok, that seems simple enough. Why is this a big thing and haven't we been able to do this already? I mean, we can clone sheep."

"Terry, I said theoretically. The problem is, HOW to remove the protons and electrons. A process called ionization can easily remove the electrons. But just removing the electron isn't enough. You also need to remove the same number of protons in order to keep the atom balanced and not an ion."

"Christ almighty Miles, get to the point!"

"As I said, the first notebook provides the information for removing the electrons. That's the simple part. It's the second part that's complicated and dangerous. In order to remove the protons, you literally would need the power of the sun. The only thing man has invented that can create that amount of power is a nuclear reaction. As you know, the sun is a giant nuclear reactor. Terry, the only way to remove protons from the nucleus of an atom is with a nuclear reaction or a particle accelerator. There's a reason this has never been successful, or at least not successful at a large enough scale to be cost effective. It's not just a chemical reaction, as that just changes the number of electrons in an atom. If Stone is attempting this, and his calculations are off, which I suspect they are, we are looking at something that can be quite destructive."

"Shit! Is there a way to stop it? Or him from finishing it?"

"Not sure. No telling how far along he is. But I can tell you this, it's even more dangerous if he DOESN'T know what he's got. Either way, we don't have a lot of time."

"How bad is this? What are we talking about?"

"Bad, Terry. It could make the west side of Palo Alto look like Barrington Crater in Arizona. More than a mile wide and 500 feet deep. And that's without knowing what increases he made to the percentages."

Eckhart stared straight ahead as he pulled onto Page Mill and up towards StoneTech. Calling ahead and alerting the local authorities is what he should do, but he also didn't need to waste that time explaining and convincing them that the threat was real. They also didn't want to do anything that would cause panic or clue Stone into the fact that they were on to him. Nope, best to get there as soon as possible and handle this quickly and quietly. He wondered how many, if any, of the employees knew what they were working on. It seemed reasonable that Benton, his friend and the chairman of the board, finally figured it out and that's why he ended up dead and dumped in Golden Gate Park. Was he dumped there for a reason? Was Stone sending a message or did he want to get caught?

"So, Miles, how do we stop this thing? Is there a way?" Eckhart asked without looking away from the road ahead.

"It really depends on what Stone is doing. If it's the ionization process which is chemical, we don't have as much to worry about. Like I said, in any chemical process, one of the compounds, or ingredients, is added last. And that ingredient is usually the one that causes the reaction. Of course, with some chemical reactions, it's the change in state that does that. Like adding heat or oxygen. To be honest, I'm not sure with this one," the professor said as he flipped back and forth through both notebooks, looking for anything that would help him understand how to stop the process. "If he is trying to remove protons from the nucleus of lead atoms, we're talking nuclear reaction, and we have a much bigger problem. But I won't be able to tell until we get in that lab."

"Great, so we'll just wing it."

As they continued down 280 and through Millbrae and then Hillsborough, Eckhart's thoughts turned to how they were going to get in the lab without Stone stopping them or even finding out. In the previous visits to the corporate buildings, he had done his normal cursory surveillance, noting the entrances and exits, the security cameras and how employees entered secure offices and the R&D labs. In the easiest scenario, they just approach security, ask them to grant access and also to not alert Stone, the company's CEO. Possible, but highly unlikely that security wouldn't contact Stone immediately after granting access. The other way to go would be to actually ask Stone to show them the lab again, but in Eckhart's previous visit, he didn't see anything that would have looked like a nuclear reactor, at least not one that was large enough to create the amount of material that Miles thought the company was creating. Which means that part of the company was either off limits to a majority of employees or in a different location. It seemed unlikely it was somewhere else. So, it had to be hidden. And if so, Stone wasn't going to just show them. No, this had to be a clandestine operation, especially since he was bringing a civilian along with him. If Miles was right, and the danger was real, there was no time for the normal channels to gain permission. It could mean his badge, but lives were at stake. Thousands of lives.

CHAPTER THIRTY-THREE

They pulled into the parking lot of StoneTech Corporation and stopped the car near the entrance to the main building. Fowler and Eckhart quickly got out and Eckhart turned to Miles.

"Stay here. I'll call if I need you."

"Terry, you don't have a clue what you're looking for. I do."

"Look, we can't risk getting a civilian involved. We have no idea how dangerous this is. You wait here. When and if we find anything, and if we need help, we know where to find you."

"Fine, but I'm warning you, time could be of the essence."

Eckhart and Fowler made their way to the entrance of the StoneTech lobby. They saw the same guard manning the front desk and approached him calmly. Eckhart pulled a folder piece of paper out of his jacket and flashed it to the guard.

"We have a warrant to search the premises. This includes all offices and labs, specifically Mr. Stone's office. We don't have a lot of time."

The guard became flustered, looking back and forth between the two of them. He picked up the phone and started dialing.

"Who are you calling? This warrant allows us access without notification. Do you understand?"

The guard quickly hung up and muttered, "I don't understand. I really should notify someone."

"It's critical we search now. It's a matter of life and death. And we need you to come with us. You'll need to provide access to any locked rooms."

The guard led them through the doors to the labs. Fowler and Eckhart trailing behind him. Fowler grabbed Eckhart's arm and held him back and whispered to him.

"What warrant? And access without notification? Do you know what you're doing?"

Eckhart didn't answer and caught up with the guard. There were a lot of areas he wanted to search and if Miles was right, a small reactor could be anywhere. He was especially interested in the door at the end of the hall that led to the storage room.

"Let's try his office first", Eckhart said to the guard. They got to the end of the hall and hit the button on the elevator. While waiting, Eckhart suggested to Fowler that he take the stairs just in case Stone uses them to come down.

"Thanks, like I need the exercise."

"Youth before beauty, or something like that."

Fowler took off through the door leading to the stairwell just as the elevator arrived. Eckhart and the guard stepped in and pushed the button for the third floor, where the boardroom and executive offices were. The elevator began its rise to the third floor.

Meanwhile, Fowler was taking two steps at a time and was already on the second-floor landing. He paused a minute to catch his breath and thought about checking the floor before proceeding. He opened the door to the second floor, peeked out, and saw no activity. Fowler closed the door and continued up towards the third floor.

The elevator had finally reached the third floor, and the doors slowly opened. The guard and Eckhart both stepped out and walked toward Stone's office. They heard a noise behind them and turned just as Fowler opened the door from the stairwell and joined them.

"You made good time," Eckhart said half-jokingly. "I take it you didn't see anyone?"

"No, but thanks, I won't have to use my stair climber tonight."

When they got to David Stone's office, the guard used his key card and slid it into the reader. The pad light lit green and there was an audible thunk as the locking mechanism unlatched and the door popped open. Fowler and Eckhart entered the office, the guard remaining outside in the hall. The office was empty, as they expected, but they had a quick look around for anything out of the ordinary.

Stone felt his phone vibrate and pulled it out of his pocket to look at the screen. A notification was received that someone had entered his office on the third floor. "What the..", he thought. He clicked on the notification and saw that the guard had unlocked his office door. He was running out of time, and he knew it. Stone pocketed his phone and continued to work on the large machined cylinder in front of him.

They left the office and headed to the boardroom to make sure Stone wasn't in there. They didn't suspect he would be, but since they were on the third floor anyway, it was worth the extra time. The guard let them into the wood-paneled room. It was empty, just like Stone's office. The guard suggested that he was probably in one of the labs on the first floor.

They left the boardroom and went back to the elevator. The doors opened immediately, and they all entered, including Fowler this time. Eckhart pushed the button for one and they rode the elevator back down. When the doors opened, Eckhart asked the guard about the door to their right that led to the downstairs storage area. He informed them that only the executive staff had access to that area. That included all the board members and all executives, including the CEO. Stone.

They walked down the first-floor hall, entering each lab. The guard using his key card to gain access. Each door unlocked with the familiar thunk. Lab after lab, they entered, looking for Stone.

Stone's phone vibrated with each access. Board room. All the labs. What the heck is going on? He was curious as hell about leaving what he was doing and going upstairs to investigate. But he knew. He knew that wasn't the right thing to do at the moment. The guard was entering all these areas, but he wasn't doing it on his own. Someone was having him unlock each room. What were they looking for? Who were they looking for? Him?

He realized that this was close to being over. He needed to press on. Once he completed what he was doing, they would all see. They would realize that what he was doing was the future. Their future. His future. The possibilities were endless. They just needed someone to be the visionary, to show them.

After checking the final lab and not finding Stone, Eckhart and Fowler went back to the lobby. "So, there is no way we can get in that storage area without one of the executives letting us in there?" Eckhart asked.

"The only other person who had access to that area was Alex Benton, the chairman of the board," the guard replied.

"Wait, I think we can get in.", Fowler said as he started going through his suit pockets. Not finding what he was looking for, he reached into the inner pockets of his jacket, fumbled around, and a smile broke out on his face. He pulled his hand out and in it was an evidence bag containing Alex Benton's car keys and… his StoneTech key card. "I forgot to turn it into the evidence room."

"I'll have to write you up for that," Eckhart said, smirking. "But for now, let's see if Stone is down there."

All three of them ran down the hall towards the locked basement door. When they reached the door, Fowler slid the card through the key reader and then they waited. Looking at each other, they realized they didn't know what the key code was.

"Fowler, any idea?" Eckhart asked.

"Hold on." Fowler says as he pulled out his phone, quickly tapped on the keyboard for several minutes, then said "Let's try his birthday."

Punching in the six digits representing the month, day and year of Benton's birth, they waited for that 'thunk' of the door unlatching. Nothing.

"Any other ideas?"

CHAPTER THIRTY-FOUR

"Try 7982" Miles Ward offered.

"I thought I told you to wait in the car?" Eckhart responded, surprised to see Miles Ward standing behind the three of them. "Why 7982?"

"The atomic numbers for gold and lead."

Fowler quickly slid the key card again, this time punching in the four digits, and they waited for the familiar sound of the 'thunk' the disengaging locks made. Nothing.

"Wait, not gold to lead, lead to gold. Try 8279."

Fowler again swiped the key card and punched in the numbers. This time, the light on the keypad changed from red to green and the familiar 'thunk' sounded as the lock opened. They pushed through the door and entered the landing above the basement floor. The lights were on, but they couldn't hear any sounds. Eckhart pulled out his service revolver, and they slowly descended the metal stairs until they reached the basement, which appeared empty. Stone wasn't there.

As they scanned the expansive room, a large cylindrical chamber sat in the middle of the room. Supported by massive steel feet bolted to the concrete floor, the cylinder resembled the old iron lungs used prior to a polio vaccine being developed. But this stood taller, at least ten feet tall and as long. Both ends of the cylinder were covered by six-inch-thick plates, one-inch diameter bolts every few inches to hold the plates on. Jutting from the side of the cylinder was a bundle of wires leading to a podium-like stand containing several controls, gauges, and a computer screen and keyboard.

"I thought for sure he would be down here," Eckhart said as he continued to search the room.

"He was, seven minutes ago," Ward said as he stared at the computer monitor. "It looks like he started the reactor. A ten-minute countdown has three minutes left."

"Three minutes until what?" Fowler asked.

"Until the reactor fires. But without knowing exactly what he's trying to do, I have no idea what that might mean. But this looks like more than just a reactor. I believe it's a particle accelerator too. I've read about these. Basically, tabletop versions of what used to require hundreds of yards to a mile to accomplish. Amazing."

"Great. Excuse me if I don't join you in your excitement. So, does this still pose the danger you were talking about?"

"Sorry, Terry. Of course, this is serious. If this is what I think it is, a combination of reactor and accelerator, then, yes, we could be in imminent danger. If Stone is trying what I think he is, and his calculations are the slightest bit off… or if he tried to alter the calculations to scale it somehow… I just don't know. Either way, this needs to be shut down, and soon."

"Look, Stone didn't go by us and we were at that door for longer than two minutes. That means there is another way out of here. We need to find it and Stone and get him to stop this. Fowler, you take that side of the lab and I'll take this side. Miles, I need you and the security guard to clear the building, just in case."

"I'm not leaving. I think I can stop this. And to be honest, based on the size of this reactor, three minutes isn't long enough to get a safe distance away." Miles was already working at the controls.

"Are you sure you know what you're doing?"

"Terry, you know me. I know a lot of things. But, no, I'm not sure."

Eckhart started checking the left side of the large lab. Fowler worked the right. They were both going through each large metal storage cabinet, looking for anything that would provide an exit from the lab. Most of the cabinets were unlocked and contained the usual lab-related items. One contained boxes of shoe booties and medical grade face masks, along with what looked like disposable coveralls. Another had several types and sizes of glass flasks. Several had large piles of file folders stored in no particular order. Others were completely empty. A few were locked with padlocks, which, unless he was a magician, he could not of used to exit the lab.

Eckhart was nearing the end of the right side of the lab, with only a couple of metal cabinets to go. Fowler was almost at the end of the left side of the lab. Eckhart was about to admit that maybe Stone had somehow slipped out the only entrance. Or perhaps started the reactor remotely, if that were possible.

"Terry, over here," Fowler yelled. He was standing in front of the last of the metal storage closets. One of the doors was open and beyond the entrance, a set of industrial steel steps could be seen.

Eckhart joined Fowler at the far end of the lab. Fowler had already started up the steel stairs. Eckhart began to follow him but turned back and looked over at Miles feverishly working at the controls. "We're counting on you, Miles."

CHAPTER THIRTY-FIVE

Miles watched as Fowler and Eckhart left the lab to chase after Stone. As he looked back at the computer screen, the blinking countdown clock had reached 2:46. What he told Eckhart was true. He knew a lot. About a lot of things. And some of those things he couldn't let his friend Terry find out. He had to stop this and stop it now. Miles was certain that Stone would be of little help to any of them now.

What he was looking at now was something he had never seen before. He was positive it was a combination of particle accelerator and nuclear reactor. Most particle accelerators needed vast amounts of space and distance in order to work. The combination of different magnets working on the beam of hydrogen atoms as they were pulled forward through the accelerator was the process that separated the electron from the atom. It was also important to keep the hydrogen beam in a hyper-vacuum because if the beam were to collide with a molecule of gas, well, that wouldn't be good.

But this contraption that Stone built was only ten feet long or so, far shorter than the mile or so that most accelerators were. He must have somehow figured out how to use a nuclear reaction to create the required speed at such a short distance. The amount of energy created from accelerating particles to that speed is difficult to contain. Add to that the energy from the nuclear reaction to push that electron beam of hydrogen and you had the makings of a powerful, yet condensed explosion. Condensed only if this thing he built was strong enough to contain it. If not, crater city.

Miles learned all this on his many tours of the Stanford accelerator. Not for himself, but as part of the classes he taught there. Most of his students were chemistry majors, a few bio-chemistry and hardly any of them took more than a cursory interest in the accelerator. Why would they? Particle acceleration was not part of any chemistry curriculum. For chemistry majors, they offered the course as an elective. Since one of the chemistry professors taught the course, students took it thinking it would be an easy grade and give them a leg up in their major. That was true of all of them except David Stone. He was the only student Miles Ward had that actually took a keen interest in the accelerator. And now Miles knew why.

But Miles knew more than that, didn't he? He knew more than he cared to at this point. He wished Stone had never taken his class, that he had never met him. But all that was water under the bridge. What he stared at now was more dangerous than he could have ever imagined. Why wouldn't Stone listen to him when he told him this wasn't a viable project? This and that insane idea of immortality.

The blinking clock on the computer screen said 2:13, each blink ticking off another second, mocking him. A second-to-second reminder of him getting involved with both Stone and Benton. Why couldn't Stone stick to making money with the circuit manufacturing process? It was making them all a lot of money, including Miles.

Focus Miles, focus. How do I stop this thing? Miles focused on the screen in front of him. There were several windows open, the most prominent was the countdown window. He minimized it so he could see the two open windows behind it. The first was a DOS window that showed an admin had started the program, the time they started it, and the program calls to three other services. One service was TMCNTR.EXE which Miles assumed was the countdown timer in the minimized window. The second was

PARTACC.EXE which seemed to be the actual service to start the particle accelerator. The DOS window partially hid that window. Miles moved the DOS window to the side and saw a complicated GUI interface that showed a representation of the device in front of him and key flagged areas on the device, which appeared to represent the sequential steps the reactor would take to start the particle accelerator.

The third line in the DOS readout had Miles stumped. ALCKOUT.EXE. Miles looked back at the GUI and saw the typical Windows tool bar at the top. File, Edit, View, Help. He hovered the mouse over each selection to see what options the drop-down menus might have. Under 'File' there were selections for New, Open, Close, and Options. Miles thought about using the 'Close' selection but was afraid that would just close the window and not stop the process. He could come back to that one later if needed.

1:55

Miles selected 'Options' and a window popped up with what looked like calibrations for the accelerator. That window had several tabs and Miles quickly went through all of them for something that looked like 'STOP' or 'PROCESS

CANCEL' and didn't find either. He closed the window and tried the Edit, View, and Help options on the tool-bar. Nothing helpful under Edit or View, but under the Help link, there were several promising selections. The one that jumped out to Miles was Cancel Sequence. YES!

1:32

Miles quickly selected Cancel Sequence and a loud beep sounded, along with a pop-up window that stated 'ADMIN LOCKOUT, ENTER CODE TO CANCEL SEQUENCE' and an empty field with no sign of how many digits or letters were required. Miles thought, "It couldn't be that simple" and entered 8279 into the field and hit enter. The system emitted a loud beep, and the window responded with 'INCORRECT CODE' and returned to the same entry screen.

1:13

"Damn it, not that easy." Miles took a step back and thought, what would Stone use as a password? He was running out of time and wasn't sure, but some of these lockout programs will only give you so many tries before you're locked out for good. But it was that or let it time out, and then what? Miles had two choices. Try anything and get locked out or try nothing and let it complete the sequencing.

He was just hoping that Stone hadn't planned that someone other than himself would try to stop the process. It was all a guess. And right now, he needs to make an educated one regarding the stop code.

0:58

All of this started with those damn notebooks that Stone found. His obsession with the past. Miles wished Stone had been more forthcoming. Stone didn't discuss what was behind his request to analyze the text and decode the chemical formulas. Miles had no idea they came from a larger collection. Stone's passionate interest in chemistry intrigued him. But when that passion became an obsession with something outlandish, Miles knew there was more behind what Stone was doing. Alchemy. ALCHEMY! Miles entered the word alchemy into the field and hit enter again. INCORRECT CODE Damn it.

0:32

Miles was running out of time, and he knew it. There had to be some way of figuring out what Stone used for the stop code. People were creatures of habit with passwords. Birthdays, pets' names, their favorite sports team, their passion. Stone couldn't stop talking about his idea of turning lead into gold, and it was theoretically possible now. But there was something else that those notebooks hinted at and Stone had been more interested in that. The whole idea of being immortal.

Immortal. Miles entered the word into the field and quickly hit enter. Again, the monitor screamed back at him, INCORRECT CODE. It had to be this; he thought.

0:10

He only had time for one more try, then it was anyone's guess what would happen if he was wrong. Obviously, Terry would not bring Stone back in the nick of time to save us. He was out of ideas and sometimes you just had to try the simplest. He stared at the message in front of him, and the blinking countdown clock. Mocking him. He kept reading the message to himself, trying to think as quickly as he could. "ENTER CODE TO CANCEL SEQUENCE. ENTER CODE TO CANCEL SEQUENCE. Crap, seriously? It can't be that simple."

He typed the four letters and hit enter. The terminal beeped several times, but it was different this time. The countdown clock stopped at 0:03 and the sound of the reactor slowly spinning down, the power eventually cutting off completely. Miles sat back in the chair and let out an enormous sigh of relief. Then he started laughing out loud.

CODE. It was right in front of him the whole time, and the system literally told him what to type.

ADMIN LOCKOUT, ENTER CODE TO CANCEL SEQUENCE

It was just the sort of warped sense of humor Stone had.

Miles looked back at the computer screen to verify everything was completely shut down. Although it had only been three minutes, to Miles, it seemed like hours.

He got up and surveyed the lab. He wished he had never got involved with Stone and Benton. What a mess this turned out to be. All for greed. Money and power. And he was just as guilty for getting involved, and that desire pulled him in, too.

Miles went to the other side of the lab, where the metal storage cabinet door was still open. He stepped in and followed the same path Eckhart and Fowler had. Hopefully, they could stop Stone from whatever else he had planned. That his old partner was now in the middle of this mess bothered Miles, but he had to see this through to the end now. It had it already gone too far.

He took the steps two at a time, climbing the four-story industrial stairway until he finally reached the rooftop access door. It was still ajar and he couldn't hear anything. He slowly pushed the door open and carefully stepped out, checking both sides were clear. He was standing right behind the massive HVAC equipment and water tank.

CHAPTER THIRTY-SIX

The stairs were narrow, and they had to take them in single file, two steps at a time. On each floor, there appeared to be an opening into a similar metal storage closet, with a lock on the inside. Eckhart suspected they led to labs or storage closets. Why would someone have these built unless he planned the need for an escape? Or used to spy on employees?

They continued up the stairs, checking each floor to make sure Stone didn't exit through one of the locked storage closets. When they finally reached the top landing, they came to an unlocked door that was partially open. They pushed through and realized they were on the roof of the StoneTech building. Obscuring their view were two large air controllers and a massive water tank.

"You take that side. I'll go this way. Be careful, we don't know what this guy is capable of. Let's try to take him alive. Miles may need help to stop that thing."

Fowler headed to the right and Eckhart to the left. Both had their guns drawn. Eckhart moved slowly around the huge air handlers, keeping his back against the sheet metal housings with his gun raised. As he neared each corner, he stopped and slowly peered around it before continuing forward. Fowler was doing the same at the other side of the building, slowly making their way past the HVAC equipment and towards the open expanse of the roof. Once they had both cleared the left and right sides of the building, they continued forward, past the equipment, and into the open. At this point, the far north side of the roof was visible. Eckhart saw him first, Fowler, soon after. There, on the three-foot-high concrete bulkhead that surrounded the roof, stood David Stone, the CEO of Stone Technologies.

Eckhart signaled to Fowler to approach Stone from the right, Eckhart taking the left. They both slowly approached the man standing on the edge of the short wall. His back was to the detectives, but he sensed them there and shouted,

"You can't stop me now. My work is nearly complete. They'll all see I was right."

"Right about what, Mr. Stone?" Eckhart shouted.

"About everything. My plans. My company. Everyone always telling me I was wrong. No one believes me. Well, now they'll see."

Stone was still dressed as he was the first time Eckhart met him. Expensive suit, shoes, and shirt. Except now, he didn't look as 'put together' or in charge as he had the last time he saw him. His tie and tail of his suit jacket were flapping in the wind, his hair mussed from the breeze, as well.

"Mr. Stone, I believe you. We can talk if you come down. I'd like to learn more from you."

"I know you're just saying that. Just like everyone else. No one would believe me. From the day I found those notebooks, I knew I was meant to find them. At the time, I didn't even know why I was looking, or what I was looking for."

"We found the notebooks, but we need you to help us understand them. Come down from there and let's talk."

Fowler moved closer to Stone, slowly inching his way toward the bulkhead while Eckhart kept him busy. Eckhart waved him back, signaling him to hold steady, not to spook Stone into moving.

"No one has ever believed me. Everyone said I was wasting my time. They didn't believe like I did."

"I want to believe you, Mr. Stone. But I need you to come down and explain it to me. I'm not as smart as you. Do you think you could explain it to someone like me?"

"You don't believe me. Do you think I killed my friend, Javier? I would never, could never, do that. And now Benton. I'm sure you think I killed him, too."

"No, actually, I don't David. I don't believe you killed anyone. Can I call you David? David, we need to stop the reactor. Can you help us do that?"

"Why do you need to stop it? It will work, I know it will."

"David, why don't you step down from the ledge so you can show me?"

"I'm not going to stop anything. The accelerator will finally prove what so many before me could not. That metal can be changed. And they are what can change us. The philosopher's stone. The fountain of youth. They aren't just myths. I was able to prove that. It works."

"Well, come down and show us. We're all interested in learning from you."

David Stone looked over his shoulder. "Not him. He never believed me."

Eckhart turned towards Fowler and saw that Miles Ward had joined them. Eckhart looked at Miles' face for a sign that he was successful in stopping the reactor. Miles signaled with a thumbs up he was successful.

"Professor Ward? I'm sure he does, Mr. Stone. Come on down and you can show us all."

"I can show you right here."

"Show me what?"

"Immortality."

Just then, David Stone slowly raised his arms out to his sides, his head dipping slightly backwards as if he were looking skyward. Eckhart knew this wasn't good. That Stone wasn't looking for god or check the weather. It was at that moment that Stone's head came forward, his body rocking back and then forward. Eckhart was too far from Stone to make a move. Fowler was closer, and he started towards where David Stone was now leaning forward. His body slowly pitched at an angle that soon would cross the point of no return, his center of gravity propelling him forward and, ultimately, down. Fowler was less than two feet from Stone when that center balance point was reached and his weight carried him the rest of the way, his arms becoming stiff as if to capture the wind under them, and for a moment it appeared Stone was suspended in air. A split second later, he disappeared from sight and the sound of two hundred plus pounds of human flesh hitting concrete could be heard.

Eckhart stopped in his tracks, almost disbelieving what he had just witnessed. "Crap"

CHAPTER THIRTY-SEVEN

Eckhart and Fowler looked over the edge of the building at the scene below. The sound that Stone's body made when it hit the concrete entryway had echoed into the main entrance, and employees were filtering out to see what had happened. The guard from the front desk made it out first and was trying to secure the area. He didn't bother checking to see if Stone had a pulse or was breathing. It was painfully obvious the life had left his body when it met the ground at 20-plus miles per hour. No airbag to cushion his fall there.

Eckhart pulled out his phone and called the Palo Alto PD. He gave them his name. That he was with the SFPD investigating a murder, and there really wasn't a hurry. He was on the scene and would make sure that no one touched the body before they arrived.

During all the excitement, Eckhart and Fowler hadn't been paying attention to Miles, who had stepped back from the edge of the building and had a look of shock on his face. He'd be OK. Eckhart turned back around, looked down for a second, then slowly raised his head and looked out over Page Mill Road to the North East and the rest of Palo Alto.

How many people went about their day, completely oblivious to how close they came to things going badly for them?

"We dodged a big one today, partner." He said to Fowler, who was still looking down at the scene below them.

Eckhart would have some explaining to do to his superiors, but it wouldn't be the first time. Sometimes it was better to beg for forgiveness than ask for permission. He finally turned around and walked over to where the Professor was standing.

"I don't understand why he would have jumped. Unless he knew there was no other way out. Knowing he would go down for killing Benton and Lopez might have been enough to make him jump." Fowler said.

"I don't think so. There's more to it."

"What do you mean? And what do you think he meant by 'immortality'?"

"He didn't jump because he killed Benton and Lopez. In fact, I'm pretty sure he didn't kill either. And the immortality comment. Maybe Miles knows."

As Eckhart mentioned his name, Miles Ward turned around and faced both detectives. His expression was unchanged, a look of confusion still on his face.

"What? I'm sorry, I didn't hear you."

"I said, maybe you can explain what Stone meant by immortality."

"I'm not sure. How would I know what he was talking about?"

"I think you do, Miles. Tell us how you turned the reactor off. How did you know what to do?"

Fowler was looking between Eckhart and Miles Ward. Now the look of confusion was on his face. "Terry, what did you mean when you said you didn't think Stone killed Benton or Lopez?"

Eckhart and Ward had their eyes locked on each other, like two kids in a schoolyard staring contest, waiting to see which one would break their look first.

"I think Miles here knows more than he's let on, don't you, Miles?"

"Terry, I don't know what you're talking about."

"You see, Fowler, Miles here knows more about this project and this company than he's told us. That's why he knew how to stop the reactor. And why he could decipher the notebooks so quickly. Or actually, didn't need to decipher them because he already did for Stone, back when he was a student. Right Miles? The first sign I had that you might know more was when Fowler and I first showed you the few pages we had recovered from Javier Lopez's phone. You referred to the notebooks in plural, asking me if Lopez had 'them' on him when we found the body. At first, I just ignored the use of the plural because I thought you were referring to the notebook and the box it came in. But when we found a second notebook hidden next to Benton's body in the park, I was going over my notes and that word 'them' kind of jumped out at me. By itself, it didn't really mean much. But then there was the crime scene in the parking lot down there."

Fowler was looking back and forth between Eckhart and Ward, watching Ward's reaction to Terry's questioning and the information he was laying out.

"Eckhart, what about the crime scene?"

"Well, there were a couple of things. First, the blood on the ground and how the pool had the indentation in the shape of a shoe's toe. Plus, the prints from the small amount of blood that leaked under the shoe. Most shoes, especially dress shoes, have smooth bottoms, which would allow a lot more blood to get under them, no matter how hard you're pressing down on the ground. Even athletic shoes, which have much more give and grip, don't create a tight enough seal to keep blood from flowing under them. But there are shoes that are specifically designed to make a fairly good seal no matter what surface you stand on. Boat shoes. Boat shoes are designed with a unique tread that allows for a good surface grip that keeps moisture, water from wicking under them. That's how you can keep a fairly stable grip on the wet deck of a boat. When the lab showed me the blow-up of the bloody print, I noticed the unique tread, unlike any other type of shoe. There are several brands of boat shoes, but the most popular one is worn by people that don't even own boats, because they are a fashion statement. Sperry Topsiders. I remember you were wearing them when we met you in class. Today you're not. I take it you couldn't get the blood off them?"

"That means nothing. Thousands of people wear those shoes. So what if I'm not wearing them today? Do you wear the same shoes every day?"

"No, I don't, and you're right, that wasn't enough to make me suspect you, but things were adding up. It was the other piece of evidence that sealed it for me."

"This is crazy Terry. You know me. Why in the hell would I have anything to do with this? It makes little sense."

"I know Miles. I thought the same thing. Why? There is always a why, and that's what kept me from going all in on you. But when I saw the piece of bloody cloth, that was the last clue. The tweed pocket. Benton ripped it off your jacket while you were killing him, didn't he?"

Miles Ward didn't respond to this latest accusation. He just stared at Eckhart. In the distance, they could hear the sounds of sirens as the PAPD and ambulance neared the scene. The crowd around Stone's body had grown considerably, employees streaming out to see what the commotion was. The guard that had helped Fowler and Eckhart was doing his best to control everything and secure the second crime scene he had to deal with this week. With this one, there wasn't any mystery about what happened.

"And I think I know why you did it. Well, not exactly why you killed both Benton and Lopez, but what the motivation behind your involvement was. Here you are, someone who had to work hard for everything you have, who started with very little, put yourself through school, intelligent, and hardworking. You end up teaching kids where a lot of this comes easy for them. They don't have to work as hard as you did, or at least that what's you think. It bothers you and rubs you the wrong way. And then a large percentage of these kids graduate and start making six figures, or even worse, start a company and become instant millionaires. But that's not what pushed you over the edge. It's when a kid like Stone comes along. He has this idea, and he comes to you to help him decipher these notebooks. And you knew there were two notebooks because he showed them to you. But after you've looked them over, you explain to him that what he's found isn't possible, that it's never been possible."

"That's right, it's not possible. Alchemy is and always was a hoax."

"Maybe so, but after he graduated and started a successful business, you were curious about what Mr. Stone was into. You looked him up and found out he had convinced his board that what he was doing WAS possible. And then when you found out they were planning on an IPO to involve even more investors, you threatened to expose him, unless."

"Unless what?" Fowler jumped in.

"Unless Stone cut him in on the profits. Miles here agreed to keep quiet if Stone started paying him. Blackmail. And things were going fine until the notebooks turned up and Benton threatened to shut the whole thing down. Benton wanted to be involved with a legitimate business, and he was perfectly happy with the business as it was originally formed. He probably wasn't part of the lead-to-gold scam. You couldn't let Benton ruin it for you. You needed to get yours, didn't you? You deserved it, didn't you? All these kids, younger than you, making millions. And for what?"

The sirens were getting louder. They were on Page Mill and would pull into the parking lot of StoneTech soon. The guard had roped off the scene below and most of the employees were a good fifteen feet back from the body of David Stone.

"I think it's time to go Miles. Fowler, cuff him."

Fowler walked over to Miles, pulled out a pair of cuffs, and put them on. Miles gave no resistance and willfully put his hands behind his back. A look of exhaustion and relief on his face. They left the rooftop, Fowler leading Miles down the steps with Eckhart bringing up the rear.

"There are just two things I don't understand. Why kill Lopez. Stone got the notebook back. He knew nothing. He was completely innocent."

"I didn't kill the gardener. I knew nothing about that. Stone probably did. He was nuts. Whatever he was experimenting with was making him crazy."

"That's the other question. What was with the immortality comment before he jumped?"

"Jumped? He didn't jump. I think he believed he could fly. Or at least that even if he couldn't, he would survive the fall. The other part of alchemy is the idea there is an elixir of immortality. Alchemists also believed that the same elixir is what could transform lead into gold. That if it was so powerful, so special to do that, then it might also change humans. Make them immortal. Stone believed that more than the lead-to-gold thing. In fact, he knew he was scamming the board and his investors, at least at the start, but whatever he was distilling and drinking was making him crazy. In the end, who knows what he believed."

They had reached the bottom of the stairs and exited the building just as the ambulance had pulled into the parking lot. Eckhart had called the ambulance knowing they wouldn't be much help to Stone, but more for body removal reasons. As soon as the ambulance pulled up near the body and the area the guard had roped off, the Palo Alto police pulled into the lot. The officers got out of their squad cars and took over for the guard. Eckhart and Fowler led Miles to their car and put him in the back seat, locking the car and then heading back over towards the scene.

As they arrived at the scene, Eckhart introduced himself to the PA officers and showed them his badge. He gave them a brief rundown of what happened, including his own involvement as part of an SFPD murder investigation. He told him they could reach him for any further questions and walked back to where Fowler was standing, staring at the body of David Stone, the blood pooling under where his head met the concrete.

"Terry, I'm still confused about Ward's involvement and when you figured it out."

"I was too, at the beginning. There were several small clues that, taken by themselves, wouldn't have meant much. But when I stepped back and looked at them as a whole, and put my friendship aside, they led me to the only conclusion. I couldn't bring you into it until I was sure, and it wasn't until earlier today, that I was certain Miles was guilty. I'm not sure I believe him about Javier Lopez, but seeing how disconnected from reality Stone was, I wouldn't put it past him to kill his old friend. Greed can do weird things to you. This entire case was about greed. Greed for power, greed to be a part of something, greed for money, and, in Stone's case, greed for immortality."

Fowler and Eckhart left the scene and returned to the car where Miles Ward was sitting in the back seat, watching everything through the window. Eckhart looked at his old partner and wondered where it went wrong for him. He was a "by the book" kind of detective, and when he had stayed in contact, Miles had been proud of his role as a teacher. He would tell Terry about the look a student would get on their face when they finally understood a lesson he was giving. He figures it wasn't until he lost contact with him, when Miles began teaching at Stanford, that things unraveled. All that money, all that instant success graduates gain without having to put in years of hard work, moving up slowly.

They got in the car, Fowler driving, and pulled out of the parking lot. Eckhart looked back at the scene and saw Miles looking back towards where Stone's body was being lifted onto a gurney and put into the ambulance. He could see a look of pain and sadness on his old partner's face, and for a moment, he felt sorry for him. It was a long quiet ride back to the Taraval station.

CHAPTER THIRTY-EIGHT

"I think you'd better see this," Brian Hackman, the M.E. said over the phone to Eckhart.

Fowler was watching Eckhart while he was on the phone. As soon as he hung up, Fowler asked what's up? Eckhart explained that the M.E. was doing the autopsy on David Stone and wanted him to come down to show him something. Eckhart and Fowler drove over to see what Hackman had for them.

When they arrived at the M.E.'s office, they headed straight for the autopsy labs on the basement floor. They walked down the long hall until they came to the double swinging doors of the lab. They walked into a room with two rows of steel tables, several of which had bodies on them in various degrees of autopsy. Brian Hackman was leaning over the body and looked up when he heard the doors open.

"Eckhart, Fowler. Come over here. I think you'll find this interesting. There's Vicks on my desk. Help yourself."

They both went to Hackman's desk and applied a small dollop of the aromatic gel under their noses. It wasn't the best smell, but it was better than decaying flesh. The good thing was, Stone wasn't at that point yet. The stuff really helped when you found that body that hadn't been discovered for a few weeks. Regardless, the lab always had a smell, and it was something that Eckhart had never gotten used to. He wondered how Hackman did.

They joined Hackman around the steel table and saw that he had already opened Stone up and had several organs out on separate trays. Along with a toxicology report, analyzing the organs of a decedent can give you clues as to their cause of death or possibly the state of mind they were in when they died. There was little question about how Stone died. Hitting the ground from the third floor will do that. But the DA had asked for the autopsy because of the way he died. Jumping off himself, almost as if he believed he was escaping and not jumping to a certain death. There had to be a tox reason or perhaps a brain disorder, tumor, or something.

Detectives rarely attend autopsies. They leave that up to the M.E. The few times they do, it's pushing for a quick turnaround, gathering some evidence that can link them to a suspect. This can be especially true if the suspect may flee or they need that evidence to get a warrant from the D.A. In this case, they already had the killer in custody, and he had admitted to killing Benton. Eckhart suspected he was also responsible for the explosion at the gardener's home that took the life of Javier and Mary Quinn, but he didn't have enough evidence to prove that yet, and this autopsy would not help. That Eckhart's old partner was the murderer made this even more difficult, but the DA handled that now and Eckhart's involvement would be minimal if he were involved at all. Fowler could take the point if needed at the trial, if it came down to it since he had no prior relationship or knowledge of Miles Ward.

But right now, Hackman had something he wanted them to see, and Eckhart was all ears. Hackman led them from Stone's body over to a stiff on a second table. He pulled the sheet off the body and Eckhart saw it was another male, approximately the same age as Stone, with a GSW to the center of his chest. Hackman explained the vic was a store cashier, shot during an attempted robbery.

"Before I show you Mr. Stone, I wanted you to see this victim as a baseline. You can see he's a white male, age 25, average to good health, other than he's dead from a bullet wound to the chest." Hackman pulled back the already open chest, and they both saw that the victim's organs were still pretty much intact. He picked up a scalpel, made a few experienced and quick cuts and pulled the victim's heart out. He weighed it and then held it up to both of them.

"You'll see the heart is of average weight and, for a male of this age and weight, in rather good condition. Other than the bullet hole through the left ventricle. There is some evidence of hypertension and probably some hardening of the arteries, and elevated cholesterol. But, again, nothing out of the ordinary." Hackman put the heart down, picked up the scalpel and made a couple more quick cuts, and pulled out a lung. He again weighed it and then held it up for Eckhart and Fowler to look at it.

"Left lung lobe, average weight. You can see some discoloring typical for someone living in the greater Bay Area, non-smoker, but just breathing the air, especially from the wildfires the past several years, it can show up in a healthy person's lungs."

Eckhart was getting somewhat annoyed. "Hackman, this is great, but can we get to the reason you called us here?"

"Sure. I'm sorry. Let's return to Mr. Stone." They walked back to the first autopsy table and Hackman picked up the victim's heart. "What's the first thing you notice?"

Fowler jumped in. "It looks larger."

"Correct detective. Good catch. Anything else?" Without waiting for an answer, Hackman said "You'll also notice the color difference, a brighter red, healthier looking, right?" he took a scalpel and sliced through the heart. "And look here, the walls of the heart are slightly thinner than our other victim. No signs of any hypertension, no signs of clogged arteries, cholesterol, nothing. Nearly a perfect specimen."

He picked up a lung that had already been removed and again asked if they noticed any difference. Seeing where he was going with this, Eckhart answered. It looked larger and also healthier.

"Yes, Terry, exactly. And like the heart, Mr. Stone's lungs look to be nearly without issue. No discoloring from breathing the air, no disease indications at all. Either of these items taken individually wouldn't be too surprising, but taken together, along with the skin and cell samples I took the liberty of having tests run on, and… well, I'm mystified."

"Mystified? What do you mean?" Eckhart said, his interest piqued.

"Have you **ever** heard of hyperplasia? It's the enlargement of an **organ** or tissue caused by an increase in the reproduction rate of its cells, often as an initial stage in the development of cancer. That's why I took some samples and had tests run to see if Mr. Stone had or was in the early stages of any cancerous growth. The test results were all negative. He was completely cancer-free."

"But hyperplasia is also the process of certain organs to repair themselves. Like your liver. You can do a lot of damage to your liver, drinking, etcetera. But once you stop, if soon enough, your liver has the amazing ability to regenerate its cells and repair itself. The same with your skin, which is also an organ. You replace all your skin about once a month. Other organs cannot do that. Your heart, lungs, they can't regenerate cells."

"So, you're saying that Stone was a really healthy guy until he took a nosedive off the third story?"

"Yes, he was very healthy. But that's not all I'm saying. I've seen nothing like this. No matter how healthy a person's lifestyle is, exercise, eating right, no smoking or drinking… your body still ages. Cells die, they can't regenerate.

Environmental conditions have a slow, definite effect on your body. And that brings me to the toxicology report."

Eckhart and Fowler both looked up from the organs splayed on the table and their attention to what the M.E. was saying became heightened. Hackman picked up the autopsy folder and removed the tox report and handed it to Eckhart. Terry took a quick glance at it, looked up at Hackman, and slowly handed it to Fowler, who did the same. The toxicology report was completely clean. Except for one. Heavy metal accumulation.

"So, you see my dilemma. Based on the tox screen, Mr. Stone should have many abnormalities with his organs. Heavy metal poisoning causes severe issues with the soft tissues of a human being, as well as several issues with brain activity. Depending on the types and quantities of the metals, psychosis, delusions, and irritability. Altered consciousness. I've had them run the screens three times."

"Doc, bottom line, what are you saying?"

"I'm saying whatever this guy was taking. He totally fucked up his brain and probably his nervous system. But his body? He has the body of a twenty-year-old. Not even. It's perfect. Seen nothing like it. Because of that, jumping off the building isn't a surprise at all. But his tissues, all his organs. They're like brand new."

CHAPTER THIRTY-NINE

Eckhart went to the kitchen and poured himself two fingers of Macallan scotch and headed to his back deck to relax. The sun still had an hour before it would finally set over the golf course behind his house on Wilshire Avenue. He sipped the scotch as he watched a group of golfers make their way from one hole to the next. Never having the desire to actually play, he still enjoyed watching. Something about the perfectly mowed lawns and the mostly silent nature of the game that was relaxing to him. It was a way to clear his mind at the end of the day. Eckhart had lowered his back fence when he first bought the home specifically so he could get a better view of the course. He sat back in the wooden Adirondack chair and took another sip of his drink.

The last lone golfer lined up his fairway shot and smoothly drove it toward the green. He strolled back to his cart and returned the iron to its bag. Eckhart could smell the grass amid the heavy aroma of the many Eucalyptus trees that were brought in centuries ago as windbreaks. He could hear the faint sound of the electric cart as it moved towards the end of the fairway, the sun dipping below the trees to the west. Eckhart thought about the golfer, spending hours on a course, enjoying his pastime. Perhaps heading to the 19th hole for a beer or maybe to Joe's down the street for a cocktail and dinner. Did he have someone at home waiting for him? Or was he like Eckhart, leading a solitary life?

Eckhart was deep in thought, trying to process what had just happened the past few days and how Miles Ward's life could have taken such a turn. He thought he heard a faint noise and figured it was a neighbor, or maybe the distant sound of the freeway. Instead, Ally surprised him as she walked out of the house and onto the deck, holding a glass of scotch. He smiled as she sat down beside him and leaned in for a kiss. Eckhart didn't expect Ally, but he was happy she was here. After the kiss, she leaned back in her chair, took a sip, and let out a contented moan.

"We got a guilty verdict in the Pascal case."

"Fantastic. Was there ever a doubt?"

"Well, you can never tell with some of these juries. I think your testimony helped."

"Part of the job. A good prosecutor had a lot to do with it, too."

She smiled at Eckhart and turned back around to take in the expansive green view. The sun was dipping and most of the golfers had finished their rounds, so the course was empty and the only noise was the rustling of the eucalyptus trees and the distant sound of the 280 freeway. Eckhart didn't know it yet, but Ally had gotten some more news today. She downed the rest of her scotch and got up to get a refill. Ally took Eckhart's glass without asking and headed back to the kitchen.

While Eckhart waited, he fell back into his thoughts regarding Miles. He understood the reason all that money tempted Miles, but Eckhart never thought he could commit murder. That was the part so difficult to grasp. When Eckhart and Fowler questioned him back at the station, Miles wasn't the same person he remembered as his partner. Those many years of seeing his students go from college classes to becoming millionaires were just too much. Not an excuse by any means. As far as Eckhart knew, none of the other Stanford professors were killing off students. What bothered him the most was that feeling of disappointment. Someone that he had worked closely with, and actually looked up to.

As he sat in that interview room, Mile's face was blank, emotionless. He answered Eckhart and Fowler's questions in an almost monotone voice, looking straight ahead, not meeting the eyes of his interrogators. Miles walked them through everything, from the first time Stone brought him the notebooks to look over. The call he got from Stone to let him know Benton was plotting to have him removed from his position with the company and how that would affect his continuing to get his cut of the company's profits. He went into detail about what he decided to do after that phone call and how he ambushed Benton in the Stone Technologies parking lot and watched the life drain out of him. What he would not admit to was the murder of Javier Lopez. And if Miles did the Lopez murder, why not just cop to it? Because Miles was being so forthright with all the information, Eckhart believed him. This bothered Eckhart because the only other suspect was dead. He didn't like leaving parts of a case unresolved.

Ally returned with two glasses of scotch and a small platter of cheese and crackers she found in Eckhart's fridge. Eckhart's thoughts turned to the present and Ally. It felt good to have someone in his life. Someone to be with at the end of the day. And someone who understood his job, respected the time it took, and wasn't looking for him to quit.

"How's the case going against Miles Ward?"

"He's got a public defender. We're still putting the case together, but it shouldn't be too long since he confessed. As long as his attorney doesn't use an insanity defense."

"He seemed sane when Fowler and I questioned him."

"Terry, you know none of that makes a difference. His attorney is going to do whatever it takes to get him off or get a reduced sentence. You've been down this road before. Remember when I was on the other side?"

Eckhart let out a small chuckle at the thought of Ally Wilder as a defense attorney. Yes, he remembered well being grilled on the witness stand by her, using every tactic she could in the defense of her client.

"Glad you're on our side now."

They both looked at each other, and he saw a sweetness in her eyes. Eckhart realized she knew his comment meant more than just being on his side of law enforcement. He was glad that she was in his life, and he was comfortable with her knowing that. But there was something else there. He could feel her holding back something.

Eckhart turned back to look at the golf course and then pointed to the left at a clump of trees and scrub oak a hundred yards away.

"See over there, between the trees and shrubs? That's where the last official duel in the U.S. took place. A chief justice shot and killed a state senator over political differences. They once were good friends and allies."

"That's interesting Terry. Why are you telling me this?"

"Because it reminded me that people kill each other for the stupidest reasons. Even good friends, two people on the same side for most of their lives, and then one slight difference of opinion, and that's how they decide to solve their shit. Why couldn't Miles Ward come to some other solution rather than killing Benton? It makes no sense to me, even though I see it all the time. And here I am, living within walking distance from a monument to stupidity."

Ally just shook her head and let out a small laugh, a more nervous response than thinking what Eckhart said was funny. She took a sip of her scotch and turned back to Eckhart, taking his hand as she did.

"I received some more news today. I'm not sure if it's good or bad, but I have a feeling I may need your help soon." Ally said.

"Of course, anything."

"Let me start at the beginning. I don't think I ever told you I was adopted. I was only fourteen months old. Of course, I don't remember a lot of what was going on then. I was too young. But as I got older, my adoptive parents filled in the blanks for me. I didn't know until later that they were only giving me bits and pieces of my past, thinking I could only handle so much because of my age. As I got older, I started pulling away from them. Not that I didn't love them. They raised me. But they were so different from me. Aging hippies, still living in the sixties. I was tired of hearing about it."

"Anyway, after high school, I moved out here to go to college, but also to get away from them. It was freeing, moving out from under the past. A past that meant nothing to me, but everything to them. I felt like I could finally be myself. I thrived at Stanford. I came here not knowing who I was and what I wanted to do with my life. I ended up finding the direction I needed and knew I wanted to be a lawyer.

Everything was going great. I hardly thought about my childhood or my adopted parents. I had little to no contact with them since leaving New Haven. We were on opposite coasts and I liked it that way. Until my sophomore year."

"My new roommate was a computer science major. We were hanging out one night and she asked me if I had ever googled myself. I didn't know what she meant, and she explained googling yourself was a way to find out what presence you had on the internet. I wasn't into social media, so I didn't expect there would be much of anything about me on the internet. My roommate was on her laptop at her desk and started typing away. She was gazing at her computer screen and then slowly leaned back and looked over at me. She asked if I was from the east coast and I said yeah. She said I can see why you never talk about your parents."

"I asked her what she meant, and she just turned her laptop towards me and all I saw were the headlines of an old article. Weather Underground Couple Convicted of Murder. I pulled the laptop towards me and read the article. I was shocked."

Ally went on to tell Eckhart about her birth parents and the life she had never heard about. In the sixties, her parents were members of the Weather Underground, an extremist group that had orchestrated several bombings of government buildings in protest of the Vietnam war. As the war wound down, most members of the Underground came out of hiding, except Ally's parents. In the early sixties, the two were involved in an armored car heist that resulted in both guards and two police officers being killed. For the next ten years, they were on the run and in 1980, gave birth to Ally. Both her parents were captured, tried, and went to prison. They had handed Ally off to friends, a husband and wife couple that were also past members of the Weather Underground.

Ally was raised by them, with never a mention of her birth parents, their past, or what happened to them. Ally never really questioned why she had a different last name than her parents. She figured it had more to do with her adoptive parents being hippies than her being adopted. After finding out about her parents, and doing more research on them and their past, she struggled with a decision on contacting them or not. In one respect, she was mad that they just handed her off to these people and never tried to contact her. On the other hand, it was probably their way of trying to give her a normal life, without all the drama and questions that would come from it.

"So, did you ever contact them?" Eckhart asked.

"Honestly, I was leaning towards never making contact. Just living my life and putting them behind me. I mean, it's not like they had anything to do with raising me. No influence in my life. It took several years, decades actually, before I could come to grips with the right answer. I decided that despite them never being there for me, I was still part of them. Part of their DNA and everything that has to do with how I'm made up. I became curious about little things. Did I look like them? What similarities did we have with things like how we talked, quirks, or things we were interested in? I was born from two criminals and my path took me to be someone that prosecutes people like them."

"So, you met them?"

"Yes. About ten years ago, I pulled their records to see where they were being held. My mother is at the Bedford Hills Correctional Facility in Westchester County, New York. She still had some time left on her sentence. My father is at Sing Sing Correctional Facility in New York. His sentence was far worse. Seventy-five years to life. I flew back there and visited each of them. It was brief, but a lot was said. I've called both of them a few times a year. The interesting part of this all was I found out my mother had a law degree and both my grandparents on my mother's side were civil rights attorneys. So, being a lawyer was in my DNA. Funny how things like that work out."

"That's a lot to go through. And you never spoke of this with anyone else?"

"Not really. I called my adoptive parents. We reconciled somewhat. I thanked them for all they did in raising me, especially under such strange circumstances."

"Well, I feel honored that you shared all this with me. You know none of it changes who you are and the person you've become, right?"

"I know. There's a lot more to the story, but I'll save the rest for another time. The reason I'm telling you all this has to do with the news I got today."

"Oh, right. The news. What is it?"

"My mother called. She's getting paroled."

CHAPTER FORTY

Eckhart didn't quite know what to say when Ally finished explaining that her mother was actually up for parole. No decision had been made by the parole board yet, but she had been notified that they were likely to agree. Her mother had been a model prisoner, using her law degree to help other inmates win their own paroles or have their court decisions reversed. She was also teaching reading and writing lessons to the less educated prisoners, preparing them for life after incarceration.

"I'm not sure if I should be there for her or not. I have conflicting thoughts, you know?"

"I can't imagine. But if it helps, I'll go with you, be there for you."

"I was hoping you'd say that."

Their gazes returned to the darkening golf course behind Eckhart's house. They slowly sipped the rest of their drinks as they sat in silence. Eckhart's thoughts danced from the previous two cases to what Ally had just told him. He didn't think Jordan would have a problem with him taking some time after the past month he had. He definitely needed to clear his head, and he wanted to be there for Ally, no matter where this took him.

Little did he know.

Ally downed the rest of her scotch and got up to go inside. When she got to the slider leading to the living room, she turned and faced Eckhart.

"Coming?"

Eckhart got up and followed her inside. She walked down the hall and past the guest room, directly to his master bedroom. Before entering, she turned to him again with a desire in her eyes.

"I need you."

A couple hours later, as Eckhart was holding Ally as she slept, he could feel his body relax. It was finally giving way from the exhaustion of the past week. From the Pascal case and the ensuing trial to the Quinn/Lopez/Benton murders. A contented feeling ran through his body and he let himself be taken over by it. He slipped into a deep sleep.

He wasn't sure how long it had been when his eyes opened wide, shaken awake when a dreamlike question invaded his sleep. Miles Ward had admitted to killing Benton but was steadfast in his denial of having anything to do with the Lopez/Quinn murders. David Stone had a solid alibi for the time when Javier Lopez and Mary Quinn were killed in the explosion and fire at their home. What did Fowler call it? Fate. Eckhart had never believed in fate. But with Ally lying beside him, he couldn't shake the fact that something had led him to her. They had been crossing paths for years, and this case finally pushed them together.

But there was something else about this case that bothered Eckhart, and he couldn't shake it. If Miles didn't cause the explosion on 22nd, and Stone had an alibi, then who did it? And why? Was Mary Quinn the actual target? Was it this mystery man from her past in Sacramento? And if it was, then this entire week was set about by a group of related chance occurrences. Lopez was an innocent victim in Quinn's murder that led Eckhart and Fowler to David Stone and what was happening in his company. Eckhart brought Miles Ward into it, thinking he was the one person who could figure out what the notebooks meant. When, in fact, he was already involved. That Stone and Benton met at Stanford and both attended Miles Ward's class was yet another circumstance that eventually caused Miles to get involved with their company. And now, as Eckhart lay in bed with Ally, fate had brought them together. A simple twist of fate.

But that still left the question of who killed Quinn and Lopez. And that was a question that Eckhart now needed to answer.

Just then, Ally woke up and asked if everything was alright.

"Yeah, just thinking about the Stone case."

"I thought that was over."

"So, did I."

EPILOGUE

The sedan drove slowly down 19th Avenue towards Lincoln Way and Golden Gate Park. The nondescript beige two-door kept its speed at the posted 30 miles per hour to match the timing of the traffic lights at each corner. As any long-time San Franciscan knows, the stoplights on every corner of 19th Avenue are timed to the speed limit to keep traffic flowing. Instead of speeding, kids were raised in this part of the City to see how many lights they could make without stopping. When he reached Lincoln, he turned left and headed towards the beach.

He adjusted his speed, first slowing, then speeding, and made light after light as he neared the beach. It had been years since he did this. He remembered riding shotgun with his dad on 19th Ave, heading to a Forty Niner game when they played in Golden Gate Park at Kezar Stadium. It was early on a Sunday morning in the late sixties when traffic wasn't that bad in the City, even on game day. Most people still rode public transportation, especially to the game, since there was virtually no parking at the stadium. But his dad loved to drive. They would find someone at the top of the park selling their driveway for game day parking, and then it was just a short walk to the old coliseum-style stadium. When the team moved to Candlestick in the 70s, they reconfigured the old stadium for high school games. He still drove by there from time to time.

Those were some of the best memories he had as a child. As he crossed Sunset Boulevard, his thoughts moved to the present and the path he'd taken over the past 50 years. He tried to pinpoint that exact moment in his life, that delta on his life's timeline, when his current path was set. When he veered from normalcy. Had there ever been any normalcy? He thinks so, yet the boundaries between the two worlds are blurred. How can one tell when they shift from one side to the other?

He slid through the light at 38th, continuing to hit the lights as they just changed to green. As he looked ahead, he could see the lights at 39th and 40th still red, but he knew his current speed would get him there just as they switched. He had made this drive many times. Practice makes perfect. Slow and steady, just like how he did his work. Cautiously, planned, precise.

There had always been that side to him. The inability to move until all the pieces were in place. He needed to research things until he was confident his decision was the right and only logical one to be made. When he was a young boy, it was just considered a quirky trait, but as he got older, that trait turned into a personality disorder and something that affected his daily life. Of course, now it was a job requirement and something that made him very good at what he did.

As his car slid through the intersection at 39th, he glanced over at the park and Martin Luther King Drive, which peeked through the overgrown shrubbery along Lincoln. A few joggers and bicyclists were heading in opposite directions, with the early morning fog already burning off. They made such easy targets with their earbuds in, their focus on what they were doing and where they were going, and very little concern for the surrounding environment. He had become quite the study of human nature over his adult life.

With each technological advancement, his ability to exploit that distraction to his benefit had grown. As people grew more introspective and isolating, their ability to focus on their surroundings waned. As a small child, he remembers being told to look both ways before crossing the street. Today, with the walking dead, their heads looking down, buried in their phones, their safety was in the hands of the drivers and not the other way around. There were days he thought seriously of just taking a few of them out. Hell, no one would even notice. They were all so self-absorbed. But, no, that's not how he did things.

As he went through the intersection at 40th and got closer to the Great Highway and the beach, he thought of those weekends he would spend with his dad in the park. Shortly after Main Drive's name changed to John F Kennedy in the late 60s, it was closed to traffic on Sundays, and his Dad would throw his bike in the trunk of their car and take him to the park to ride down the middle of the vast expanse that ran the length of the park. They would usually start at the bottom or west end of the park and make their way from the soccer fields, past the bison paddocks, and end up at Spreckles Lake. Most of the lakes in the park were man-made, and Spreckles was his favorite. He loved watching the old Italian men sailing their large toy sailboats from one end of the lake to the other. They used long poles to recover their boats when close to shore. Otherwise, they were left to the whims of the wind to make it from one end of the lake to the other. On any weekend, there might be hundreds of expensive toys tacking back and forth on the shallow waters of the artificial lake, vying for space among the ducks that the intruders barely bothered. He had dreamed of one day having one of those boats, whose masts were as tall as he was at 10.

As he passed the lights at 41st, he watched as a young jogger entered the park via Chain of Lakes Drive, clad in the typical uniform of today, skin-tight yoga stretch pants and only a sports bra. They leave nothing to the imagination. If this were a different day, he might have followed her in. But no, not now. He was looking forward to the beach and the peace it offered. Besides, he wasn't a spur-of-the-moment guy. He left that to the nut jobs that wandered the City looking for vulnerable women.

He drove through 42nd and then 43rd, leaving just six more blocks before he got to the Great Highway. With the windows open, he could smell the ocean and hear the waves in the distance. He was getting close to the playground at 45th that his dad would take him to on those weekends when he had custody. The old equipment, made from steel pipes and sheet metal slides, was long gone and replaced with the plastic and wood jungle gyms that were much less likely to elicit lawsuits from overprotective parents. How he missed those giant swing sets, wide leather seats connected with thick metal chains. We all thought we could swing high enough to loop the chains over the crossbar. It never happened. Although he had heard tales of older kids who had accomplished the feat, he had never witnessed it. The best he had ever achieved was to get high enough to launch himself beyond the bark base and over the concrete rim onto the lawn.

When he hit the intersection on 44th, he could see that playground to his left and a few small children playing. Their parents barely pay attention, with their focus on their phones. They make it so easy. Not that he would ever consider a child. No, that wasn't him. But there were those types out there. If these parents actually knew how many sadistic fucks were roaming amongst us. They'd never leave the house or let their kids walk a few blocks to school.

With the windows open, he could hear the innocent laughter and screams of joy as the kids scaled the equipment like little chimps. It reminded him of Monkey Island at the zoo just south of where he was. He had probably spent as much time there with his dad as he did at the park. Nothing like some stale pink popcorn and a hot dog before being sent home to Mom.

He passed through 45th just as the light changed to yellow and picked up his speed to make it through 46th as it stayed green. Two more blocks before he came to the only street without a number before the Great Highway. The sound of the beach was louder now, the smell stronger. It was still morning and a weekday, but the number of people he saw increased as he got close to the beach. He was tired, not because of the past couple of days but the years. He needed more time to catch his breath lately. More solitude to think. To clear his mind. The thoughts didn't come as often, but their intensity was overwhelming. What used to be cloudy and disjointed visions, coming in small batches that his mind wrestled with to avoid or piece together, now came as blasts in vivid, high definition. Long sequences appeared to be more like memories than things to come. If he tried to avoid them, their intensity and periodicity increased to unbearable levels until he acted on them to make them real. Only then could he tuck them away as memories left in that part of his brain for later recall.

He made it through 47th and then 48th with no problem, but when he came to La Playa, the last block before the Great Highway, he hit a red light. It was still early, and there weren't many cars out, but no sense running the light just to finish the drive as he had planned. He didn't need to be stopped by a cop this morning. I mean, nothing in the car that would tie him to anything, but he avoided law enforcement at all costs. No need to raise a flag or put himself in a situation that might get him tripped up by saying something weird.

As he sat waiting for the light to change, La Playa to his left and Martin Luther King Jr Drive entering the park to his right, he let his mind recount the dates, locations, and details of his past jobs. Let? Not really, more like force. It was his way of exercising his brain. Like remembering what you had for breakfast a week ago on Tuesday, what you wore to dinner a month ago on Sunday. It wasn't much of an exercise. For whatever reason, he could remember insignificant facts like these just as well as the large, very significant facts anyone would remember. Birthdays, anniversaries, and major news stories took the same amount of space and importance as his path from home to a job thirty years ago. What someone was wearing and what they said were as clear as what he saw right in front of him today as he waited for that damn red light to change. It was a curse as much as it was a gift. But it was a gift he cherished and was proud of. Recalling details of obscure events to others was something he enjoyed. He thought it made him more important than he was. On those rare occasions, he actually spoke to other people.

The light changed, and he navigated through the wide intersection and made a right on the Upper Great Highway, heading north to the large parking lots that dotted the west side near the access points of the beach. He drove along the Park's western boundary and past the Beach Chalet soccer fields, where he could hear the different ethnic voices of the men playing in the cool of the morning before the sun rose to bake the fields. He could see the Beach Chalet restaurant and bar, which once housed changing rooms for beachgoers in the 30s and 40s. The building closed and fell into disrepair during the 60s and 70s. After an extensive renovation project, they reopened it in the 90s in its current iteration. The views from the second-story restaurant at sunset were incredible.

He passed the end of the Park at Fulton and drove by the large, ugly apartment buildings where Playland at the

Beach used to be. His Dad had lived just two blocks from Playland after the divorce, and they spent many of his weekends riding the old roller coaster and diving bell at the beachfront amusement park. He wished it was still there. The smells of the Hot House Mexican food still wafted in his memories. He remembered his dad and him sitting in the car, watching people go by as they ate a burrito or enchilada out of a paper container, listening to the insidious cackling of Laughing Sal in her glass box at the entrance gate. He wondered if this was where he got his penchant for observation and human psychology. His dad's game of trying to guess who people were and what they were doing was still fresh in his mind.

He smiled as he made a left across traffic and into the mostly empty parking lot facing the ocean. Those were happy times. He pulled into a slot away from the few other cars, one that pointed towards the large concrete abutment that attempted to keep the sand from the beach from covering the highway and etching the paint of the homes across the street. The parking lot sat ten or fifteen feet above the beach, access provided by concrete steps on the other side of the abutment. Fifty years ago, those steps numbered three times as much, buried in the unrelenting forward progress of the sand as the wind pushed it against the concrete and slowly covered it step by step. Over the years, several city-funded programs attempted to uncover the steps and keep the sand from advancing. Nothing worked, and it appeared the City had given in to nature.

Not long after his parent's divorce and those days spent with his dad at Golden Gate Park, Playland, and the zoo, that's when he knew this all started. It's when the visions began. Faint and barely discernible, but clear enough for him to interpret. That first one, the one that troubled him so deeply, haunted him for over a year before he acted on it. It was disturbing on so many levels, but especially since it involved someone so close to him. But it was unrelenting, like the sand covering the steps, inch by inch. He didn't know what DNA was or that things like hair color or personality traits could be hereditary, but looking back, he knew that he had to have something to do with all this.

The arguments before the divorce, his mother questioning his dad. None of it made sense. Looking back, he guesses the clues were there. Being gone for days with no explanation. His Dad staring at the TV even though it was off. Locked in some deep thought. And then in later years after the divorce. At those times, his father left him alone for hours in the apartment. Wondering when his dad would come home. Looking back now and seeing that, he found himself caught in those same deep thoughts, time passing quickly, so quickly that when he came out of it, hours had passed. And the only memory he had of it was the movie that had been playing in his head and what he knew would come to pass. Did his dad have those same visions?

At the time of his mom's death, he justified it in his head as her continual attacks on his Dad. She just wouldn't stop the accusations and the constant recalling of every argument and supposed lie his dad told. It was exhausting. He kept telling himself that was the reason. He was defending his dad, and he had to make the noise in his head stop. But now he knew the truth. Well, he knew the truth shortly after his mom's death, when he had to do it again. By the time he was twenty, he knew for sure that it had nothing to do with his dad, at least not defending him. A chip off the old block? Maybe. But what he truly knew were the visions. The only way to stop them was by making them real. That's why he had to kill his mother. The only reason.

He stared out through his windshield and watched the waves; the people walking their dogs, bundled up against the cool breeze of the morning air. He slowly looked down at the newspaper on the passenger seat of his car and the headlines about the Silicon Valley CEO who jumped to his death. Apparently, the police had him as the prime suspect in the murder of the Golden Gate Park gardener. If only the police had known what really happened. He wondered how much the executive denied the murder as he stood on that ledge, waiting to jump to his death. They probably were looking at him for the murder of the company's chairman of the board until that Stanford professor copped to it.

But the poor Mexican? Hell, he shouldn't even be dead. He smiled to himself, thinking that he actually helped the cops to uncover what was going on at that company. Had it not been for the connection between the gardener and the company's CEO, they wouldn't have had a clue. That was his own fault. An obvious mistake he had made, his usually excellent and carefully planned operation gone awry. The last time he had made a mistake like this was in his twenties. And if the police had the same technology as they do today, that probably would have been the end of his career.

No, his visions and need to make his visions come to pass involving the girl, not the old Mexican gardener. He had been watching her for some time, planning, perfecting how he would do it. But he made a mistake. How could he not know someone else was living in the same place? He queued up the memory like you would an eight-millimeter film. Visiting her at the bank where she worked, following her for weeks, watching her every move. The visions got clearer and clearer about what he needed to do. It was the only way to stop the visions. Make them real.

The police thought the girl was the innocent victim, and the gardener was the killer's primary target. But they had that wrong too. That and who the killer was. He was tired of this.

Riley Richmond looked back up and out the windshield to the grayish-green water of the waves. He knew this had to end. He was getting tired. Tired of the planning. Tired of the entire process. And especially tired of the visions, getting stronger and stronger every day. No, there were only two ways out. And he planned on taking both with the help of Detective Eckhart.